"Once again, Dwight Wilson essential history about our cou are looking the other way, captivated by his tales and characters from our shared past. " — Laura Danforth, Head of School, The Masters School, Dobbs Ferry, NY.

"The Resistors" is a reminder that time does not separate us from our ancestors, but instead connects us — their errors, their sorrows, and their redemptive acts of courage. Telling stories of people who lived, breathed, and suffered long ago, Dwight Wilson brings them to life in his readers' hearts — and somehow in the process we comfort their spirits and they comfort ours.— Paula B. Chu, Ph.D.

"To call our ancestors forth to witness is a noble pursuit. Through characters, real and imagined, Wilson gives us the wisdom of ancestry and the gift of story. It is our stories that carry us through the danger water and heal our broken places. This human rights parable is a sweeping trek through the American historical landscape that brings us to back to center." — Carla R. Young, Director of Community & Multicultural Programs, Cranbrook Schools

"The author has woven an exhilarating and heartwrenching re-creation of a specific time in our shared and shadowy history as a nation. The pages are filled with a pageantry of pain and a parade of hope. In many ways, for each reader, this work will feel as if you are discovering pages either lost or torn from the family photo album. The confluence of cultures, politics, finance, and family is so enthralling; the reader feels as if he or she has been teleported to the actual cotton field, shanties, or battlefield. As such, it is extremely difficult to conceptualize the atrocities my foreparents endured in their quest to be seen and respected as human beings, not as chattel. I simply wasn't prepared for the emotional rollercoaster laid out in these pages. This work is guaranteed to inspire, empower, educate, and convict. This is fiction only by title; its truths are anything but fiction." — Kendall C. Wright, "The Actualizer", President /CEO Entelechy Training and Development, inc

"If history textbooks were written like these stories, perhaps our students would engage in our heritage to a much higher emotional and intellectual level. Even if every word isn't factual, these accounts of stealing and owning human beings, both Africans and Native Americans, and the struggles to live feely even after they were declared free, reveal incredibly long-lasting pain. No wonder we're having such a hard time getting over it." —Sylvia Graves, retired educator and former General Secretary of Friends United Meeting

"The Resistors, stories of historical fiction, written as of memories that are passed down through generations, has an astonishing ability to bring alive the individuals who endured our collective history of enslavement of one group of peoples by another. The well researched stories detail day to day experiences of, among others, the ancestors of author Dwight L. Wilson. Captured are testaments to resilience and heroic responses to oppression through imagined but very real conversations of the peoples of succeeding generations. These conversations take place within the context of events occurring during periods of America's history, deepening an understanding of the significant effect an individual can have during one's own time and for subsequent generations." — Penny Corbett, Owner, Jorn Court Associates

"John Hope Franklin, when referring to American history, once said, 'We've got to tell the unvarnished truth!' One cannot read Wilson's latest work, The Resistors, without seeking the unvarnished truth about slavery and those who emboldened themselves to disrupt, in   some manner, this 'peculiar institution.' Wilson's novel challenges a host of false notions that many Americans hold as pure truth. Indeed the characters in The Resistors—the escaped slave who risks her own freedom and returns to the south to find her brother; the Quaker family whose daughter accompanies her on this dangerous mission; the slaveholding Cherokee elder; or the 'good' northerners who would rather look the other way as injustices are meted out against their unwanted 'neighbors'—will make us all do what good historical fiction is designed to do: pique our curiosities to seek the "unvarnished truth." Esther L. Williams, Ph.D., Retired Educator

"In The Resistors: A Collection of Stories, Dwight L. Wilson depicts the hardships and endurance of the ancestors of present-day African Americans from their compelled departure from the shores of Africa until the days when freedom looms before them. The stories focus on the enforced subjugation of a race of people who view their imprisonment and treatment through varying prisms. Wilson's book reveals that these victims of displacement perceive their "pecular institution" based on their relationships with religion, each other, and the enslavers. The stories are told from the viewpoints of the people who travelled the Middle Passage and their descendents. The reader is also provided with the perspective of the Quakers who, in general, saw the slaves as human beings but had in their ranks members who were not willing to see them as equals. This book provides an extensive examination of African Americans and their sustaining experience in America." — Colleen Lloyd, retired professor of English and Coordinator of English at Cuyahoga Community College who has taught African American Studies over 40 years.

THE RESISTORS:

A COLLECTION OF STORIES

By Dwight L. Wilson
Edited by Lisa Diane Kastner

Published in North America and Europe by Running Wild Press. Visit Running Wild Press at www.runningwildpress.com Educators, librarians, book clubs (as well as the eternally curious), go to www.runningwildpress.com for teaching tools.

ISBN (pbk) 978-1-947041-36-3
ISBN (ebook) 978-1-947041-37-0

Printed in the United States of America.

AUTHOR'S NOTE

The author spent nearly fifteen years researching the time period and geographical areas into which these stories are placed. This is a work of fiction peopled by many real characters, most of whom play cameos, and some of whom are the author's relatives. None of the dialogue is actual and many of the events are created. Nearly all situations were possible.

The Resistors is a parallel sequel to 2018's *The Kidnapped.* It focuses on blacks, whites, and Native Americans resisting pre-Civil War oppression while attempting to establish dignified identities. It is also in the voice of Sarah, one of the author's direct ancestors. She was the daughter of Esi and Kofi two fictionalized Fante kidnapped from West Africa in 1795. With the help of Quakers, together with two brothers, Robin and Dan, Sarah escaped from being enslaved in Culpeper, Virginia and settled in Warren County, Ohio where she met and married the Scots-Irish Quaker, Charles Ferguson. It is imagined that Sarah was primarily educated by her father who himself was taught reading and writing by Nathan Prescott, his slave master, and secondarily through nearly three years of education at Goose Creek Friends School, a Quaker school in Northern Virginia, renown for being integrated prior to Nat Turner's revolt which led to state laws forbidding the education of people of color.

The short stories are chronologically arranged slices from American history in which many characters appear multiple times.

WIDER UNITED STATES TIMELINE

Year	Chapter Titles	Elsewhere in America
1795	The New World	The Naturalizaton Act of 1795 specifies that citizenship was reserved only for free white persons
1808	The Freeing Game	The act prohibiting the importation of slaves comes into effect
1820	The Foundation Story	Maine and Missouri become states (Missouri Compromise)
1823	Hope and Defiance	President James Monroe forbids European nations in Americas
1827	Pinching	*Freedom's Journal*, first Black owned newspaper published
1827	Navigating Limitations	Baltimore & Ohio America's 1st commercial railroad begins
1828	Four Different Ways	*Cherokee Phoenix*, first Native American language newspaper
1829	The Original Jim Crow	Andrew Jackson begins as President of the United States
1832	A Call to Leaving	Cholera Epidemic Reaches New York City
1832	Because We Are Divided	Black Hawk War ends
1832	Dispersed	First Wagon Train (Bonneville's) crosses Rocky Mountains
1833	The Stand	Oberlin College is founded as nation's 1st integrated college
1835	Three-Fifths	Unsuccessful attempt to assassinate President Jackson
1836	Where Love Rules	Battle of the Alamo

THE NEW WORLD

Mother did not believe the sea was always storm tossed, but the air-tight lower level of the slave ship and frequency of upset stomachs on both sides of the powerless aisle made it seem there was neither stillness nor peace. Nurturing her inner disturbance was the frequency of white men violating black women, sometimes with their chained husbands witnessing repeated outrages. More than one of these women and several of their husbands found ways to throw themselves over the side or starve themselves despite being forcibly fed.

Weeks chained together had helped mother and Sofoase, a Borno woman, form a common language. They wanted to believe their words were closer to what their ancestors had spoken centuries before their people had divided. Was their new construction correct or imagination? Mother did not know, but I am convinced it helped them survive, especially when they used their conversation to pretend that the hateful things happening on the ship were nightmares instead of reality.

According to my sister Fannie, who told me this story, the division between Esi's Fante ancestors and Sofoase's Borno forebears was because as the Akan population grew in their journey from East Africa, the land could not bear their numbers. Rather than fight among themselves, the elders advised a series of divisions and laid out the proper way of going in separate directions without fighting among themselves. The People lived off the land with some learning to farm and others the value of mining gold.

The longer the evil journey across the Atlantic, the less attractive the idea of separation became to the two kidnapped women. Deprived of their families, they wanted each other's company to last until death. If that were not to be, they determined to maintain their dignity no matter what befell.

They were talking softly in their reformed language when a sailor who had failed at hanging himself called out, "We are home! Soon I will be a rich man and you niggers will begin a new life."

"He might as well be speaking the language of the jackals," said Esi.

"Remember, before I was purchased for this ship I worked at the fort and learned their language," said Sofoase. She translated his words, adding, "Do not fall for his lies. Home for them is not home for us."

"I pray that wherever we go we will go together."

◊◊◊◊◊◊

Perhaps 150 of the original 300 slaves who had been loaded on the ship in Africa were still alive and well enough to be sold soon to the highest bidder. Those who had not died but were too sick to stumble or bring a sufficient price, would be kept in a special stone cell until they were well enough for the auction block. They had arrived nearly naked at Sullivan's Island in Charleston Bay. Once the time came to disembark, Esi prayed in Fante. 'Nyame, I have a dream that one day I'll be free again. But if not me, my children.' A few moments later, she saw the male line of slaves walking a separate gang plank.

Briefly she linked eyes with her twelve year old suitor, Kofi. He straightened his back. The movement gave a guard an idea. He hit the nearest man in the stomach with his stick, forcing him to also walk more erect and screamed curses at the rest of the men to march like moving trees. Spying him was fine, but she and Kofi had never touched each other, and Mother was eager to see if another ship was carrying her parents. She scanned the shore in all directions. Theirs was the only slave ship nearby. Had some from her village been taken to Cuba? Jamaica?

Brazil? In all the time I was with her, Father was the only other person she met from her home village. Fannie, who related most of this story to me, was with her longer but before writing this book I never asked her if she knew otherwise.

A new team of slaves brought sack cloths for them to wrap around their bodies and water with which to bathe. All the while the caretaker slaves vainly searched for relatives. Mother realized that she was a 12 year old, lost and lonely in a new world.

"Sofoase, where are we?"

Her friend had no answer.

◊◊◊◊◊◊

A few days later, still in chains, the newly arrived were bathed again and examined by white physicians. A boat took them ashore. When they were marched to the Old Slave Mart, whites on either side examined them, called them wild, and laughed at things even Sofoase could not comprehend. My sister reported that Mama's breasts were still uncovered as they would have been back home in Fante-land. She was amazed, that despite summer's heat, she saw white women dressed in a superabundance of clothing and black ones trying to imitate the clothing of the ones who ruled.

The slaves waited in an overcrowded upper room, fighting fear until the heat of the day lessened. Outside they could hear the streets filling. People were coming out to enjoy the cool of the evening and search for late day bargains on fruits and vegetables at the markets run by urban slaves.

"I will care for you," Daddy called to Mama through the wall separating females and males. "Never doubt me."

It was odd that a commoner such as the man who would become my father would see himself in chains yet imagine himself worthy of Mother. He always smiled at himself when he told me this story but never tried to explain his determination. I have wondered if his courage was always there. After all, as a boy he had chased a lion out of the village. As our life on Fruits of the Spirit Plantation would reveal, American slavery is more ferocious than any lion. I have mixed feelings that I was not present on the day that he admitted as much.

Before dusk, two groups of local Charleston slaves entered. The first group washed them down again and greased them. Most treated them as though they were livestock. One exception was an older woman who spoke Fante. She was greasing Mother's back when she noticed next to the slave brand there was a tattoo of the Fante stool.

"You are a member of the royal family?"

"What is royalty to a slave?" Mother said.

The woman dressed her hair with more attention than she did the other women. She also offered counsel. "My name is Akua. I am told there are worse places in this new world, but this one is bad enough. Many of us are broken, but you must not be. Keep in mind that even as a slave, how you carry yourself will influence the people and must impress the barbarians. You are a chosen one. Your responsibilities are unending."

Akua's words made such an impression that when Mother had children, she told us all we too had to carry ourselves with special dignity.

"You never told me you were of a royal house," said Sofoase.

"As I told her, what is royalty to a slave? I also never asked about your family. Here we only have each other."

◊◊◊◊◊◊

No one had the vaguest idea of what it meant to be a slave in this world. Esi recognized a well-designed terror and pretended she was walking through a forest where letting wild animals smell one's fear might be a grave mistake. She told Sofoase, "We have resisted committing suicide, and many have survived failed rebellions. We are survivors not victims."

"Thank you for the reminder."

They called on venerated ancestors for assistance not because they were seen as gods but because their deaths did not end their love. They asked powerful animals to appear and attack the ones with ghost-colored skins, not because they had been seen wandering the streets of Charleston but because dreams had been known to come true. They petitioned various deities to take them home again not because they had recently been in touch with the enslaved but because their spirits were their only real hope. Suddenly an auctioneer screamed. "You niggers rise!"

On the block she stood with consummate grace, held her head as high as her Queen Mother grandmother when she walked through village streets in Fante-land. A planter from the Danfuskie Island was the first buyer to examine my mother. He placed his hands on her breasts and squeezed as though they were fruit. She had already experienced worse uncivilized behavior. She pretended that he was not there polluting the air with his tobacco laden breath and touching her without permission. He spit away from others, pried her mouth open and felt her stomach. The auctioneer said, "I certify this wench is capable of producing untold numbers of pickanninies."

"She appears to be little more than a child," said the buyer.

"All the better, Mister Barnwell," said the auctioneer. "She has decades ahead of her. In the right hands you can expect a new nigger every 13-15 months."

While Esi waited for the bidding to begin, Sofoase translated the exchange. "What does he think we are that we can produce babies so fast?" said Mother.

"In their minds we are little more than breeding beasts."

The auctioneer appeared undisturbed that he was helping to break up both recently arrived families from Africa and some, who as units, had been sold south from Maryland and Virginia. Fortunately Barnwell and his armed guards purchased both Kofi and Sofoase. In total this man drove two dozen slaves out of Charleston, boarded them on two small boats and brought them to an island near Beaufort.

◊◊◊◊◊◊

My parents slaved on this Sea Island from 1795-1801. When they were each 16, my father said, "You know I love you, and I know if we were still in Fante-land a man of my stature could never hope to marry you. Will you have me as husband?"

Father reported to me that my mother smiled and said in Fante, "There is no better man here or at home. I would be honored to call you husband and be the one who helps make this new world your best world."

Barnwell died and left his estate in such poor condition that his heirs sold all the slaves to an agent of Nathan Prescott of Culpeper, Virginia. They arrived while Prescott and his wife were at church. The overseer arranged them in the manner Prescott always reviewed his slaves. The original slaves were still within sight when Father said to Mama, "Stay near me, dear, and all will be well."

"You are too trusting, husband. All will never be well here." said Mama. "Sofoase knew this truth. That is why she died so young on the march to this place called Fruits of the Spirit."

"Without hope, how can we go on?"

"Hope without opportunity is a seed that grows into bitterness."

"I am too strong and sweet to ever become bitter."

She knew the warrior was trying to convince himself. Mother said, "Whatever evil befalls us, I will resist being reduced."

In front of everyone on Fruits of the Spirit Plantation, Prescott fondled Mama in more places than her breasts the first time he saw her. Instinct told my father this man deserved bodily pain. Common sense told him anyone who can be purchased can also be sold away. Mama's assurance that nothing could take away her humanity allowed him to protect his family. Daddy willed himself still and searched for a way out. Later he often said to me, "Your mother has taught me that knowing when to resist with force and when to attack wisely may mean the difference between freedom and perpetual slavery."

THE FREEING GAME

The Quaker abolitionist, Patience Starbuck was as close to an aunt as I ever knew. One snowy day, as we sat in her parlor knitting for my twin boys, she told me this story about her childhood on Nantucket. I recorded her words in my journal and later refined my hearing when I was allowed to review her own journals.

Jane Boston looked in at Peter and Adelaide Starbuck's ten year old daughter Patience. Jane had just fed Adelaide broth, changed the sheets, and held the bed pan that she would empty in the outside privy. Patience heard Jane return and anxiously asked about her gravely ill mother. Mother and child had been denied the ability to speak for almost two days. She was told her mother was sufficiently awake for a visit.

Patience jumped up from her game that she had named "Freeing the Slaves" and hurried upstairs. An hour later she found Jane in the kitchen preparing dinner.

"Mother was so weak she went back to sleep almost as soon as thee brought back the bed pan. I sat in silence praying for her well-being, hoping she would at least open her eyes. I might as well have been waiting for southerners to free the slaves."

"1608 or 1808, dying in a foreign land must be a hard reality for a Frenchwoman."

The two had been speaking about the coming death for weeks. Upstairs, Penelope, Patience's older sister, was still in denial. To Patience it seemed that aside from figures, Penelope was impervious to most things.

Patience was silent a while then said, "My freeing game falls short. Mock Congress, the President's White House, the Supreme Court, the people I sneak into the south to free slaves... Long after the War for Independence there is still slavery, and my games offer so little promise."

"Please don't tell me, little miss, that a certain ten year old Quaker girl still thinks the French army should invade these shores."

"Well—"

"Thy father forbids that thee even think of violent games."

"Who can control my thoughts?"

"I was instructed to control thy practices."

"Thee cannot control Penelope," There was nothing Jane needed to say. Even Peter Starbuck found his older daughter headstrong. "As for my actions, Father may be thousands of miles away."

"I know thy behavior, and a charge to keep I have."

Patience left the kitchen in a huff.

Jane paused only a few seconds before following the child into the room where she held her brown doll and brooded. Jane glared, and Patience pretended she was invisible.

Jane cleared her throat and as she would never do with Penelope, she said, "disrespect is unbecoming scum let alone a Quaker lass."

Patience put her hands over her mouth. "Oh no! Never would I disrespect thee on purpose."

"Then come to me."

Patience ran to Jane. The two embraced. When they separated, Patience said, "I am almost as tall as thee!"

Jane smiled. "What is height among friends?"

◊◊◊◊◊◊

The next day was the sabbath, the day that Jane claimed mostly for herself. Jane prepared breakfast and was relieved by a sister of Patience's father. Although it took longer, as always, on her way to religious services at the African Meeting House she walked along the seashore. She once explained to Patience that the sea called to her, and no whites silently demanded she yield to them the right of way. "Double love wins every time."

Jane's brother John kept a room for her. Since she typically spent each night at the Starbuck house she seldom used it for more than a nap or if she was sick and wanted to keep from passing some illness on to the family for whom she worked. Over dinner John complained bitterly about the Quakers' refusal to allow his children in their schools. "Do something, sister!"

"The father is at sea, and may be there for who knows how many more months, and I have all I can do to help the mother die without getting aggravation when I come here."

"Without good schools we ain't got no *home*. If we had one my children could have a good school. I'm a damn resident when I should be a citizen."

"We just came from church," said Jane.

"A colored church 'cause them Quakers don't mind helping us escape slavery but don't want us in their church!"

After the third meal Jane returned home. Patience played with a Quaker doll in the White House while arguing with the President over slavery. Penelope visited with her fiancé's family.

Mentally exhausted from her own argument with her brother, Jane sat down and watched the girl play. In time Patience asked why she was so silent, and Jane gave her what Patience assumed was a well edited version of John's words. In subsequent years Patience could see rage in John's face each time their paths crossed. She smiled and spoke. He grinned and grunted.

◊◊◊◊◊◊

Almost nine months later Peter Starbuck and his two sons returned from whaling. Jane disclosed that his wife, Adelaide, had died four months earlier. Upon learning of their loss, the three men left for the graveside.

Although Penelope was invited to come, she told her father it was more important to make ready the business papers. "Mother is dead," said Penelope. "What can an old colored lady do to change that?"

Jane was tempted to say something but held her peace.

"Jane, would thee care to accompany us?"

By the time the four of them returned from the graveside, Patience was home from school. Patience was appalled but not surprised when Jane reported Penelope's words. Peter heavily sat down. His eyes were still red from crying when Jane brought him a glass of water and he said, 'I knew thee would not *mux* the job, Jane. Thee has done a good job rearing my girls."

"Rearing?" said Penelope. "A colored could never rear me."

Patience bit her lip for only a moment. "With mother dying and more so since she passed, Jane has been our mother!"

"Shahh," said Penelope. "That is like a huckleberry chowder."

"*Bring to!* I will not have this unkindly speaking," said Peter. "I am the captain of my ship on sea or on land. Without my trust in Jane we would have no business. Apologize, Penelope."

"I will later."

"Thee will now! Thee embarrassed her in public. Apologize in public. That is the way of Friends."

Following a reluctant apology, Peter said, "Now Penelope, take us through the books. This time Job, James, and Patience will all stand at the work table."

Patience clapped her hands for this was a time she had long awaited. Penelope vainly tried to dismiss the thought but Patience was almost 12 years old and obviously precocious.

The family went to the office where Penelope demonstrated that with the earnings from the latest whaling trip the family's wealth had grown substantially. However, there was a serious problem with her report. Absalom Bernard, Penelope's future father-in-law and Peter's business partner, appeared to have paid less than his fair share of a major expense.

Peter was still steaming when the family came to feast on lobster and mainland beef as well as several kinds of vegetables.

"This beats *fu-fu.*" Job, the oldest brother spoke of the mush and molasses that they had eaten while at sea.

The meal had almost ended when Peter said, "Tell me, Jane, what has concerned thee most in my absence? I have had my own burdens, and a new one has reared its ugly head. Might thee also have some burden?"

Penelope tensed, wondering if this would be the time she would inform Peter of her consistently unbecoming behavior. On the first day of return, in the presence of his children, Peter always asked the same question whether his voyage had been 10 months or three years.

Jane said boldly, "I have nephews who would love to attend the school where Patience studies and her older siblings have finished."

There was a long silence before Peter said, "When I address the Elders over my problems with Bernard, I will also speak about this separation of colors."

Penelope flushed red. "Father, I am sure the coloreds prefer things as they are. They live among themselves in New Guinea. They attend their own churches, and they should attend their own schools."

"That is not what Jane has suggested. Speak more please, Jane."

"My brother and others believe their children would receive a better education in the schools where white children study."

"That is race mixing," said Penelope, "which is outlawed in this state and most others."

Peter peered at his sons. "How can it be that I am less than a day on land and in my own house a child dares teach me about the law?" Neither son ventured an opinion. He looked at Penelope. "I have the greater lay and I will use what little I have to speak in favor of justice." He turned to Patience. "Now that I am home, Penelope marries soon. Shall I place thee with my brother Joseph's family or with our sister Mary?"

Patience said, "I am content to stay with Jane." There was a deep silence. "Uncle Joseph's household is too busy. Aunt Mary is a traveling minister and often away. Jane is everything I could want when thee is absent."

The silence continued until Peter replied, "I am open to *boiling* thy idea until I leave with thy brothers in a few months. Until then, let us see if what has worked in my absence will continue working in my presence."

THE FOUNDATION STORY

For much of this story I am indebted to a brother who once was lost and heard more details than I knew or could imagine.

◊◊◊◊◊◊

My parents were in love as deeply as any couple I've known. Their only pronounced differences were in how they saw the New World. Sadly that filtered over into what they said about the Original World — Fante-land in West Africa.

Back home Daddy had once challenged a lion. He called himself forward-looking and never spoke of anything to do with life before slavery. It was Mother who repeatedly told the story. On the day of the famous incident, most of the people who were in the Fante village were taking a midday rest from a sweltering sun. Only a few old men who were barely able to walk, women and children were present. Men in their prime were either on a hunt or with the almost-warriors who were being initiated into manhood. Kofi was returning with two friends from a mission to deliver food to the initiation group. One of the trio spied a young lion walking toward the village. The two friends fled. Kofi took a spear from the front of a nearby house, then trailed a few feet to the rear. He followed the prowling lion. A row of huts between them and imitating a lion's roar, Kofi rushed out of his hidden place. The lion froze which afforded a clean shot at its throat. Kofi hurled the spear with all the force in his ten year-old arm, jerked the knife from his breech cloth, and stabbed the lion's neck with all of his power. The startled lion ran out of the village.

My grandmother, the Queen Mother, heard the commotion and was the first to arrive at the scene. My mother was right behind my grandmother. "What have you done, my son?"

"Mother of us all, I have bloodied myself."

My mother cherished this story. She would let those who imitated Daddy's love for America ignore all other stories of Africa, but she called this one "the foundation story." Was this the day she fell in love with Daddy? Now that they are dead, the questions never asked are assigned to a sewing box that should be marked, "permanent mystery." What we do know is when life weighed most on him, or some child's eyes questioned his heart, mother shared this story.

◊◊◊◊◊◊

Nathan Prescott owned the plantation where we were enslaved. Daddy knew that he was a better man than Prescott, and yet his blond-haired, blue-eyed master defined manhood not only for Fruits of the Spirit but also for the American continent. Daddy's spirit was always willing to stand up against Prescott, but his flesh was so powerless that after a savage beating and threat to be sold apart to the Deep South, he had surrendered all ideas of preventing Prescott's attacks on Mama. He searched and believed he had discovered a way to use Prescott's energy for the betterment of our family. Of course I did not realize all of this as a child. In those days, I was certain that Jehovah had ordained our treatment and wondered if Mama's Nyame and Anansi, the trickster deity, had become his body servants.

Although I am sure each slave master has a special place reserved in Hell, Prescott was not the worst. Against Virginia law and his neighbors' counsel, he taught Daddy how to read and speak "the king's English." I believe guilt was the prime motivator, but it may have been loneliness. On Fruits of the Spirit, other than Hackley, the uncouth overseer, he was the only white man. Prescott had made Kenneth as much as Kofi had transformed himself. But I worshiped my father more than I cared for Jehovah, and I know that Daddy was always a double-sided man: a Fante warrior dressed in a slave's rags; dignified while disgraced.

Most did not realize it, but Daddy had pushed himself to ask Prescott to teach him Latin. Prescott had looked at Daddy and finally said, "If the northern nigger wench, Phyllis Wheatley, can learn, I think you can learn. Then I'll have someone to polish with." Prescott's wife, Miss Anne, whose Catholic background included five years' study in Latin, was frustrated because not only was she without child but also because she had to share her husband's attention with people who should be beneath building relationships. Often in Daddy's presence she told her husband much of what he did with slaves was outlandish and teaching Daddy was reprehensible. But she did not have to deal with being tormented for claiming Christian behavior while repeatedly violating the wife of a loyal serving man.

Among the Fruits of the Spirit slaves were several who were related through Prescott or Hackley. Neither white man called someone son or daughter. Likewise, none of their offspring called a child born of another mother, sister, or brother. At the same time, anyone who suspected a kinship with one of the mixed race children steered clear of possible incest. In this painful dance, it was always easier for people to pair off dark-skinned with dark-skinned or dark-skinned with light-skinned.

Light-skinned with light-skinned couples were frowned upon on two levels: slaves condemned incest, and anyone suspected of trying to produce a lighter next generation could be accused of assuming superiority. The cuckolded men silently accepted rage and self-doubt. Will their pain ever be addressed?

At some point, Miss Anne realized that just as whites are not identical, the same is true of colored people. She began studying faces like an art student in a museum. She was an astute detective.

◊◊◊◊◊◊

Over the years, many of us have discussed the subject, and the only ways that anyone remembers Mama openly defying Daddy's wishes were with her refusal to master the English language, the trappings that came with it, and in her feelings concerning his choice to turn away from the practices of the old world. To some it appeared to be a comfortable truce, but I studied them. The tension was there until the end of their relationship.

Everyone knew what was required but with great fanfare, each Wednesday afternoon, Daddy was ordered to leave the fields and study Latin with Prescott. Years of three-hour lessons with the son of a man who claimed that he had been driven into the plantation life when his preference was to teach theology and Latin at the College of William and Mary or the University of Virginia, made Daddy confident in the language of the Caesars. As long as he remembered never to look Prescott directly in the eyes, was silent if the master went to side-talk, or fawned about any subject, Daddy believed he was moving closer to his American dream. My brother Robin once claimed that Daddy had sold out. I pointed out that not only was he not being paid but also he had no choice. For his part, Prescott steered clear of mentioning Mama or any other member of our family.

Mama was a natural skeptic. "Don't let 'im steal your soul," she often pleaded.

"My soul belongs to Jehovah," Daddy would answer, "but Master owns us and might as well own the language if we do not appropriate part of it. If I can learn it well, we can all be free."

The Latin lessons had been preceded by months of lessons in English. Prescott believed that black people's struggle to pronounce "th" was because we spoke a "primitive, if not savage tongue." Prescott claimed that initially he had wanted little more than to be free from hearing at least one slave say "dhe, dhem, dhat and dhere." But once Daddy was successful in rarely saying "dh", Prescott found that Daddy's voice was as fine and mellow as imported chocolate. To shape the mind it was necessary to teach reading and writing. I suppose Prescott decided that a brain-washed education was the most efficacious way of sustaining the status quo for he chose Bible verses without hint of themes dealing with justice. He wanted passages that taught servants and slaves the virtues of obedience. The Bible he gave to Daddy must have been privately designed. It had no verse numbers and freely used the word "nigger." In his own teachings Prescott advanced to the laws and legal decisions of the state of Virginia, each of which reinforced a slave-based society. He rounded off Daddy's English education with the writings of noted slave apologists, preferring selected excerpts from the sometimes self-contradicting Thomas Jefferson and Prescott's pastor, Reverend Thornton Stringfellow. For good measure, Prescott added a little Plato in translation. Having exposed Kenneth to what he believed was irrefutable knowledge that slaves were born to be inferior, he turned to teaching his beloved language, Latin, never realizing that Daddy refused to see himself or his children as inferior in anything but earthly power. "Never give up the high moral ground," Daddy told his family.

Miss Anne criticized Prescott yet again. "This is a dangerous strategy."

Prescott answered, "Danger lies not in reading, but in what is read. So long as I control the medium, I control the man."

That he would have the audacity to say this as though Daddy were not present only underlines his hubris.

When Daddy repeated this to Mama, she said, "Ain't I done told you, ain't nothin' good in that man?"

He brushed it off. "All Jehovah's children have some good."

"You supposin' he's somethin' he ain't."

Daddy decided against replying.

Before a notable lesson, Prescott said, "With the selling of your last shoes to the ex-slave who has the temerity to call himself 'Judge' Grimes, you have earned enough to purchase your own freedom plus that of your three youngest children. As you know, the order of which I will sell the others is youngest up, Esi last."

Daddy had spent sixteen years of non-field time earning money making shoes for the slaves on the plantation and selling the excess to Judge Grimes, a greatly admired freedman. This was the first time Prescott had given an accounting.

◊◊◊◊◊◊

After studying Ovid, Daddy returned to our shack. He spoke one of his favorite lines, "Thank you for thinking there would be that which will sparkle for those who travel the threshold of the right thoroughfare thoughtfully."

This was in 1820, the year after Charlotte and David had died of influenza. Only Mother, my younger brother Luther and I were present when we heard his approach.

Our parents did not hide their love for each other. Thus I was not surprised when Daddy entered our shack and Mother walked into his arms. Years later, long after three of us escaped, a brother found Daddy in Philadelphia. Daddy told this brother he had thought about withholding some love but, "Chances are, as followed nearly everything I did on Fruits of the Spirit, that would have blown up in my face."

Daddy was about to kiss Mama when she said, "Look deeply, Kofi."

He stopped the kiss and searched her eyes. "What do you see?"

There was something fearful in her tone but Daddy was the eternal optimist. "Brown eyes."

"You should see Africa and love. That's all you need to know 'bout." He was silent. "I can tell you ain't heard."

"Pardon me?" He stepped back from their embrace to study better for an answer that he doubted he wanted.

"While you was up there with the master, the overseer done lashed Robin."

Unable to hide his anguish, Daddy said, "Why? Why?"

"Hackley claimed he talked back and looked 'im in the eye 'like he was white too'."

"Who gave him the right to lash my son?"

"Honey, you know their ways good and well. In their minds we all belong to the Prescotts: toes, knees and backs."

Daddy bit his lip. "Where is Robin now?"

"Hackley wouldn't let me tend to 'im. I sent the older gals. Had she not died of white sickness I would've sent Charlotte, but Susan and Fannie together can do near 'bout good as her."

"Heaven help us all."

"That's what I keep telling Nyame. Come quick and lift this burden. Mercy that's what we need."

"Dearest, Esi, once more, Nyame has nothing to do with this new world. Jehovah rules. If we are to have any hope, pray to Jehovah."

"The day I pray to a mean, spiteful, lazy god is the day you can bury my soul."

◊◊◊◊◊◊

The next night, after we had all come in from the fields, Daddy immediately began working on his cobbler business. We had just settled when Robin walked through the door doing his best to hide the pain that came with each step. Robin was the hardest man I have ever known, and I loved him for his strength. He silently headed for the corner where his mat lay beside Dan's. Before he could lay down Daddy looked up from his knees, and set down his work . "If you can walk, why did you not join us in the fields?"

"They already done got my pound of flesh, Daddy."

"Do not speak smartly to me, Robin."

"I'm sorry, Daddy. I'm just tired."

Daddy stood up. Robin recognized the silent signal to come nearer. The two stood in the candlelight with Robin not daring to look into Daddy's eyes. "Sometimes, Robin, I think you enjoy being beaten. What am I going to do with you, son?"

Daddy was aware that my freckle-faced brother Robin lived to hear himself called 'son'. "Did you hear, my son?" said Daddy in his voice that usually brooked nothing that permitted a hint of defiance.

Mother answered what Robin may have been thinking, "Love 'im like you do all the others in this family."

Daddy shrugged his shoulders. "Get yourself some sleep, son. We have a long day tomorrow."

◊◊◊◊◊◊

Friday was a long day. Our work in the morning was delayed by the selling of Robin's main love, Eve, and two men who had been deemed expendable. With the money, "in his pocket" as slavers love to say, Prescott seemed to have second thoughts. He removed the money. "Kenneth, put on your best clothing. I am sending you to Richmond to deposit this money in my bank."

I watched Daddy's face. It took a few seconds for his eyes to go glassy. I imagined nearly thirty years of unchecked oppression passed through his memory. I turned to Robin whose eyes flashed with such hatred that only Mama's silent warning made him soften the daggers he sent Prescott's way.

This was not the first time Prescott had sent Daddy to Richmond. Daddy was the only colored man I have ever known who had a permanent pass. "The bearer of this pass answers to the name Kenneth. He is almost 6' tall, dark as an ace of spades and has on his left shoulder the brand DT, beneath which are my own brand NP. He is free to travel at will." Prescott had even considered renting Daddy out to work as a city slave allowing him to come home from Good Friday through Easter and Christmas to the New Year. By then Anne Prescott had figured out who had fathered the light skinned children living in the homes of Kenneth and Esi as well as Gabe and Eula. She stopped Prescott's scheme before it was put in play.

From hard experience we knew that while Daddy was away, Prescott would have us children sleep with Eula's and Gabe's family while he spent a portion of the night violating our mother.

Hackley had to have known the game; still his face showed astonishment that a white man would trust a colored man with a single dollar let alone over $3,000. A paltry sum compared to the worth of Daddy's family which ostensibly was being held hostage. In fact, if Daddy had chosen to run away, I doubt that Prescott would have minded.

I was only six years old but wise enough to know both that true warriors cannot be tempted and to pray that Daddy would ride the old nag he had been given for transportation as fast as a strong wind travels north.

HOPE AND DEFIANCE

March of 1823 was in the midst of the term of slaveholding Virginia governor James Pleasants, who, like my master, came from a family that was once good Quaker stock but chose money over religious practices. Initiating a turning point in my life, the Hoges, a family of practicing Quakers wrote a letter asking Nathan Prescott if he "might spare my services.

Eula's daughter Mae was the first among us to learn of this news. She heard Miss Anne say to her husband, "Nathan, I have heard your witless cousins waste money on an Irish girl who spins and churns butter and the like, but why ever would practicing Quakers want to rent a slave?"

"They'd be expelled from meeting if they actually *rented* services," said Prescott. "They know I don't need her now so they'll feed and clothe her for a time. Money will not change hands between us. The money shall go into an account to be included in my estate."

"I would ask why you are so generous toward this particular servant but her light skin speaks volumes."

Prescott ignored the insinuation and said to Mae, "Now girl, take the letters and the money for their postage on the far table to the waiting postman. Then send to the fields for her father."

Mae informed Daddy that, as I had been with my brothers a few years past when the flu had ravaged Fruits of the Spirit Plantation, I was being sent away. However, this time I would go alone.

"Why?" Mama demanded when Daddy told her.

"Like Jehovah, Master does not give me explanations."

Mama called me to her side.

"Yo' daddy say Prescott's sending you back to the Hoges."

"I don't want to go, Mama," I said.

"And I don't want you to go, but ain't neither one of us too old for our wants to hurt us." At the time the idiom made even less sense than the coming exile. Tears filled my eyes. "Don't start that now, Oseye," she said using the name she had given me at birth, only to see Daddy change the Fante for an American name. "You a big gal, almost ten and working in the fields. This ain't no time for crying over what dumb white folks do."

◊◊◊◊◊◊

Through Daddy's efforts, I returned to the Hoges with more education than the average American white child possessed. Mary Pool Hoge said to me, "Sarah, thee hast intellectual capacities that have outstripped where I thought thee would be. Thy father must be a gifted teacher. What does the Creator think of the potential wasted through slavery?"

Silence hung until Tyler said, "There is no joy in this southern Paradise."

"I understand thy dislike of our surroundings," said Mary Pool Hoge to her husband, "but once more I say that I will not run with the others to Ohio. The Creator has need of us here among the slave holding heathens. Does thee think our presence is an accident? If the Ninevites can repent, so can our Virginia neighbors."

I learned that the Quakers had their own school at Goose Creek and begged the Hoges to let me visit. At first they disagreed, Mary Pool wanting me to go, and Tyler believing home schooling was safest. The disagreement was decided in her favor.

The first day that I walked into the brick school house, I was amazed. A single male teacher was addressing almost seventy boys and girls from all the local faiths. The children were seated on long benches behind double rows of desks. Not only were there whites but also a few people of color! Comly's spelling book held their attention. Back at Fruits of the Spirit, we were relegated to scraps of discarded paper fished out of the trash by my father. Here everyone used lead pencils on "foolscap paper" approximately 13" by 16". In the scores of conversations with the Hoges, why had they not told me about these free colored students?

Mary Pool said during afternoon tea, "Would thee give serious consideration to attending this school as a regular student?"

I clapped my hands and answered, "Yes, Aunt Mary Pool."

For the next few years, I studied at Goose Creek Meeting School. With the exception of Sundays and two weeks for the harvest, most students attended school even on Christmas, one of the 365 holy-days a year celebrated by Quakers as an opportunity to practice perfection. In addition to our school work, we were required to attend Fifth-day afternoon meeting for worship with members of the local congregation. I was one of the few students who enjoyed the silence and was thrilled when a Quaker would occasionally rise to speak in a sing-song voice against slavery or in favor of "loving thy neighbor."

The first time I ever held money was in school when the teacher taught multiplication tables by using both Federal and English coins.

Mary Pool had allowed me to become a serious student in an academically challenging school. At first I measured myself against girls my own age and a few years older. Obviously I was intelligent but none of them had my hunger for learning. Next I looked at myself against the boys. The teacher kept a motivation list at the head of the room. Soon only older students ranked ahead of me. I was a proud sixth overall. Who knew that after Nat Turner's rebellion the school would be closed to us colored people?

During this period I asked myself as a slave on loan, "What will I be?" I was without a free woman of color who might serve as a model for my secret dreams. However, I refused to accept the silly notion that my destiny was to be a perpetual slave. I longed to write my parents, but I knew slaves were not supposed to read and write. Of course, Prescott knew I was literate, and he might have given a letter to my parents. He certainly would have opened it and learned what Daddy called *arcana imperii*, the secrets of the empire. I would rather have died than become open to that hateful man.

◊◊◊◊◊◊

Of course, the Hoges owned no slaves. What they did own was a stand of maples, one of peaches, and another of apples, two milk cows, six horses, an ox, several chickens and numerous marked hogs that ran loose in nearby woods. Unless we were on our two week vacation of the school year, I rarely helped with farm work for more than a few hours a day. I helped harvest fruit and sometimes with cooking, but my only regular chores at home were fetching water from the spring about 100 yards below the house, feeding chickens, washing dishes and keeping my own room clean. Still they placed money in a secret account for chores done beyond assignments. They also placed money in Prescott's estate account for the time he did not have use of my services. Moreover, they encouraged me to learn as much as possible reading Shakespeare and an uncensored Bible, one in which they had marked verses opposing the exploitation of workers and the value of all people.

Mary Pool taught me to make Maryland biscuits, apple dumplings, cider cake, and since Uncle Tyler wanted pie daily, I learned to make custard and various fresh and dried fruit pies. As Mama told tales of Fante-land, Mary Pool reminisced about the Philadelphia area Quakers. "They call it the city of Brotherly Love and the Holy Experiment. It is head and shoulders above Virginia, but I'm afraid Friends there draw hard lines between whites and coloreds." Despite my curiosity I never asked what she meant. My father had placed so many of his dreams into Philadelphia, the city of his dreams, that I feared making him more melancholy than he deserved to be. That said, I must admit she watered a seed in my mind that Mama was correct: there was no place where we colored people would be appreciated.

I came home from school and found that the Hoges and Eileen, their Irish servant, were in the backyard. I was barely inside the house when I heard and answered a knock at the door. An elderly gentleman with a bowed back and few teeth greeted me. "So, miss, you must be that 'pretty l'il smart one' they all talkin' 'bout."

I hesitated a moment. "Excuse me, sir, do I know you?"

"We ain't yet met, but when I seen you come to this here yard I had to follow you." Perhaps he could discern his words made me uneasy. Before I slammed the door he said, "All the white chillen been talkin' 'bout you. Say you smart as a whip and call you 'Shinin' Sarah'." I relaxed. "My wife used to call me Kanem. Nowadays I call myself Ned Marble. I come for to see Miss Mary Pool Hoge, but if you don't mind I'd like for to touch you. My luck ain't what it's supposed to be, and I believe you can change it." He was respectful and I stood frozen by his words. I could see hope in his eyes and respectfully he kept his hands beside his torso. I put caution aside and extended my open hand half-way toward him. He reached out and gently touched my palm.

"I just wanted a l'il," he said with a slight nod. "Thank you, l'il ma'am."

By this time, Aunt Mary Pool was entering from the rear door. She saw him. "Good afternoon, Ned Marble. I had heard that thee was in the vicinity. I'll take two of thy well-crafted brooms, please."

"Yes ma'am," he said before being paid and hobbled away to bring back a selection of his craftsmanship from the cart in the yard.

Mr. Marble had yet to return when Aunt Mary Pool said, "A dozen years ago, his former slave holder turned him out for being a burden. He had been used up in the fields. Now he survives by making the best brooms in Loudon County. We have found him to be a kindly soul."

"He treated me with respect." I thought, 'And he gave me hope.'

◊◊◊◊◊◊

In the spring of 1826, members of the meeting decided that I was being kept "under false pretenses." I had been with the Hoges for almost three years, and had nearly forgotten that I was still a slave. I am afraid that I knew little of the real world. I was so foolish that I imagined I was on a road that led to a mountaintop. Perhaps one day I could become an admired teacher at Goose Creek Friends School.

The Hoges and most other abolitionists saw justice as indisputably the first of all Quaker practices, a subset of following the witness of Jesus, the once imprisoned and Roman-crucified Lord. The Quaker elders elevated their integrity above my desire for justice. The eldering process took two monthly business meetings to run its course. On the heels of the death of both the Yankee John Adams and the Virginian Thomas Jefferson, one Founding Father who had compromised our freedom for the sake of an illusion and another who had left his slave mistress in bondage, we prepared for my return to Fruits of the Spirit.

For the dispirited trip home, Mary Pool dressed me in a new light blue cotton dress, processed by North Carolina Quakers, and a pair of shoes almost as finely crafted as those my father made for adults. I was a slave, but Ned Marble had shown me that I was much more.

Although I thought of myself as a Daddy's girl, while riding along the road I realized my mother had an undeniable lure. Once or twice I strained to make sense of the Africa in Mama's tales, but even when I wanted to appreciate them more, they struck me as simply prosaic, antiquated, and repetitious. They might be fine for someone like my brother Robin or my sisters, but I had seen the new world and wanted to be fully a part of it. Wasn't mine the best of all brands of luck?

An hour from Fruits of the Spirit, I made a request, "Aunt Mary Pool, could you please send a message to tell Mama I am here, so I can see her first?"

The Irish servant boy who accompanied us went ahead. We turned onto the long driveway, and it occurred to me that I would miss Mary Pool. I became confused. In the past three years, I had spent more time with Mary Pool than the previous years had allowed me with Mama. How much would parting cost us both? Was loyalty only for slaves? Why did she not defy the Quaker business meeting?

It was a Sunday. Mama waited under a shade tree, she wore a loose fitting dress with a rope for a belt. She heard us before she saw us and ran up to embrace me when I saw her. I jumped off the stopped wagon and met her half way. "You almost a woman, now, my Oseye," was all she could say.

We looked at each other until Mama's heart filled. She whispered in Fante. I lost all but the love and the beauty of her words to my ears.

Later she translated. She had said, "If it should all end tomorrow, my loving child has returned. Nyame, I am happy. If it's your will, return us to our true home."

I looked around and saw that Mary Pool wanted to hug me one last time, but her husband gently held her back. Neither of us wanted to damage Mama's moment. Mama sensed it all and whispered, "Go to her, baby. Let her know you care." I obeyed.

From our embrace Mary Pool whispered, "Never forget what Ned Marble showed you."

◊◊◊◊◊◊

Bright and early the next morning, I went back to the fields, worked beside Daddy and made him proud. Once, with his head bent over his work, Daddy said to me, "Sarah, the most difficult thing in life for me is seeing my children being raised as slaves. As a child it never entered my mind that my babies would be slaves."

It dawned on me that up until he was my age, my father had been free. This epiphany took me out of feeling sorry for my own loss of freedom. I had only tasted what Daddy had grown up and had took for granted.

We had not been in the fields three hours when I was summoned to the big house. Why did he want to see me, this man whose only heretofore gift was the fact that he had never spoken to me? Even as a child, I knew his measuring tape was more than an inch short and his scissors as dull as moldy molasses.

Shortly after I was sent away, Mama had become the big house cook. She greeted me at the back door and whispered, "Be careful baby. The man is a poisonous snake." I believe she could have said more, but Mae came to guide me into the parlor. Mama often warned us to be careful around Mae. "She tells all the Prescotts' business. Anybody who tells other people's secrets will surely tell yours. With that one listen and learn, don't talk and regret."

Prescott rested in the biggest chair I had ever seen. I stopped in the doorway. Because heretofore I had avoided looking at him, I had never seen his smile, but I recognized it. The familiarity nearly unbalanced me. "Come closer," he said. I remembered whose child I was. As I assumed Mama would have done, I walked boldly into the middle of the room, daring to look him in the eyes despite everything I had been taught to the contrary.

He started by asking me what I had studied in school. Although I was surprised that he knew of my time in Goose Creek School, I answered without hesitation.

"Give me ten valuable lessons for each course," he demanded.

I was twelve years old and had yet to meet the test I feared. I answered in both sentences and paragraphs with such specificity that another might have grown bored. He hung on every word as though each were a clue to the Holy Grail. As I had desired, he was impressed.

Leaving me standing at attention, Prescott lit his pipe. He scrutinized without undressing me. I tired of the inspection and nonchalantly looked around the room. It was as opulent as the Hoges' was simple. 'We made all of this possible,' I thought. My hatred swelled, and yet I came close to forgetting that Mama had called him poisonous.

"What do you think?"

I had thoughts that I believed a white man, especially one as evil as

Prescott, would never understand. I turned my face back to him. "That I would like to sit down."

He laughed and pointed to a chair. As I sat, the air in the room changed.

In a voice as soft as royal velvet, he slowly said, "I suppose you are wondering why I brought you here." I said nothing. "Do you know who I am?"

My heart heard Mama's voice, 'A poisonous snake.' My lips said nothing. It was at this point that I realized it was not I who was being tested. I was a slave, but I had power. I decided that if I chose to speak again I would mimic him by speaking softly and slowly and never let my eyes blink. Silently I recalled my own dictum, "All games are preparation for life." The thought of power went to my head, and I decided on this day of days I would follow my hope and act as though I were free.

Prescott rang for Mama. She entered, eyes on him, but clearly also watching my face to see if she could gauge both sides.

"I will have lemonade," he said. "Make that two."

I was not surprised that he had not said "please" but I was taken aback that she did not say, "Yes sir," as we had been taught to address whites.

"Tell me more about your stay with my cousins."

I thought, 'If they are your cousins, they must be distant indeed.' This time my speech was lethargic, almost flat. I touched on surface things that I hoped revealed as little of my inner self and the Hoges as possible. In the midst of my rambling discourse on what crops they planted, animals they kept, the lay of their land, and the details of their place of worship, Mama returned and handed him both glasses.

"Would you like a lemonade?" he asked me. Mama had deliberately placed the undoctored glass in his left hand—although when I later learned what she had done, I told her I would not have minded her saliva. "The spit weren't the problem; it was the gall I put in it."

In Prescott's stifling parlor, I was thirsty. "Yes, sir," I said to his question.

Mama handed it to me.

"Esi, I would like for you to leave the house," Preston said. "And take Mae and any other servants who might be inside with you. Go until I summon you."

Both of us heightened our guard. As if reading my mind he said, "My wife went to call on a neighbor and won't be back until tomorrow."

I prayed not only to Jehovah but also, for the first time, to Nyame.

"I have much to say to you in private," he began. He went on to tell me that a business associate had watched me while I was living with the Hoges and that he had predicted the Hoges would put me in Goose Creek Friends School.

"You are a smart girl, Sarah. I do not believe that this condition suits you well."

I could not help thinking, 'And who do you think should be a slave? Perhaps your depraved self?'

He continued, "It would be much easier for all of us if instead of waiting until he can purchase you all, Kenneth would stop acting selfishly and purchase himself. Instead he pretends to be the dulcet father when he could make much more money as a free man."

Prescott knew I was smart, but he also thought I was a fool. If Daddy purchased his own freedom Prescott would guarantee his expulsion from Virginia according to the laws of the state. Then what would be the chances that before reaching old age Mama would ever know freedom? Should he grow bored with what aging might do, might he replace her with one of my sisters?

"You have influence with him. I love you, Sarah." He stopped and waited for me to say something. I held my peace and he repeated, "I love you, and I want you to love me as your mother loves me." He paused before adding, "Do you know what that means?"

I thought my face was inscrutable, but perhaps he read my thoughts, 'Mama despises you.'

"Why you hussy!" he said in a sudden rage. I thought I was smart. I held my precious peace. He stood, walked quickly over to me and slapped me so hard that I saw stars, my head rang, my knees nearly buckled, but I did not go down nor did I break the glass Mama would have had to clean up. Some thirty years later, if I close my eyes I can still feel his porky right hand as it struck the left side of my face.

He was standing frustrated over me when my mother ran into the room. "I want my baby outta this house right now!"

Prescott was flabbergasted at the interruption. "Didn't I send you away?"

Mama brought out her butcher's knife and waved it menacingly. Neither of us knew if she would actually use it.

"Go. Go," said Prescott.

I fled fleeing back to the fields.

I had thought of Mama as Prescott's victim. Through this act, I realized she was our protector. With this enlightenment, I came to understand that she had always been more of a warrior than a sacrificial lamb. The revelation shamed me and gained added weight because I could not tell others that my mother had threatened the master.

PINCHING

Although the site was named after his great grandfather, to my knowledge, only once did the fourth African-Shawnee to wear the name Caesar attend meeting for worship at Caesar's Creek Meetinghouse. That occasion was in 1827, a few days after he and his wife had rescued my brothers and me from slavery and delivered us to the Fergusons' Underground Railroad station. From the midst of a deep silence, a man in the congregation stood up. "Because we treat them like the humans they are, never has a member of our Religious Society been killed by Indians."

I was impressed by the Quaker's words: not only had Quakers proved themselves friends to me and my family but they also appeared loving to Indians. When all other whites I had met held us in open contempt with men more rapists than Christian, and women complicit in every way, I felt such relief that I promised myself never to stray from the side of members of the Religious Society of Friends.

I still basked in the glow of false safety when at the supper table, Caesar said to our hosts, "Clark and Mary Crispin, I thought truth bearing was the Quaker way."

"Have we spoken falsely?" said Mary Crispin.

"Then let us make amends," said Clark.

"Not y'all," said Caesar. "That old man in meeting told a bald-faced lie. I fought with men that would have made him the first Quaker killed if it was possible."

My oldest brother Robin hit the shoulder of Dan, the middle sibling at the table, and smiled. I glared at his rudeness.

A silence ensued until Mary Crispin said, "I suppose thee is referring to what happened to the Slocums of Wilkes Barre."

"Them's the best known, but there were others before and after," said Caesar. The table grew deathly silent. I had never seen Caesar this angry at anything beyond slavery. Perhaps the same was true with the Ferguson family who had known him much longer. "All Quakers ain't been friends to my people."

"As for Frances Slocum," said Mary Crispin in her consistently calm voice, "when I was a child, she and the Lenape stopped by our home in Chillicothe."

"That home, like this one, was built on land stolen from us Shawnee. Took our land; kept our name."

"I understand thy points," said Clark, "but those soldiers who fought in the Revolutionary War were given the land by the Federal Government."

"Did it not seem wrong that without consulting the tribes," said Caesar's wife, Monni, "their land was given away?"

"My father said he always regretted that," said Mary Crispin. "He had defied his meeting for worship in New Jersey by joining in a war that our cousin Richard Stockton, signer of the Declaration of Independence, said would make all people free. For fighting, father was disowned."

"What's that mean, ma'am?" said Robin.

"It means by taking up arms—no matter for which side— he had broken our discipline and was no longer seen as Quaker."

"He was still a white man, though, wasn't he?" said Robin.

Instead of answering my incorrigible brother, Mary Crispin turned to Caesar. "Soon Father learned that slavery would remain even in New Jersey. Fed up with such poorly stitched fabric, he brought us to Ohio when I was a small girl. No one had told him his new land on the frontier was displacing those with older claim."

"Did he think that it was empty?" said Caesar.

Mary Crispin was a seamstress and often used metaphors that sprang from her work. "My father was not a hunter. He was a farmer. Although he never explained the whole cloth, I believe he thought there were enough checkers that he could settle on a small square, and whoever else lived on the frontier could settle on other squares."

"Should my father-in-law, a poor man, have taken his family back east?" said Clark, addressing Caesar.

"Is the east you are referring to New Jersey or England?" said Monni in a voice that sounded more naïve than I knew her to be.

The question brought a tense silence that Caesar eventually broke. "Those Lenape who took Frances Slocum were only in Ohio because their land already had been stolen in what y'all call New Jersey and Pennsylvania. As I recall, when y'all left England the big boat landed in Pennsylvania and then y'all moved to New Jersey. "

The exchange fascinated me, not as it thrilled my brother Robin who loved hearing anything negative about whites, but because I was young and hungry for knowledge, good or bad. Even in Goose Creek Friends School I had never heard of the Lenape. Were they kin to the Shawnee as the Ashanti were kin to the Fante, or were all Indians the same but called differently by those of us knew no better? Could I, a colored girl, now think of "us" and include any white folk? Monni explained that Lenape, Shawnee, Miami and many others were Algonquin. Robin added that many more than our ancestral Fante and the Ashanti were Akan. It bothered me that he was able to teach things about our original homeland that I had refused to learn. Even now I cannot remember all the names he listed.

"My father and others chose to remain but resist further evils," said Mary Crispin. "That is why every child in his family learned to speak Shawnee, and we have sheltered Shawnees as well as blacks."

Here was a portion of my answer. At least with these Fergusons, as with the Hoges before them, I could align myself with more than American slaves.

"I have not forgotten that I stayed here, and you nursed my wounds after The Battle of the Thames," said Caesar in a more conciliatory voice.

"We have been thanked many times," said Mary Crispin.

"Quaker born soldiers were there too," said Caesar. Robin almost laughed out loud but I gave him a look akin to our mother's dagger-glare, and he stifled himself. "But as for you Fergusons, I for one am happy to have *this* family here."

"That means the world to me," said Mary Crispin. Following a head-spinning silence she said, "Since thee guided her here, Caesar, thee knows Frances Slocum came later to this very house with her husband Shepoconah, 'Deaf Man'; her daughter Kekenakushwa, 'Cut Finger Comes Again'; and son-in-law Jean Baptiste Brouillette, whose father was a Frenchman."

"They needed a safe place to rest. Where better to send them than to recommend you Fergusons?" said Caesar.

"I told both mother and daughter how much I admired their silver rings and hairpins and embroidered dresses with silver broaches. Frances offered to exchange dresses with me, but I told her I might be disowned from our congregation if I were to dress so fancy, and someone might frown were she to dress so plainly. Instead of smiling at what I had intended as lightness, she seemed to become more cautious. Too late I remembered my mother saying refusing an Indian woman's gift is usually seen as a slight. I accepted later when she offered one of her rings. With her inspiration, from that time I have dressed a bit more gaily."

The pale orange dress Mary Crispin wore obviously had been made by a highly skilled woman—herself. Admittedly it was brighter than the Quaker-gray I had seen both in Virginia and the ones worn by others at that morning's worship service. Still it fell short of my definition of *gay*.

I learned that I was not nearly as smart as I had thought. "Did I miss something? From your earlier words I thought Frances Slocum was also born a Quaker?"

"That very day she revealed her heritage. Frances told us that being in our simple home reminded her that her family was Quaker. She obviously saw nothing important about such a birthright."

"It's not the birthright it's the do-right," said Clark who had converted to prove himself worthy of marrying Mary Crispin.

Mary Crispin smiled. "After we have cleaned the kitchen, Caesar, would thee tell us more of Frances Slocum's story?"

"If I can have some more of those summer peas," said Caesar in his joking way.

I laughed more than the occasion called for, and passed the peas. "Before we do our work, I would like to know if Frances acted more Indian or Quaker?"

"I would say," said Mary Crispin, "That people are people, but all in this room know that is the untruth. Ma-con-na-quah, which means in our words, 'Little Bear' was a white woman, who once was the Quaker child Frances Slocum. As an adult, she was fully Indian, Miami to be precise."

"Nothing of her former self remained?"

"I do not know her former self. The woman I knew had received her name because she could hunt, ride, and lariat horses as well as any man."

"Ma'am," said Robin. "I knows you is a good Quaker, but how can a woman do anything manly as well as the best man?"

"Manly?" said Mary Crispin, "I am not sure what thee means."

Robin retreated in himself, and the moment passed. The smallest child was nearly finished eating, signaling clean-up time. Mary Crispin pushed her chair back, and I said to her, "Another question, please. Did thee write to her family and tell them Frances Slocum had been found?"

"I like a woman who asks 'manly" questions," said Mary Crispin pausing to smile so kindly at Robin that he did not feel that he had been put in his place, at least until I teased him later that night. "As I said, Frances was fully Miami. Clark and I discussed the matter. Tell them what thee said, dear."

"I am from Scots-Irish stock. I have no desire to be drug back to

Scotland or Ireland. Now and until I die, I am an American."

"From her standpoint," said Mary Crispin, "the child born Frances Slocum was Ma-con-na-quah, the Miami."

◊◊◊◊◊◊

While clearing the table and sweeping the floor alongside Elizabeth, the oldest Ferguson girl, I reviewed what I had heard. It appeared to be a world unseamed. I cannot pretend I understood all, and it has taken years to tease out some truths that fell into crannies. Cleaning up quickly passed, and I went into the great room, settled in between my brothers so I could secretly signal to Dan what I deemed important and Robin when he might be better served by silence.

Caesar spoke to us. "My grandfather told me much of this story. In 1790 he was part of the Shawnees, Lenapes and Miamis who had defeated General Harmar. Although primarily an interpreter, he too had killed men, taken scalps, and freed some of the slaves traveling with the enemy. Grandfather was on his way to the great battle with General St. Clair when he stopped by a village on the Mississinewa River. Like many others I have known, this village had members from several different tribes: Pottawatomies as well as Shawnees, Lenapes, and Miamis. We love each other; should we not live together as friends? He and three other warriors were guests in the home of the woman born Frances Slocum and her new husband, Deaf Man who though he had lost his hearing during the battle, was made a war chief for his courage."

"You're a war chief, ain't you?" said Robin.

"A war chief needs warriors to lead," said Caesar.

After a short silence Monni said, "Little Bear's first husband was a Lenape. They were only together a short time before he moved west because he feared the Americans. Her second husband is a Miami resistor as my husband is a Shawnee resistor. Men need not kill and scalp to be men."

"But they do need to free slaves to be men," said Robin more as a pronouncement than a question.

"Yes," said Monni, "the same is true for women."

Language has always interested me, because our bored slave master had taught my father Latin as well as English. My father in turn had taught those of his children who wished to learn. "Then she spoke many languages?" I asked.

"Like my grandfather and his father before him, I too am an interpreter," said Caesar. "Most people I know speak many Indian languages. Grandfather said that because neither of Little Bear's husbands spoke English, she had lost most of her original language while learning at least four of ours."

"My parents were kidnapped in Fante-Land." I said, "Was she kidnapped in Pennsylvania and made a slave?"

"A Lenape who was there said that one of her brothers had fought against them," said Caesar.

"From that," said Monni, "they concluded Quakers not only were land thieves, they were also were liars to be feared as much as any other whites."

Caesar continued his story. "It was my grandfather who told Frances that soon after she had gone with the Lenape both her birth father and her mother's father were killed by Lenape. Her elders were Quaker members of a family that had betrayed our trust. This is well known. Why the man who spoke in meeting said otherwise I do not know. But unlike your parents, Sarah, she was not stolen to be a slave. She was adopted by a family whose daughter was about her age when the Americans raided a Lenape village and killed her. She was even originally given that child's name. By the time my grandfather reached her village on the Mississinewa, she had been taught to mistrust whites. She asked Grandfather, 'Are you a black white man?' Grandfather said, 'I am a Black Shawnee.' She smiled and said, 'I have known Black Lenape, Black Wyandot and Black Miami'."

"I bet she didn't say, 'I'm a White Miami,'" said Robin.

"She claimed no whiteness," said Caesar. My freckled brother clapped his hands then quickly grabbed my wrist before I could pinch him.

Caesar went on to explain that his own grandfather would not have claimed blackness because he had been born to a Shawnee mother and had always lived among them. We learned that almost 100 Christian and unarmed Indians had been massacred in 1782 by whites at a place in Ohio called Moravian town and that the story of that tragedy had been passed down among all of the tribes. Little Bear knew this but never expressed shame, for she no longer understood herself as white.

I said, "Where is she now?"

"She is still on the Mississinewa in nearby Indiana."

"Is that the end of the story?" said Dan.

"How can the story end when we are still here?"

I believed this was an appropriate place to end the night because Mary Crispin had already demonstrated that females in her home were expected to rise before dawn.

"Didn't you say your granddaddy was on his way to a battle?" asked Robin.

"He was," said Caesar. "And what a battle it was. A combined army of Miamis, Shawnees, and Lenapes defeated General St. Clair's army. It was our greatest victory. Nearly 1000 Americans were killed."

"How many scalps did you take?" asked Robin.

"I was not yet born! How old do you think I am?" I heard a few chuckles. "I was born at the time of our defeat at Fallen Timbers where Tecumseh's brother was killed."

"Did the tribes' British allies really close the gates to the fort to the Shawnee?" said Clark.

"We were allied with many tribes, but the Americans had Choctaw and Chickasaw scouts who had spied on us. Yes, the British betrayed us, but they were not the only ones. If tribes like the Choctaw, Chickasaw, and Cherokee had stood beside us, this land would still be ours, and the Shawnee would not have been split between Tecumseh's warriors and

Black Hoof's followers who decided to lay down their weapons."

"I would have gone with the warriors' side," said Robin.

"Me too," said Dan.

I surrendered to my desire to control my brothers, "And you, Caesar, which side did you choose?"

"I fought my first battle at The Battle of the Thames where Tecumseh was killed and my last at Horseshoe Bend where Jackson tricked the Cherokee nation into fighting against us. Now I am a man of peace, one who rescues those held in slavery. I do not kill, but I am still a man who fights evil."

"It is through my husband's resistance, that you three escaped slavery," said Monni. "And it is through her resistance that despite many Miami being pushed west, Frances Slocum remains on the Mississinewa as Little Bear."

Caesar turned to Robin and smiled. "What besides that a warrior may sometimes be pinched by a sister, did you learn?"

Everyone except Robin laughed. Deliberately he said, "I'm a resistor." Some stared at him until he added. "I resisted slavery before I was free, and now that I'm a free man, let some fool try to take me back."

NAVIGATING LIMITATIONS

After a storm aided flight from slavery we had arrived in Waynesville, Ohio, a Quaker enclave. Other enslaved peoples had made the trip from our home state of Virginia, Kentucky, and points deeper in slave territory. Some had continued on moving further from the slave line, many to Indiana, others to Michigan and even Canada. At age 13, I was the youngest of the three escaped children of Esi and Kofi, but I was also the most self-assured and the only girl. I liked the Ferguson family that had taken us in and was in no hurry to try life among strangers who would probably either be hateful whites or fearful colored folk. Caesar and Monni the Shawnees who had led our escape were clear that kidnapping was prevalent everywhere we went, but Quakers were the whites most likely to resist the catchers and treat us like humans.

We had just received our forged free papers when Mary Crispin Ferguson said to her son Charles, "Here is a list of things I would have thee pick up from the open air market in Waynesville. Thy father and older brothers are using the wagons to take produce to Springboro, so thee can take our new friends on foot to help carry the bags."

Robin, my oldest brother, had never been to town. That did not stop him from being in the lead, walking the same way as people off to market. Dan joined him, and I walked beside my brothers while, despite his mother's directions that he "take" us, Charles brought up the rear.

On the way, my brothers openly scoped women and whispered judgments on their merits. They were often sickening when it came to such opinions, so I followed my usual practice when they were on a roll: I ignored them and daydreamed about who I might become if America gave me half a chance.

I had just ended a fictional chapter of my life when Robin said, "The ones I seen look a bit better than the Virginy gals."

"I haven't seen a one that can stand up to Zephyrine or Eve," said Dan. "Some of them don't even seem to know they're pretty.""

"Don't be no fool, Dan. Ain't a pretty woman on this here earth don't already know she pretty."

I said, "You boys would not know beauty if it were standing next to a hog."

"If you's the one you calling 'beauty'," said Robin, "most *men* I know would saddle up next to the hog."

"I can see you are in one of your teasing minds." I increased my gait.

"Look at them little spindly legs go! Thin as a pin, narrow as a sparrow," said Robin.

I acted as though I didn't hear him and continued heading in the direction of the small crowd of walkers and wagons. Before we had fled slavery I could have remained beside them simply by threatening to tell Mama about both their conversation and a few other pieces of information that I always made certain they knew I had in my possession. Trying to outrun the pain of having no mother to protect me, I increased my gait yet again.

"Slow down," called Dan.

"I'll be happy to walk with thee!" said Charles in a loud voice.

"I know you will," said Robin, "but you won't! She okay by herself long as I can see her."

I was several yards ahead and about to pass five white teenagers when one said, "Hey, Meg, can I stroke your leg?"

I do not know if Robin heard him, but when the others laughed and he approached me, Robin hurried to my side. "That's my sister, cracker."

"What do I care about who you are?" said the teenager who had addressed me.

"If you set foot on my farm you better have 'nough sense to watch how you step," said Robin in a low growl.

The teenager pushed him. Before we knew what had happened Robin hit him in the jaw, and the attacker was out cold. The downed teenager's friends rushed to revive him. One asked the others, "Should we jump the nigger? It's five of us."

"Five? Richard is just coming awake."

The four turned to see my brothers and Charles standing at the ready. "It's still only two Nigras and a Quaker boy in his beaver hat."

We were shocked when Charles said, "You want to try this Quaker." He assumed a boxer's stance.

Richard had sufficiently shaken cobwebs from his brain. "I am to blame. I approached their sister."

"You boys just saved your own lives," said Robin. They stood aside. This time I walked between my brothers. Fortunately they chose to speak more respectably in my presence.

◊◊◊◊◊◊

A few weeks later, Mary Crispin watched me cross the yard on my way to water garden vegetables. I sensed I was being observed and turned and met her eyes. The sun shone, I was safe, far removed from any bully boys, and certain Robin's unseemly behavior had been spread far and wide. I smiled and waved more at the world than at the loveable mistress of the farm. Then I skipped over to the house with the water bucket still on my head.

"Thy bucket never lost a drop," she warmly said.

I laughed. My brother Dan is so agile that he once ran several steps up the side of a barn. I never complimented the show-off but I did appreciate his skill. "Compared to Dan's physical tricks, this is nothing, Miss Mary Crispin—"

"Please, dear Sarah, thee knows we don't stand on the formal. Thee and thy brothers are with equals at the Ferguson home. My heart would be enlarged if thee would use but 'Mary Crispin'. Surely, thee did not call Mary Pool Hoge by some title?"

'No ma'am. She was 'Aunt Mary Pool'."

"And I do not merit 'Aunt'?" Mary Crispin laughed. Left unsaid was the fact that she had given us sanctuary and work when we were fugitives from injustice. I also did not touch the fact that Aunt Mary Pool was the first white woman to prove to me that they could be civilized both in deed and word. First is special. I did not need Robin to trumpet that truth.

Robin had overheard my conversation with Mary Crispin because he practiced his trade outside the little house we three siblings shared. Later he said to me, "It'd be better if'n she coulda said, 'equals in this here *world*'."

"Are you never satisfied?" I asked.

"As long as we be living limits, we ain't living whole. Quakers think if they make it right on their piece of ground, it's right ev'rywhere and them that's being stepped on oughtta shut up! That's why I had to knock some sense into that fool's head when we got sent to town."

Robin was restless, sure of nothing but his ability to make excellent shoes, fight, please the average girl, and need to be wary of everything white. He even managed to maintain clear distance between himself, the Fergusons, and Patience Starbuck who paid him to make shoes for any barefoot runaways or common wanderers who might come our way. How could we hope to realize Daddy's dream of being accepted Americans if we insisted on constructing walls?

Dan was easier with Ohio because it was not slave territory. He was not totally blind because we had discussed Caesar's and Monni's warning that unless people of color were among Quakers, the state rarely pretended to be welcoming. My brothers had already ventured to nearby Cincinnati. There, they said, people of color lived without illusions of being accepted even in their own homes. We were north of the Ohio River but well south of Eden. My brothers informed me that group attacks, individual lashings, and slaver raids along the main streets were daily occurrences from Cincinnati north to the Canadian border. Dan was literate and read any newspaper he could get his hands on. He said any newspaper's report on an outrage was more pageantry than balanced. They spun stories to make the victims take the blame in a self-induced tragedy whose final scene they wanted to occur on our return to the African continent. Never did they mention that we had not come here willingly. We had been kidnapped and not paid for making their lives more comfortable.

Mary Crispin and Patience Starbuck told me that the Quaker communities in Warren, Clinton, and Highland Counties were anomalies. By the late 1820s, they sheltered more than two dozen safe havens for escaping slaves. This fact was like water in a drought for Dan and me. Robin wanted more. He wanted equal rights and justice, not merely a desire for the gradual, peaceful abolition of slavery. He longed for Quaker commitment to take up arms and fight for emancipation. Most Quakers he had met fell short of his demands. He even told us privately that if a fight had occurred, he doubted Charles would do more than hide behind his back.

"Surely you recognize Quakers are on the cutting edge," Dan pointed out.

"That 'cutting edge' sounds good," Robin had grumbled. "But I wanna be edging on slicing not just be cut up like some wormy tobaccy."

They would argue the nature of our place in the world. Then the tension would ease with a good-natured wrestling match or me breaking into a work song whose lyrics I had changed. For one such song, I sang both lead and chorus. Originally it was "Shuck That Corn 'fore You Eat." I renamed it, "Let Your Mind Dance, Make It True."

> All the freedom you have dreamed,
> Let your mind dance, make it true.

Life can make the milk be creamed,
Let your mind dance, make it true.

When you're ready for the right,
Let your mind dance, make it true.

Don't let sadness cover light,
Let your mind dance, make it true.

We're the three that made it out,
Let your mind dance, make it true.

Welcome grace; don't sit and pout,
Let your mind dance, make it true.

While singing my song, I always laughed, lifted my skirt and danced a quick-paced African-flavored version of a stomp dance that I had learned on Fruits of the Spirit from Eula who had once been a Cherokee slave. The first time Robin heard how I had transformed the lyrics from a work song that he had despised as a slave, he actually laughed and clapped his hands in time. Later he caught himself humming the song and became angered. Having convinced himself that life was his principal opponent, he was committed to killing hope.

Dan sat between Robin and me, sometimes humoring me by joining in my Latin studies, although his mastery was well below mine; loving me although more than once he called me "hopelessly naïve"; chasing women with Robin, although his energy in that capacity far outstripped that of our older brother; empathizing with him, although he knew clearly that economic success could never be found by railing at the world. Like both of us, he was haunted by the loss of every other person we had called family.

"What would Mama and Daddy say if they were here?" was a

question Dan and I frequently asked.

Sometimes Robin mused along with us. At other times he would snort, "If 'if' was tobaccy, we could smoke Washington."

◊◊◊◊◊◊

One Saturday afternoon Mary Crispin and Patience worked together on a patchwork quilt. They were easy with Mary Crispin's greater dexterity and Patience's penchant for daydreaming. Mary Crispin's hands worked non-stop. She could sew, nurse a child, or discipline one of the older ones while carrying on a deep discourse. Sometimes Patience would simply stop her work and stare out the window or speak about ways to improve the world. I was in the room, quietly working on the morrow's meal. During one of the many pauses in conversation, Mary Crispin said to me, "Why so contemplative this bright afternoon?"

"I was thinking about the way you and your husband touch."

"Is it new to thee?" asked Patience.

"My parents touched often, but seldom in public. And because of how they were worked, it was rare for them to see each other in daylight. If it was more than a moment, it usually was Sunday, Christmas time, or Prescott's birthday."

"Did their touch make thee uncomfortable?" said Mary Crispin.

"No. It was just their way."

"And touching is our way."

"Mary Crispin, what does 'our' mean?" I asked. "I've spent years around the Hoges and other Quakers; spent my life watching the Prescotts and other white folk. In my experience, whites hardly ever touch unless it's shaking hands. You're the first two white people I've ever seen who give evidence of feeling passion for each other."

"Then the non-touchers are all slaves!" said Mary Crispin.

"How so?" asked Patience.

"Slaves to appearances and voluntary at that."

"What a notion!" said Patience.

"Tell me, Friend Patience, did thee see touching and such in thy home?"

"My mother was sickly, died young, and my stepmother was as stiff as a table."

"Thee had other relatives and neighbors. Did they touch?"

"They would sooner have danced in meeting than let their brood see them touch."

"And from whence doth thee think that 'brood' came?" said Mary Crispin.

"I am unmarried not innocent," said Patience.

We all laughed and returned to our labors. I finished plucking the third chicken and said, "Ma'am, who is to cook these birds?"

Before Mary Crispin could answer, Patience said, "I thought I would take a hand at stewing them with those fine onions, summer squash, and tomatoes the boys brought in."

"If you don't mind, Mary Crispin," I said, "may I use the little flour left to cook one of the chickens the way my mother taught me how to fry them in oil? She was a fine cook."

"I had promised my sweet-toothed children I would bake a cake tomorrow morning," said Mary Crispin.

"I heard your promise; I've already set aside more than enough flour for your cake."

Mary Crispin clapped her hands and said, "Why then, let there be fried chicken!"

"And biscuits?" I asked. "It seemed to me I could make a couple of dozen biscuits and the chicken, and you could do the cake before the milling."

"Why, child," said Mary Crispin, "thou art on the way to being a woman, with all of thy figuring." Again we laughed. I recognized that there was a special bond between us and said a silent prayer that it would last throughout eternity.

◊◊◊◊◊◊

Mary Crispin and Patience walked to the porch swing where they fanned themselves from mosquitoes and enjoyed the night breeze. I finished my chores and seated myself on the porch watching fireflies, reminiscing about Sunday nights on Fruits of the Spirits. Background to all was the younger Ferguson children playing night games and simply listening to the crickets and frogs.

"I love summer nights," said Patience. "But sometimes I get lonely."

A child's obviously affected scream pierced the air and Mary Crispin said, "May I offer thee three or four or five of my finest?" After laughter, she added, "I implore thee to rear them to be great whisperers and trust that even if they should not obey, thee will never be lonely."

Patience laughed. "Thee knows that I was not made to be a family woman."

"I know no such thing," said Mary Crispin.

"Oh, I was fine as a sister to brothers, maybe even as a daughter, but Nantucket and her whaling took family out of me the day I learned my father and two brothers went down."

"It's a hard story, thine." Mary Crispin placed her arm inside Patience's.

"Not as hard as that of the three self-stolen siblings." My ears perked up.

"To compare pain, Friend Patience, is to do ourselves a disservice. There always seems to be some soul more unfortunate. We need not have our Ahab to have our downfall."

"Truly, but those poor children have such a cross. Where is their crown?"

A line had been crossed. "Excuse me," I said, "but are you talking about me even as I sit here?"

"Have we offended?" asked Patience.

"Only in behaving as though I am absent as you thread through my life."

"Then the fault is mine, Sarah," said Patience.

"Thee was not alone," said Mary Crispin quickly. "I too offer an apology. We have acted outside of proper respect."

I was so taken by having the two white women apologize that I was speechless. To my knowledge, in all my years on Fruits of the Spirit Plantation Miss Anne had neither apologized nor thanked slave nor overseer.

"Are we forgiven?" said Patience.

I regained my composure. "Only if you continue sharing *your* story."

Mary Crispin chuckled and leaned back. "Thee should have been a mother, Patience."

"The last time I saw my father," said Patience, "I told him I wished I had been born a boy. I am too soft to be a mother or a wife, Mary Crispin. I watch thee rule this Ferguson clan, and know I could not imitate thee in obeying the Creator and serving my family."

"An imitator is not a child of the Light!" said Mary Crispin. "Thee thinks too highly of my little and too little of thy greatness. To be Patience, thee must have faith *and* patience."

"Does thee have an opinion on the topic, Sarah?" asked Patience.

I had insisted on redirecting the conversation, but it took a while to find something meaningful to say. "We people of color will have our crown one day. I will not go to my grave a nonentity." I waited to see if they would say anything to this brash statement by a fourteen year old with neither credits nor surname, but they were silent. "As well," I added, attempting levity, "I agree that patience is a good thing regardless of one's name."

They laughed before Patience said, "I have a new batch of letters waiting."

She left and Mary Crispin studied me a moment while I pretended not to notice. Then she said, "Come, child. Sit with me for a time."

I had always thought that the swing was reserved for Mary Crispin either with her husband or Patience Starbuck. None of the Ferguson children sat on it unless their parents were out of sight. I walked over and stood quietly; perhaps she would change her mind. "Would thee care to sit, or am I presuming too much again? I know thee, but I do not know the ways of thy family."

I was pleased that she did not say my 'people'. I thought I knew myself but was aware I did not know the world. I knew well only people in a corner of Culpeper County, and even though I had studied for a time with a handful of colored children in Loudon County it did not make me an expert on their ways. Without saying anything, I sat down. Mary Crispin said, "Would thee like to swing?" Before I could answer, she pushed off the floor with her feet. I found myself enjoying a new sensation, moving as free as a white woman, unburdened by invisible walls and feeling I deserved happiness. Our laughter melted away.

I waited, thinking we would have a natural Quaker silence. Instead, Mary Crispin said, "Thee came poor and empty into our family, and yet thee hast a mild, peaceable spirit. If way opened, Sarah, who might thee be?" Forswearing spending life as a nonentity, I had opened the subject, it was I who led us into fresh silence. I bowed my head and retreated within. Mary Crispin allowed the shortest silence that I have ever shared with a Quaker. Again she said, "Who might thee be?"

"I am who I am, and I will be who I will be.'"

A less secure woman might have been offended. But Mary Crispin laughed. She knew I was not trying to be disrespectful. "Yes." She hugged me. Touch is as marvelous as nature's various nighttime songs. Her hugs were softer than my mother's, not even as firm as Mary Pool's, but in warmth they were equally comfortable. I trusted her and knew she loved me. Mary Crispin sat back, retaining her smile. I felt easy with answering her original question.

"I don't now know myself. My fears are that the world is more magnificent than I will ever know, and that the attempt to find my way through it will bring more pain than joy. Perhaps I should remain where I'm safe."

"The Spirit has knit and united us together. Child, as long as I breathe, in the flesh, or in thy heart, I pray that Mary Crispin Ferguson may be with thee through thy great work and that safety may not become a beacon. Only the Light has the power to fear nothing and can provide true safety. Resist all evil that would limit thee."

FOUR DIFFERENT WAYS

My sister Fannie was sold from Culpeper, Virginia by Miss Anne Prescott to a slaver who took her to Washington, D.C. and sold her to a western Kentucky breeder. The Kentuckian made his fortune by selling offspring down river to Mississippi and Louisiana. Fannie said that daily she and the other women on the plantation had to convince themselves that they were human and of more value than the horses that were the master's pride and joy.

Fannie chose the right moment and fled. On the way north an untamed white Kentuckian named John Fairchild aided her. He was on one of his frequent rescuing forays through the south hoping to free slaves and make life hard for wealthy whites. Fairchild happened upon her in central Kentucky then sent her to a colored woman who sneaked her all the way to Covington, Kentucky, just across the Ohio River from Cincinnati and non-slave territory.

◊◊◊◊◊◊

Fannie inched along a dark and rutted street. At a black oak tree, distinguished by scent and feel, she did as Fairchild had instructed and turned left. Stepping through puddles and offal, she arrived at a tiny, windowless log cabin. She knocked in the magical one-two-three-four pattern. Inside chatter went quiet. She waited a while and repeated one-two-three-four. All three residents met her at the door and greeted her warmly.

"Nobody comes to see us but the Lord's children," said Samantha, the unofficial leader of the trio.

Nothing that Fannie had heard before taking flight on what would one day be named the Underground Railroad suggested that three old colored women on the jagged side of the border might be conductors.

Over pork fat back, neck bones, and grease on biscuits Fannie learned that the trio's masters had conspired at a ball to maximize their profits by each freeing a woman far beyond her prime years. The unholy trinity of masters would, "Bear a part of purchasing the cost of a shack and donate a month's worth of food." Judging themselves responsible providers, they could hold their head up in the white community as role models.

"I heard it all," said Trudy, "and all I said was, 'Choose me'."

"Did they give you any money?" Fannie asked.

"They 'gave' us $2 each," said Trudy.

"That's all?"

Samantha said, "Carrie's master dared to say, 'Now you got incentive to work or die'."

"I don't know what they Hell they thought we'd been doing for more'n 150 years," said Trudy.

"You don't have to cuss," said Carrie, "and that many years is counting all three of us."

"You too good for your own good," said Trudy smiling wanly. "It was two winters ago when Master let me go. The sadness in this house weighed me down, and I'd heard the ice on the Ohio River was so thick you could walk across to Cincinnati. I upped and tried. Some young bully boys threw snowballs with rocks inside at me. What was the use? I turned back."

"Them or their fathers was probably born in Kentucky," said Samantha.

"Right there in the middle of the ice," said Carrie, "her longtime dream melted."

My sister had dreams that she intended to fulfill, not melt. Trudy chose otherwise. She turned back and settled in with the Carrie and Samantha.

"You don't need Cincinnati to be free, Fannie, not if you can find a way to get some free papers here…But finding a Kentucky judge to help would be like finding newborn pea seeds birthed in a pail of pig piss. Me? I have my prim and proper papers, and I've settled my mind to stay put. Look what happened when I tried to run."

Carrie told her a story of being born in New England where her grandfather was kidnapped during "The War for Their Independence." He was taken to New Jersey then on to Maryland where she was born to his third family. As a teenager she was sold to Virginia and then to Kentucky. I have heard of peregrinations with more stops, but Fannie said few have been told with more sadness. Relatives and friends were lost all along the way. When Fannie asked her where she had lived in Virginia she learned that it was in Winchester, a town I knew but my sister did not. Trudy had been a slave in Richmond, the city where her mother had been brought after being kidnapped. Neither woman had heard of Culpeper, the place where we were born.

For the rest of the evening they exchanged names of relatives, searching for the lost ones who they hoped were also searching for them, recalling plantation names chosen to sound like pieces of heaven, when, in the four women's minds, they were little more than Satan's domain. The time came to blow out candles. In the morning each said that she had slept more fitfully than normal.

Carrie spent most of her days rocking in a decrepit rocking chair that had been retrieved from someone's trash. She sewed rents in clothing, smoked, or let her pipe hang tobacco-free as she chewed on the ends, like a woman biting her fingernails. Sometimes she spoke of things my sister did not even want to imagine. One day, interrupting the conversation of others she said without apology, "It's best not to talk 'bout them days."

The room grew quiet in anticipation. "Them days when such happened to us that ought to be brushed from rememory." Rejecting her own counsel, she continued, "My son runned away with my secret blessing. Patrollers caught him and brought him back. He was beat everywhere 'cept 'tween his toes. Then he got sold to Mississippi. I expect I'll see him one day in the great up yonder."

Fannie was surprised when, without comment, the conversation continued where it had been left. How could things like the weather and a preacher's sermon take precedence over a woman's heartbreak? She dropped out of the conversation and listened, wondering if there would ever be a time of freedom.

In what passed for a lighter moment Trudy said, "From the time I was a l'il gal, people was lousy. I wasn't no more'n four when my introduction to work was morning, noon, and evening, picking lice off the damned master and his family. Mama said they wasn't better than us, so at night, I did the same thing for all my kin folk. Then Mama done me. Mama was as clean as they come. You couldn't even think 'bout climbing in her bed without washing yo' feet, and she made her soap with wild rose petals. Smelled so good I bet Satan wanted some."

Carrie said, "Satan might've wanted some, but my Mama said the Good Lord wouldn't give that slimy rat anything that could ease."

Trudy said, "Yo' mama was right. I recall a song mine used to sing.

Once upon a time you said a vow,
telling my dear Mama and all the rest
never in this world should their kin be sold,
not for pieces of silver nor for gold,
so long as the Lord's sun goes east to west.

"Hardly a single year has passed now
That we ain't watching go down the dusty road
a loved one bound to the deep south.
We trusted words from yo' own mouth.
Master, oh Lord, too heavy is this load.

"I sure 'nough wish I could understand how
to gather and clutch to this breaking breast
the loved ones I was given to birth and growed."

"There must be ninety eleven songs in the world," said Carrie. "Why'd you have to sing that one?"

"I sing to ease and hope to please," said Trudy in a softer voice than Fannie had heard her use. She paused briefly. "It helps to know you ain't the only one been wronged."

"Let the church say, 'Amen'!" said Samantha. "And let the church not be so melancholy."

Once when Fannie mentioned how much she loved her father, Carrie was moved. "My pappy lived a few miles away. We seen him on Sundays in good weathers, but when the cold weather set in we'd do good to see him more than once a month. He'd say, 'even love don't like cold.' He used the word love with cold. I seen it as proof he loved us."

The story fell short of Fannie's measure of love. Wanting to make a deeper impression, Carrie added, "Child, you wanna hear how I caught my husband? He was always eyeing me, but I never paid no never mind 'til one day I said, 'Ed, every morning I come out to slop hogs I look up and see you eyeballing something. Could it be you in love with one of these sows? Point her out, and I'll be happy to make the introductions.' He was so surprised he almost wet his drawers."

This time all of the women laughed, and Carrie said, "I been saving that one up. These two ladies thought they'd heard it all. Wrong! Stick 'round; I got more where that one come from." They laughed again. "That's 'xactly what I told Ed. Many is the night I wet his drawers for real."

"Religious folk also have a sense of humor?" asked Samantha.

"Jehovah is a God of love not hate," said Carrie.

◊◊◊◊◊◊

Sunday was the third day. The trio put on the best of their dresses and flowered hats and went to church. Without a free paper Fannie was confined to the hut. To come this far and be arrested when Nyame could be worshipped anywhere made no sense. In their absence, Fannie gave the house a thorough house cleaning and prepared a chicken pot pie. Mid-afternoon they returned from worship with a young woman carrying an extremely light skinned baby.

Fannie wanted to ask the new woman if she were no longer a slave how had she won her emancipation or did she have to leave before curfew to return to her master? Those questions were as forbidden as, "Who fathered your baby?" South or north, no colored woman controlled her own body in 1828. More than thirty years later, it's still true. We live knowing even our husbands have no recourse beyond being lynched or standing aside when we are assaulted. Violation is commonplace, yet I have never heard of a white man being tried for, let alone convicted of, raping a black woman.

While the older women played with the baby, Priscilla said to Fannie, "They need new life to bring them joy." When Fannie did not comment, she said, "I brought some new life for you." From a gunny sack bag she withdrew a neatly folded dress and handed it to Fannie.

"I can't accept this. We don't even know each other."

Priscilla smiled. "We're about the same size."

"Size ain't the problem."

"Do you think you're the first somebody to accept kindness from a stranger?"

"Get on up and try it on," said Trudy.

"Do child," said Samantha.

Fannie was still reluctant until Carrie said, "Priscilla has her part just as we do. We're in this world together."

◊◊◊◊◊◊

Samantha put down her Bible and suddenly said to Fannie, "You don't read letters do you?"

"I didn't really wanna learn. Daddy invited me many a time, but I was a Mama's gal and she ain't had a use for letters."

Samantha explained that reading allowed her to think new thoughts. One was the wrongness of stripping memories of Africa from her parents' minds. When Fannie said that she had been one of our parents' children who knew the old stories, Samantha said she had sensed as much and then added, "For a colored woman, reading might free your mind, it won't free your body. And there's many a master who will not tolerate a reader."

She had been taught to read by, "A old white man Christian named Alexander Joiner. He taught me with a Bible, his only book. I'd sneak out of the quarters barefoot and gather pine knots. I'd take a bunch of pine knots, and we'd light them to serve as candles. That good man taught me to read as some somebody taught him when he was apprenticed as a joiner. He was one of the indentured white men."

"Truth be told," said Trudy, "a indentured white man ain't no more than a slave who knows his sun will rise."

"I ain't doing a good job of it," said Samantha. "Least ways, you ain't catching on. Now that I know reading no man can snatch it away. You cannot learn now because Joiner ain't here, and I don't want you to linger long enough for me to teach you. Lingering is like too much whiskey: it clouds your mind. Ours is a sad life not meant for a youngster like you. Here, you can't even to go to market when we mind poor white folks' stalls who wouldn't be caught dead selling next to a colored person. You could not even go to church last Sunday. Leave. And soon as you get over, Fannie, get some kind soul to teach you to read and find some brand new thoughts that'll lead to a better world than this shadowland."

"I got you some new shoes," said Trudy. "Payment for working a stall for some poor white lady. Too big for anybody else I know, but you can have 'em in freedom with that new dress Priscilla gave you." She went to the corner where her few possessions were kept and returned smiling.

Fannie was at a loss for words.

Samantha said, "Child, don't you dare leave here feeling bad for us. We will not be dying in slavery, and each breath you take up north will be a whole free pie split four different ways."

THE ORIGINAL JIM CROW

Fannie trembled in the cellar of her two-room shack. Fading light filtered through the weathered boards. Dusk was at last descending on August 15, 1829. It had been a while since the last scream had made her clutch closer her little dog Taffy. Now the only sound was the occasional curses of varying sized groups of bully boy who cursed and congratulated themselves as they roamed the streets in search of other ugliness. My 17 year-old sister exhaled and closed her eyes, hoping to nap. Not long afterwards she heard singing.

> "Come listen, all you gals and boys,
> I'm going to sing a little song,
> My name is Jim Crow.
> Wheel about and turn about and do just so.
> Every time I wheel about I jump, Jim Crow.
> I'm a monkey shinin'
> dancer of the galoppade;
> and when I'm through
> I rests my head on shovel, hoe or spade."

This was no nightmare. Her little dog whined and moved closer. Down the streets of Cincinnati came a man who she would later learn was named Thomas Rice. His song was destined to become an anthem. For the next several days, with painted black face, he presented himself as what he deemed a typical black man: he staggered as though drunk; bellowed as though disturbing the peace was his birthright; assured those who hate us that their behavior was well-founded.

The last strains of "Jump Jim Crow" trailed away. Near midnight Fannie and Taffy emerged and went into the body of the house along Deer Creek, close to the slaughterhouses. The heavy, blood-weighted breeze nearly gagged her. The earlier human screams had forewarned her that more spilled blood and guts than that of pigs, chicken, and cattle layered the air.

Removed from sight, a child sang the minstrel's song. 'Nyame, how many lyrics can the mind hold?' thought Fannie.

With less compassion than a butcher might have shown in carving a nameless beast, the bully-boys had taken her neighbor Mr. Smith's life. Had they despised him for taking her in or being a successful store owner? Had they hung him for teaching her how to read and write? What would have happened to her had she not moved out of his house after her laundry business got off the ground? If she had encouraged him to leave in the spring when the politicians said they were going to enforce the Black Law requirement that colored people post a $500 bond against the first time they might be arrested, would he still be alive? When the Cincinnati Daily Gazette ran all the hateful editorials, should she have counseled him to leave? Should she have left herself? Where safe could she have gone? Where was Nyame? Was He back in Fante-land sipping coconut milk under a palm tree, or scratching his head befuddled? Did Nyame simply refuse to supply answers or at least those that brought ease? Did he even care? Was questioning without the possibility of sane answers worth the effort?

Fannie had seen Mr. Smith drug from his house toward a lynching tree. His wife tried to stop them until two men nearly ripped her dress off, and Marie screamed to Fannie, "Run!"

Country born and bred, Fannie knew that nature is both creation and self-destruction in motion. Teachings of Esi, our mother, jarred Fannie back to dealing with the present. The unseen child was singing louder and obviously heading in the direction of her house. "I cut so many monkey shines, I dance the galoppade; and when I'm done, I rest my head, on shovel, hoe or spade."

Ignoring her own safety Fannie ran out of her house and grabbed the child's arm, "Honey, don't you know that hateful song is making fun of us?"

"Ma'am, I like it."

"But it doesn't like you."

The boy thought a few seconds and said, "What should I do? Them bully boys done drug my daddy away, and I don't know where Momma is. I been back home four times. They trashed it and I'm all alone."

She brought the boy into her house and turned her energy to comforting him.

◊◊◊◊◊◊

Fannie's beau, Ethan Jefferson, saw the trouble earlier than most. In the midst of his milk delivery rounds, he stepped off a porch only to be surrounded by armed white men. "Here's one of them niggers that's taking all the good jobs then being paid so little we can't make enough to live on," said a scruffy bully up from New Orleans. "Let's beat his head 'til it ropes like okra." Ethan was pummeled, kicked and spat upon.

"Stop. Stop I say!" shouted down one of Ethan's customers, running from his house in response to the screams. "This nigger works for Wiedermann who owns that big dairy in Price Hill. He's the first delivery boy I've known who always gets my milk here on time. There's a hundred niggers that needs beating more than him." To break the tension he added with a laugh, "None of you sorry rascals will help me feed my 13 kids."

The bully boys grabbed a large canister of milk, took long drinks, perhaps hoping to cool all of the whiskey inside, and moved off, seeking another target. Ethan limped to his cart and carried his rescuer's milk into his house where he deposited it before returning to the dairy. Unilaterally he canceled milk deliveries. Fortunately for him, Adalbert Wiedermann was compassionate. "Why risk your head and my milk?" he said to Ethan. "Stay home until I send for you."

Even sadists tire of beating, maiming, shooting, lynching, and raping, and this mob was made up of ordinary citizens. Ethan waited for the quelling and sneaked out to search for Fannie. Fearing the worst, he knocked more softly than usual on her door. She did not answer. "Fannie! Fannie darling! It's me."

Here was Fannie's knight come to rescue. She weighed in ascending order what she knew of Ethan together with what she thought the present moment seemed to reveal were his virtues: he was caring, handsome, clean, ambitious, patient, assiduous, and free. 'How blessed I am to be loved in times like these,' she thought. She rose from her place in a corner and removed the rope latch from around the nail. Taffy growled before trotting off to relieve himself.

"Who is that crouched in the corner?"

"It's Tommy. He hid with me. Come here, Tommy. Meet my man."

"He look white to me!"

"I am only almost white," said Ethan.

"Mama said 'almost white mean all the way nigger'."

Ethan blushed. "You should run along and find your mother."

"Is it safe out there?" said Fannie.

"If it were not I would not be here."

Tommy gave Fannie a hug and ran out the door.

"What was that about?" said Ethan.

"He hid in here with me because we were both afraid, and he thought I could protect him."

Ethan laughed at the thought that his delicate fiancé could protect anyone. Fannie settled on a chair at the table. He spent the next hour telling her about his exploits and finally asked how she had fared. When she told him her escape from harm was mitigated by Mr. Smith being lynched and his wife both raped and dragged away, Ethan said, "An old woman was ravaged but nobody touched you? Were you hiding?"

"Of course I was hiding."

He appeared disgusted as though an assault might have validated her worth. Fannie was momentarily dazed more by his questioning her being untouched as though undesirable.

"Will you look for Marie?"

"Surely you jest," said Ethan. "I almost was lynched while minding my own business. I wouldn't risk a pinky busying myself on some stranger's affairs."

◊◊◊◊◊◊

Half the colored residents of Cincinnati began an exodus from the city. Hundreds would end up in Canada. Others would become refugees in the Ohio countryside or head west. A few even went east, and at least one—the Smiths' next door neighbor—sought safety in Kentucky. The misprision of city officials went unchallenged. Legal or even political ramifications for not protecting victims of color would only be realized in the dreams and private conversations of colored people. Each time someone in Fannie's presence whispered they wished the roles were reversed she said, "If we were them we'd act civilized."

"Them?" said a friend. "Most of the ones we thought was Cincinnati's best either looked the other way or joined the mob! I've told you more than once, we need to get outta town just like our friends did."

"I may not love Cincinnati, but I do love myself," said Fannie. "When I leave, it will be with my self-respect, not because the evil ran me out."

A CALL TO LEAVING

Caesar's Creek Friends Meeting gathered on June's first First-day of the month, 1832. Dressed in silk, Patience Starbuck was the only woman in the assembly not wearing linen and together with Mary Crispin Ferguson she also did not wear a plain gray dress. Both sartorial rebels enjoyed quoting Margaret Fell Fox that uniform dress was "a silly poor gospel." Mary Crispin was in a new two-toned dress made of leftover greens from my illegal wedding to her son, and Patience Starbuck wore Mary Crispin's latest work, a high-collared ivory colored dress. Both had tried to convince me to free myself from the regimented clothing, but I said, "I am a colored woman, sufficiently different without wishing to be in meeting for worship calling more attention to myself." My dress was simple, black, and as beautiful as I, an ex-slave turned professional seamstress, could have made it.

Midway through meeting, Patience rose to her feet and said, "No one claiming to be a Christian has the right to say, 'Here am I;' accept and store bounty from the Divine; and then conclude, 'send someone other than me'. As we pray and work for slavery's end, let us each reach out to our African-ancestored neighbors: make them Americans, prove ourselves worthy to be called Friends of the Light."

My heart raced at the realization that a wealthy white woman who was close to me could look beyond her considerable privileges and publicly trumpet my cause.

Following Patience's words, there was a true silence before many others spoke in favor of manumission, abolition, love, and justice. I thought it was what Quakers call a gathered meeting. Worship ended. Outside, we discovered my brother Dan, smiling wearing a white silk suit under a cockily angled straw hat, sitting astride a prime palomino, surrounded by giggling young colored people, women who, seated at the rear, were the first out, and men, many of whom had never bothered to enter. I had not seen him or even received a letter from him in nearly three years.

One of Dan's friends, a hired man from another farm, reached up to shake his hand saying, "My man, Dan."

"How you been, Jake?" said Dan.

"I'm just tryin' to get what you got!"

Dan cackled, reached in his pocket to finger what only he knew was a small remnant of money that Patience had sent him with her last letter. He said, "I ain't got no money." It was an inside joke that brought laughter from all the men, and a look of surprise from those who had never heard him use common speech. He saw me approaching and added, "I'm just trying to maintain, Jake. I'm just trying to maintain." All of the colored people laughed. Here, in the midst of hard times, was the picture of success saying that he was just like everyone else.

I ran to him, parting the group of admirers. He laughed. "I thought it would be best to bring your letter in a 6'2" form."

He climbed down from the horse, but before I could take him from the crowd, he had set up a rendezvous with a woman I did not know. I told him to come to my house later and went back to where Mary Crispin and Patience stood. Mary Crispin noticed that Patience was sullen. "Friend, what troubles thee?"

"I was eldered by Clara Hoover," said Patience.

"I am clerk of Elders and know nothing of this. Without a formal meeting, thee could not have been eldered."

"Thee knows what I mean; Clara is an Elder and she spoke harshly about my words in meeting then added, 'All can see that thee dresses inappropriately. I have also heard it said that thee hast a stained glass window and even reads frivolous poetry. Such behavior is out of unity'."

"What did thee say to her inquiries?" asked Mary Crispin.

"I heard them as statements and framed them with silence."

Mary Crispin laughed despite herself. "Patience, thee once spoke of thyself as too soft, and I am beginning to understand why. If she had called thee 'God', would it have made thee the Creator? Poor, poor Patience, thee must not be blown about by every thin wind that enters the yard. Whatever will thee do in a storm?"

"Thus far on my adult journey, my life has seen few challenges. My only excitement came in sneaking around pretending I am not bound by our Book of Discipline."

"Embrace Truth, Patience," said Mary Crispin. "More is within thee than sees light."

◊◊◊◊◊◊

We honored Dan, the latter day prodigal, at supper. He set the evening's tone by declaring that in honor of Mary Crispin Ferguson he had taken her birth name as his surname. She was so breath taken that when she regained her composure, she actually walked over and kissed his forehead!

All of the Fergusons and Patience Starbuck were regaled as Dan told epics of his heroic adventures in the northland where he and our older brother Robin had fled when in 1829 half the blacks in Cincinnati had been expelled and made refugees. Screaming cougars, and rabid beaver, and charging bears, oh my! He became so carried away that he almost forgot that he had scheduled a nocturnal meeting. Coming to his senses he said, "Please forgive me, friends, I have to skip dessert today. Please save me a piece. I'll be back for it tomorrow morning."

"Thee knows we stay up late on First-days," said Mary Crispin. "Come by when thee finishes thy business."

"I would not want to bother you good people. Good evening. The food was the best I've had since I left here."

My husband and I arrived at home a few hours later and found Dan on the porch swing that Charles had recently made for me.

"Well if it isn't the black knight himself, my big brother Dan Crispin."

He ignored my comment and said to Charles, "It feels odd calling you brother-in-law."

Before Charles could respond I said, "I thought thee was planning to spend the night out."

"Forgive me, sister. It's your time I want."

I thought, 'She must have a vigilant mother,' but said, "Please, Charles, change the baby's wetness. Then I will feed her as I talk with my brother."

Apparently traveling alone had given Dan new found appreciation for silence. We sat in silence until upon Charles's return to the porch, Dan held out his hands. I nodded, and her father handed Susan to him. He kissed his niece. "She's almost as cute as her Uncle Dan."

Observing that he did not understand timing, and believing he was probably only trying to amuse, I chose to hear his words as pure arrogance. As I knew would happen, Susan cried, making him think she disapproved of him. Of course, the baby was unable to measure this wayward uncle; she was simply ready for her meal. Charles left us, and I began feeding the baby. Dan waited until he was certain my husband was out of earshot. Without addressing his unforgivable years without writing, he explained that despite the grandness of his earlier entrance, he was almost penniless. He had hitched a ride as far as Monroe, Michigan. Under cover of darkness, he had "borrowed" a magnificent horse and saddle from a former customer of the store owner for whom he had worked. He had ridden to Dayton and used most of the remaining money Patience had sent to purchase new clothing so that he could arrive appearing prosperous. He disclosed all with minimal prodding, claiming, "A Detroit priest once told me that 'a quick confession frees the soul of all encumbrances'."

"If thee, a hater of priests, confesses so easily, why the pretense of prosperity?"

He looked away and refocused. "I know whatever befalls, you'll accept me, but I could hardly come back looking beaten to whites."

"Is that what thee hast become: beaten down in spirit and a thief as well; a man who pretends genius but lives the life of a fool?"

"That's the kernel of my problem. I'm tired of living double." Dan told me pieces of the truth about his experiences. Somewhere in Central Ohio our brother Robin had been kidnapped and taken back into slavery. This I knew from a letter he had written to Patience who had sent money to Wilberforce, Canada where she had learned the refugees had fled. This was not the time for me to hear more about the theft of my "beloved brother." Declaring this bitterly, Dan moved on to his time in Canada where he had abandoned because she was moody a woman pregnant with his child. Later he left a Wyandotte woman in Detroit because he felt there was more opportunity somewhere down the road.

Dispensing with what Quakers refer to as 'plain speech', I said, "How could you treat women like slaves?"

"I'm a lover, not a fighter. I've never beaten a woman."

"You beat hearts, and as soon as someone learns to need you, you disappear. That's not how we were reared."

"We were reared on a Virginia plantation watching our mother taken by our master."

"Our state had nothing to do with our spirits. We were taught morals by our parents. Their genius was that neither Esi nor Kofi was made less by the Prescotts."

"You mean Kenneth."

"Don't try to distract me, brother. Our father was Kofi before he was Kenneth, but either way, he was proud, and I don't see your pride, except in a stolen horse and a suit that you can ill afford. Don't imperil my thoughts of what a man can be."

"Excuse me." Dan walked out into the shower that had just begun to fall. "I need to clear my head."

It shames me to say, but my brother needed spiritual clarity more than a walk.

My conscience bothered me all night. At breakfast I apologized to Dan for my harsh words. When he accepted, I handed him my just nursed baby. He seemed surprised when Susan went smilingly to him. Despite his unfortunate inexperience with holding babies he appeared a natural.

◊◊◊◊◊◊

After the following week's meeting for worship, Patience Starbuck spoke words that would change generations. "Sarah Ferguson, thee hast a living brother who is a part of thy life. Join me, and let's search for Robin. Why hesitate?"

"Hesitate?" I looked first at Patience and then at my mother-in-law. "I'm a wife and mother. My personal life is a study in hesitation! I'm not free to act without regard to my family responsibilities. And however could a fugitive search the south for a lost brother?"

Mary Crispin said, "I've been praying, and know I can nurse both babies. I've milk aplenty, and what I may lack, the Lord will provide. I also have, in Elizabeth, a beloved daughter who, save nursing, has promised to help me in all things great and small."

After recovering from the shock, I said, "What says thy youngest daughter?"

"Lucretia is nearly sixteen months old; she must learn to share the Lord's bounty."

Her husband Clark intensely listened. "What is thee thinking?" he asked in a voice we had never heard. "Mary Crispin, thee hast a good estimate of my love, but what will Friends say?"

"The Book of Discipline does not advise against feeding my grandchild. Thee knows that I am willing to suffer anything for The Truth. Sharing the milk of my body is not suffering."

Patience said, "Then it's settled."

"From whence cometh this new steel, Patience?" demanded Clark. "Steel that leads thee to interfere in my household?"

"Thee shares this house with me, Clark Ferguson. Patience has leave to speak her mind."

"Then speak it. In *our* marriage, she is not *my* superior. Even in the name of friendship, she should not tell me what is settled." To Patience, he said, "I rue the day thee came here."

"Husband, Patience is my dear friend, nay, she is my sister. Thee must make amends, for a rupture I will not abide."

Clark searched vainly for words. After several seconds he threw up his hands and stormed away. I had never seen this side of him and was embarrassed for having witnessed the exchange. For two nights, he slept upstairs on Charles's old bed. The next day he went to see Patience. She met him at the door and said, "I have wronged thee, Friend Clark."

"Thee hast wronged no one. I spoke like a man. I've been called to be a little less than an angel. There are principles of Truth that I allowed myself to deny."

Having achieved a sustainable peace, Clark went back home. Mary Crispin did not look up as he entered the room. He started to leave but instead walked over to their daughter Elizabeth, who was playing with Lucretia. "Daughter, would thee take the little one outside? I need to talk to thy mother."

"She has heard us talk," said Mary Crispin.

In a quiet voice, Clark said, "I would have it as I would have it."

Elizabeth picked up Lucretia and did as directed.

"I did not come to argue," said Clark. "I've already behaved poorly in thy presence, but before coming home I apologized to Patience Starbuck; now I am apologizing to thee. Will thee forgive me?"

"I do. Will thee forgive me?"

"I grant it freely, but what am I overlooking?"

"That I pretended that thee was without say in my life."

"Thee hast never made such pretense," Clark said taking her hand.

"Then forgive me for including thee late instead of first."

"'First the Lord'," he said, quoting her from their courting days. She smiled, and the kiss that she gave him, she told me later, was as deep as the one she had desired at the conclusion of their wedding vows when he had held back for fear of embarrassing their parents.

◊◊◊◊◊◊

Charles casually pointed out that aside from small portions of Culpeper and Loudon counties in Virginia and Warren County in Ohio, I had seen little of the world. Searching for Robin must seem to be a grand adventure. I said nothing. After a lengthy pause he asked if I were jealous that he was far more traveled. The thought had not occurred to me so I said nothing.

Annoyed at my silence, he blurted out what was really on his mind. "Sarah, how can thee even consider going on a search for thy brother? Doth thee not know that thee too can be taken back into slavery?"

"We escaped together," I said softly. "I owe my brother at least an attempt."

"This makes no sense. Women who journey into Hell may be singed by the Devil himself."

"The Devil has unfocused flames. What he burns in Mississippi he singes in Ohio."

I would have been content if Charles had left me alone until the moment of departure, but he was desperate. "I cannot have my wife gallivanting about the South looking for a brother who is not worth half her bootlace."

"Don't speak to me of what thee can have as though thee owned me. Nor do I suggest thee put a price on my brother."

"I'm sorry; I overstepped—"

"Yes, thee overstepped. Charles, my head is splitting, the baby is fretful—"

"Thee dare speak of a baby that thee intends to abandon?"

"Please, don't say I abandon my child. I leave her in the care of thy mother."

"Thee abandons! Thee abandons! Thee abandons!"

Like the desperate 18-year old he was, Charles repeated himself, jumping up and down as though he had found the magic key to making me stay. I began crying and still he screamed, "Thee abandons! Thee abandons! Thee abandons!"

"Touch me, Charles," I pleaded. He could not hear me for the sound of his own voice. "Touch me, Charles." Still he ranted. "Then kill me," I said cold as April snow.

He stopped between words and fell on his knees, as I remained seated, trying to soothe Susan who was stunned by being amidst such unfamiliar antics. Grabbing his heart and breathing deeply until he regained self-control, he said, "Kill thee, Sarah? I want nothing more than to love thee. For thee, I would kill death itself and abandon the peace testimony."

"I'm not asking thee to kill or abandon anything. Charles, I only desire that thee understand I'm a sister, and sisters never sever."

His head was in my lap. I stroked his disheveled locks even as I held our baby to my breast, kissing her reddish hair. He said, "Whatever thee wants, I want for thee."

I was still angry and thought, 'Is that a gift, an admission, or a punishment?'

In bed, we were both sleepless. Near midnight I said, "Lovely Charles, sleep."

He pretended to be already asleep, but I knew the way he sounded when he slept. "Then hold me as though I leave tomorrow."

Charles came out of his stupor and obeyed. Almost by accident he began stroking my back as though it were covered in gold dust. Making concentric circles, delicate undulations, windswept plunges and smooth rises, he was careful not to lose a single grain of the fantasized essence. Then he quit abruptly. "No," I said, "don't stop."

Inside a moment of mutual epiphany, we knew that whatever the name for the turning point, although he might from time to time forget to remember, only death would make him cease and desist, settle for being less than I needed. Would it be enough to sustain the glow? Would I always honor his clumsy attempts? I was 17. What could I know above what I had witnessed?

◊◊◊◊◊◊

Dan was anxious to talk with me. He had heard about the rescue attempt through younger Ferguson children asking if he were going. Feeling that he had been disrespected, he found me and angrily said, "Have you lost your mind?"

"Hast thee lost thy courage?" He was dumbfounded. "I would do the same if thee were the one stolen back into slavery. Would I be wrong in caring about thy freedom?" He paced but said nothing. "With or against me?" He laughed.

"What's so funny?"

"Being against you is more foolish than going back into Hell." I smiled. "I didn't promise Mama to look after you thinking we would have to go on such a rescue, but I did promise her."

◊◊◊◊◊◊

We women put together our plan of action, beginning with Mary Crispin's plan to nurse both her own daughter, Lucretia, and her granddaughter, Susan. No one had second thoughts about turning the American practice of interracial wet nursing upside down so we moved on. Patience explained the travel outline. She would pretend to be a slave mistress traveling with me as maid and Dan as driver. We would find out from Quakers living along the Ohio-Indiana border where the slave catchers had taken Robin, trace the trail of sales, and purchase him back. I wondered why, if these Quakers knew the kidnappers' path, they had not stopped their egress and was told they would never use violence even

76

against the violent. I have yet to recover from that lesson.

Our simple plan began to unravel when Patience said to Dan, "Among others speak little, and if thee breaks thy silence, don't use thy normal tongue. Thee must speak as a slave, or thee will be discovered intelligent, thus intimidating without power to effect positive change. Let them think of thee as they will."

"You mean let them think I'm a fool?" said Dan.

"If thee were a fool, thee would consistently act ridiculous. We cannot appear as we are. Allow me to speak even more plainly. Thy skin makes thee a suspect thief, rapist, fool and worse. Say nothing around whites other than 'Yes, ma'am or no ma'am'. Expect nothing bordering on gratitude and step to with alacrity."

"Brother," I added, "doth thee really think that speech mirrors intelligence? Our own mother refused to speak as she might have spoken."

"I spoke as I do now on Fruits of the Spirit Plantation. This isn't right!"

"Nathan Prescott, a kleptoparasitic leech, taught thy father the overlords' English as well as Latin, and thus thee and Sarah, to speak his language. Why should he be intimidated by his own teaching?" said Patience.

"Are you trying to strip me of all I really own: my self-respect?"

"What I'm trying to explain is that I cannot act wholly Quaker, and thee cannot be wholly articulate. What we undertake has nothing to do with a right world, full of freedom and liberty. It has everything to do with finding and bringing back thy brother, something I could not do when mine were lost at sea. Thee must not let thyself be diminished."

"I'll be diminishing myself by not looking whites in the eyes, acting a slave again."

"Dan, doth thee want thy brother or thy pride?"

He paused before answering, "I'm sorry."

"Thee is not *sorry*. Thee is a *man*. Resisting evil sometimes costs more than appears reasonable."

"Dare I ask," said Dan. "Are you pursuing justice for my brother or because you lost your own brothers?"

Patience paused yet her countenance changed but slightly. "I am not sufficiently clear in my own mind to answer so weighty a question. What I do know is a wrong has happened in my circle and the Spirit demands I pursue the right."

BECAUSE WE ARE DIVIDED

When I escaped from slavery with my brothers Robin and Dan, we did so under the leadership of Caesar, a Shawnee who also had African, Creek, and Cherokee ancestors. His mother was born a Creek but had married into the Shawnee nation. Some accused him of having divided loyalties, but I understood him as a man who owned himself, yielding only to his understanding of the will of the Supreme. On this day in 1832 he led the Lion and the Lamb coach owned by Patience Starbuck into Head of Coosa. Patience was a headstrong Quaker committed both to women's suffrage and the freeing of the slaves. When my brother Robin was kidnapped back into slavery, Patience had voted with her person to lead Caesar, Dan and me on a great odyssey in search of my brother.

Head of Coosa was the birthplace of Caesar's Creek grandparents. The Cherokee had seized it during the American War for Independence and made it their northwest Georgia stronghold. When last Caesar had seen Head of Coosa he had been a young warrior traveling with the great Tecumseh trying to forge a confederacy of all the great Indian nations. In those days it was a village but when we arrived it was a respectable town.

Patience's well-appointed room overlooked a manicured garden whose grass was maintained by a team of perspiring slaves using watering cans. Because my mother's best friend Eula had been born a Cherokee slave, I knew they kept slaves but was surprised that all were not from

African peoples. On our long trip through the south, Caesar and my brother Dan were pretending to be slaves of Patience. Both were taken at gunpoint to the colored men's dormitory. It was a long log cabin with ample room. A Cherokee guard escorted me to the much smaller dormitory for enslaved women. When he discovered it was already full he offered me a space on the floor with a tattered blanket. Because I too was pretending to be a slave, I drawled, "Sir, I'd rather be posted in a chair outside my mistress' room. Case she need something or wake up in the night and have need of me." I was led back to the hotel where I settled down in a chair at my mistress's service. Nearby two other black women were similarly posted outside doors. We spoke our greetings without me explaining I was only pretending to be a slave.

Meanwhile, believing that he was in one of the few remaining areas in the east where his dress preference could be appreciated, Caesar changed from his coach driver's uniform into his normal buckskin clothing with loose fitting shirt and pants, covered by red leggings and armband. He tied one red scarf around his neck and, turban-style, placed another on his head and fitted shell earrings with matching nose ring. Once he had added a single eagle feather to a headdress, he looked into his sack of gifts and extracted two for relatives he intended to visit. Then he knocked hard on the door. The guard was shocked to learn that not only was Caesar's Cherokee perfect, he also had a free paper. Satisfied that the seal appeared official and certain Caesar's dress was a clear indicator of authenticity, he allowed Caesar to go out.

Caesar was surprised how the town had changed over the years. As far as the eye could see were fields of cotton, corn, squash, pumpkins, melons, sweet potatoes, cabbages and beans. Most of the workers were darker than Caesar who was himself only a few shades lighter than Dan. When Caesar came upon Cherokees, some were dressed traditionally, with a few wearing feathers, small animal tails, and leaves in their hair as well as having red paint in various designs on their faces. However, a high percentage were dressed like whites. Caesar said he spoke with several men and women including fellow members of the Panther clan. Nearly all of his clansmen were considered relatives, even if their nations were different and any blood connection went back past most people's memory.

His first stop was at the home of Lanyi Bushyhead, a distant cousin who was one of the Cherokees who for a time had lived in Ohio and fought beside the Shawnees against the American invaders. Caesar came to Lanyi's five-room log house and said to himself, 'My cousin must've changed.'

Black slaves were everywhere he turned. A teenage slave girl used bark to dye cloth in the back yard. Nearby, a small slave girl stirred a huge pot of stew with ground cornmeal, field greens, pork, wild turkey, deer, chicken, squash, sunflowers, catfish, turtle meat, and kernel corn. Beneath the pot rested roasting green corn and ash cakes. At Caesar's approach, an older slave came out, pretending to supervise. She actually tried to ascertain if he might be an assassin. Caesar saw the outline of the butcher knife beneath her skirt. To set her at ease, he smiled warmly and said in Cherokee, "Good day, honored friend." She merely grunted and fell behind him as he walked inside.

Lanyi was cleaning his weapons. The only thing distinctly Indian in Caesar's cousin's appearance was the color of his skin and his ear slits where silver rings made from ore originating in a Kentucky mine that recently had been appropriated by whites from the Shawnees were catching the sun. Caesar said in Cherokee, "I've arrived, the Stalking Panther known as Caesar!"

Lanyi jumped up and said in English, most of which had been learned from contact with colored slaves, "You old Shawnee roamer. I done heard you was in the area. How come you don't look a day older?"

Ignoring his pot-bellied cousin's question, Caesar reached out to him with their traditional hands-on-arms greeting and said in English, "So you done gone American?"

Caesar extended his favorite skinning knife, and Lanyi said, "Thank you for this fine weapon." Although it could certainly have been used for scalping enemies, Caesar had never used the knife for anything but gutting freshly killed wild game. His cousin should have recognized as much but busily trying to change himself, he had forgotten. "I haven't gone all the way American," pointing to his head shaved completely except for a single row across the center.

"Are you too far American to feed me?" Caesar smiled.

"Grab a bowl, and go help yourself." Lanyi laughed.

Caesar took one off the table and frowned at the metal forks, spoons, and cloth napkins. He returned from the yard eating the thick stew with his hands.

"They can take the Shawnee out of Ohio, but they can't take Ohio out of the Shawnee," laughed Lanyi. "From time to time I hear about your travels. Why don't you settle down?"

"I've got a house tucked away in the woods, but I'm hardly ever there. It ain't to my liking being available whenever the white man wants to grab me."

Lanyi looked up, but quickly went back to his work. He had put away his pistol and cleaned one of many rifles. A fourth slave of mostly Creek heritage rocked two baby cradles while Lanyi's wife weaved alternating strips of white, yellow, and brown. Caesar said in Cherokee, "I-yo-ka, your food is as good as you remain beautiful."

He had guessed correctly, I-yo-ka had yet to assimilate. She replied in her first tongue, "I may still be beautiful, but my husband's slaves cooked the soup."

"I was hoping," he said to his cousin in English, "to see Uncle Pathkiller. Got any idea where he might be?"

"That's right, Major Ridge is your great uncle. You done forgive him?"

"I try to dance life; grudge over a loss you can't change is death."

"The Ridge is bigger than ever. Over on the Oostanaula River he's got a mansion, ferry, plantation, general store. If you can get past his guards, he'll be glad to see you."

"Guards? He's in prison in his own land?"

"Ain't you heard they tried to kill him in '26," said Lanyi, "and times are more dangerous now. Yeh, him and all the big men's got guards."

◊◊◊◊◊◊

While crossing the Oostanaula River on his relative's ferry, long before the ferry docked, Caesar could see The Ridge estate high on a bluff. It overlooked the water and the Blue Ridge Mountains, ignoring the fact that many felt the owner had abandoned the People by lusting for power and living ostentatiously.

A small squad of Light Horse Patrol Cherokee policemen met Caesar at the gate. "What's a damn Shawnee doing in these parts?"

"I'm part Cherokee," said Caesar.

"From here it looks like you're more part nigger."

Caesar kept his calm and went through his lineage highlighting the Cherokee tie, ending with, "And I'm part *African*."

Another distant cousin suddenly remembered a story his own father had told him about Caesar's father. Caesar thought he was free to go, but someone asked, "What weapons do you have?"

"I have a knife." Two of the guards argued over taking it. Ending the dispute, Caesar unsheathed it and said, "I'll be back for it." They apologized, but he said he understood.

The grounds were replete with oaks and sycamores which were maintained along the lengthy entrance by a team of six well-trained slaves. The plantation itself had a huge pasture with milk and beef cows and magnificent horses. Marked free-range pigs wandered here and there. The plantation was more than 300 cultivated acres with over 1500 peach, apple, quince, and cherry trees as well as corn, wheat, indigo, cotton, tobacco and various potato fields. Caesar noted two long rows of slave houses. Each was a log cabin without any windows. Doors were open to flies and mosquitoes. Most of the little children running around were considered blacks, but there were also a few Creeks. The majority had ancestors from multiple cultures. Within view of the slave hovels were fine vineyards, an ornamental garden, a smokehouse and two stables.

A uniformed butler met Caesar at the door of the wrap-around porch. He was told to go to the back entrance. "Friend," Caesar said in Cherokee, "The Major is my great grandfather's cousin-brother." He was tired of playing the slave.

The 61-year old Ridge came to the door cursing in broken English, smoking a cigar, dressed in a frock coat trimmed with gold lace, and wearing his teased, long white hair in the Jacksonian style. Caesar said in Cherokee, "Kah-nung-da-tla-geh, it's good to see my great uncle."

"The Stalking Panther! I heard you were with Quatawape giving away some more Shawnee land."

"Like Tecumseh, I've never set pen to a treaty."

"Anyway," said The Ridge, "provided you don't have that red war club, you're just in time for supper. My wife and the children have gone visiting in Pile Log. I was afraid I might have to dine alone."

Caesar regretted the disparaging remark concerning the club of justice the Red Sticks had carried. Pretending not to notice, he sullenly observed The Ridge's ceilings and walls made of hewn logs and the floors of hardwood. A finely designed arched triple window was at the curve of an elegant staircase. In the dining room were well crafted and highly polished chairs around a long table. The slave waiter brought in smoked pork chops, potatoes, and French-cut green beans. 'This is a white man's meal,' Caesar thought. 'Lucky I already had real food at Lanyi's.'

The two had not seen each other during peace times, a period of almost twenty years. In fact, the last time Caesar had seen The Ridge, the older man's horse was trampling on a Creek toddler. Only the Shawnee's lack of ammunition had saved his relative from instant death.

Supper ended, and Caesar reached for his *piitaaka*, saying, "Uncle, I brought tobacco and my calumet. Would you share a smoke?"

"Put away your old fashioned tobacco and keep your gift-pipe. We're not at war with the Shawnees, and I'm not at war with my nephew," said The Ridge with a laugh. What had happened was past, and it was presumed that Caesar realized had the battle of Horseshoe Bend only been between the Cherokees and Creeks, the goal would only have been to prove the most honorable nation. It was white presence that had encouraged The Ridge to kill six Creeks and the united army to pursue massacre. Accepting a peace pipe as though balance had been restored could indicate a prologue that the more powerful man might regret. Silently Caesar placed his tobacco and pipe back into his travel bag. "You really should set aside the old ways. I smoke cigars now," said The Ridge. "It's more civilized. Can you imagine George Washington smoking a three-foot-long pipe?"

Caesar could not imagine George Washington doing anything. He looked at The Ridge and wondered if he too was haunted by the 1814 pyrrhic victory of the Cherokee dupes at Horseshoe Bend. Caesar had been with the remnant of the overmatched Red Stick Creeks and their allies who had fought their way out of the lethal snare. Female survivors had reported that the Cherokees had helped Jackson by participating in his order to take a literal nose count by cutting off the nostrils of fallen enemies. Next they stripped their skin below the waist, in order to make bridle reins for the American dragoons, and boot legs for the infantry. They had taken the strips and sun-dried them as though they were pieces of wild game. Caesar had heard that The Ridge himself had taken at least one Red Stick scalp. Once upon a time, he also had taken scalps. Seasons change, and so do some men.

Caesar reached behind his back and brought out a carbine from his belt and offered it as a gift to The Ridge. "I thought you were searched," said his Great Uncle with a smile.

"They were only half serious. Do I look like an assassin?"

"Assassins only look like assassins in campfire tales," said The Ridge.

Puffing away on his cigar, The Ridge thoroughly examined the gun. "Thanks, I'll keep the carbine. Nephew, I hear that the *Unakas* are sending more Shawnees west in a few months."

The Ridge's information was correct. At the Battle of the Thames, more Shawnees had fought with the American army than with Tecumseh and an even larger number had claimed neutrality while their relatives fought to save the land of the ancestors. Less than twenty years later, Jackson was the President and on the verge of expelling the same co-opted Shawnees from Ohio.

Caesar wondered if The Ridge's primary concern was that the Cherokees might lose yet another group of Shawnees serving on their frontier as buffers against invaders. They ate in silence until Caesar said, "Uncle, explain the keeping of slaves to me."

"Let us speak in English," said The Ridge switching to the language of the overlords. "Dolly, where you at? Come on in here and interpret."

The slave appeared and took her place, within a few feet of both men, waiting to answer her master's glance should Caesar speak any words that might be confusing. "My son's sure the practice will do us both some good."

Caesar knew that one of the jobs of the house slaves was to use their bi-lingual skills to improve their masters' English. Another was to be displayed as conspicuous powerlessness. Instead of speaking to these facts, he said aloud, "I don't know the good it will do to speak a barbarian language; there are no whites nearby." The Ridge ignored the observation, and Caesar switched to English. "If'n you wanna be speaking their tongue, it's your house. Uncle, explain all the Coosa slaves to me."

"Cherokees don't like the word slaves. I prefer to call 'em servants or 'unpaid workers'."

"Unpaid workers?"

"When've you been a wage man?" said The Ridge laughing.

"When's the last time somebody told me what to do and I said, 'Yessir, Master'?"

"As I recall once, before they got all broke up, the Shawnees kept servants, including Cherokee servants."

"Shawnee slavery weren't like white folk's slavery. The few we had were honored as folk not animals. Nearly all married into the nation. Many rose to be chiefs. From where I sit, y'all trying to be just like whites."

"Nephew, 'fore he got hisself killed, Tecumsech ever talk to you 'bout unpaid workers?"

"Tecumseh steered away from white ways and did not keep slaves. Anyway you know I weren't no big man able to counsel Tecumseh."

"I thought you Shawnees claim y'all's equals." Caesar said nothing. The Ridge smirked, "If I'm wrong, tell me who are the Shawnee big men these days? I forget."

The Ridge knew that the Shawnees were dispersed, nearly decimated. Although many of Caesar's contemporaries claimed to be a war chief, both men discounted them as puffed up pretenders and knew they could not lead men on a raid, let alone into war.

"Did you see my servant quarters? Finest around! If the next tobacco harvest pays like I think it will, I'm giving each a glass window, something few of your Creek cousins have in their rundown shacks wherever they're hiding." Caesar was clearly unimpressed, so The Ridge added, "Not only on my plantation, anywhere in Cherokee territory you see somebody being beaten, let alone tortured?"

"Do you break up families?"

"We're civilized now, Caesar. We're 'bout profit."

"Considering the fortune you made off the Creek treaty with Washington, profit's surely been a guest at your table," said Caesar. He waited for a denial that the Cherokee had sold thousands of acres of Shawnee land in Kentucky that the Cherokee had never owned. The Ridge simply blew smoke upward. "I hear now you have a law against letting slaves learn how to read," said Caesar.

The Ridge looked at Dolly who interpreted, "Y'all's got 'nough profit." Realizing from the frown on her master's face that her tone might have shown a bit more servility, she quickly added, "Sir."

The Ridge turned to Caesar. "I'm supposing you understand that the surest way for a man to profit is to master what the white man loves. That includes speaking and reading the language. You don't appear to understand profit so I'm guessing you can't read a lick."

"I can read and write Cherokee," said Caesar. "Ciphering Sequoya's symbols only takes a few days to learn."

"It ain't Cherokee I need to learn," said The Ridge. "I didn't think you knowed 'bout reading English. I know 'nough to know the white man is right: if a unpaid worker reads enough, he'll think keeping him down low is 'gainst the laws of nature."

"It is."

"Like I keep trying to learn my people, nature is power," said The Ridge patiently. "Ain't a bit a diff'rence 'twixt and 'tween the two. I can't speak for Shawnees and Creeks, but losing is 'gainst Cherokee nature. For example, we took Head of Coosa from the Ulibahali Creeks when the Master of Breath saw even He couldn't help such pitiful warriors and abandoned 'em. Us Cherokees is a nation of laws now. We ain't savages running through the woods ignorant of progress. In our own tongue, we write and constitute like civilized folk. We could've passed a law that all unpaid workers had to be Nigras or even all had to be Creeks. We make the laws we want. You may dress like a Shawnee and pray to Moneto, but don't you have as many Creek relatives as Cherokee? As I recall, you even have more Creek relatives than Cherokee. Anyway, we Cherokees could've made 'em all slaves."

Caesar, who had once been a trusted messenger between the warring peoples, ignored the ludicrous boast that the Cherokees could have enslaved all Creeks. The Ridge and his faction had allowed the whites to inflame long-time animosities, exploit shortsightedness, and conquer their enemies and allies alike. If when they met at Tuckabatchee, Tecumseh, the most articulate man Caesar had ever met, could not convince The Ridge that his way of analyzing white behavior was lacking, why should he even try? 'But,' thought Caesar in Shawnee, 'I owe it to Tecumseh to try. The vision of freedom should not die with the man.'

"If the Cherokees lose—and you will—should your old friend Jackson make y'all slaves?" Without waiting for an answer he added, "Uncle, you look at the white man and see what y'all got in common. He look at you and see what's different." The Ridge frowned as though he did not understand.

Dolly interpreted, "Ya'll see kin folk; the white man see suspect."

The Ridge said to Caesar, "I'm Cherokee and gotta watch both sides."

"Your land is rich without the gold everybody knows is here. Now it's just a matter of time before the crackers kick you outta these parts. You know good and well they don't operate on loyalty. As soon as you helped 'em beat us at Horseshoe Bend, they stole from y'all on their way back to what they call Tennessee."

"They was starving," said The Ridge interrupting.

"When did starving justify stealing from friends?"

"I may dress fine, Caesar, but I never stopped being a warrior. You see that buffalo headdress on the wall?" Caesar had taken in the complete room when he had entered, but, deferentially, he looked again at the symbol of authority. "The horns may not be on my head, but they're always in my heart," said The Ridge, pausing to sip a cup of coffee that must have grown cold. "I let you speak to me in ways a Cherokee could not, nephew. A wise man needs all the good counsel he can find. Since there's nothing for you to gain, I have to figure you wouldn't try to snow me."

"I wouldn't try to snow anybody in this heat. But I got plenty to gain, Uncle. My dignity is a gaining not a losing proposition. If the Cherokees lose, I lose."

"Well said, son, but on my back is the whole Cherokee nation. I'm trying to do what's right for everybody."

"I believe you, and 'though he died before I was born, I know your father/uncle and my great grandfather woulda been proud of the power in your hands, but look at what's happening all over the country. The first ones of us have been pushed out and now live far beyond our ancestors' graves. Y'all doing well here, but the Cherokees have already lost most of what y'all owned in Georgia, Alabama, and Tennessee. Why even mention Carolina where they stripped y'all cleaner than a deer's ass in a fire?"

"Do you remember what the peace chief used to tell your daddy?"

"I recall many Cherokee sayings, but not all."

"Crests the Flood taught, 'Tensing up, the snake uncoils'."

Caesar took advantage of the fact that the phrase was spoken in Cherokee and answered accordingly. "I've had years to consider that one."

"So whatchou think 'bout it?" said The Ridge, trying to return the conversation to English.

In Cherokee, Caesar said, "Watching closely, the panther leaps to safety."

The Ridge narrowed his eyes slightly to indicate that he wanted the conversation to stay in English and Caesar switched back to English. "Life made me find an antidote to his warning."

Dolly interpreted, "Things made him find a cure before he got hurt."

"Shawnee running would have to change a man's view," said The Ridge laughing.

"My cousin says that the white man just made the Cherokees sign another treaty. I know that even now your son John and Buck Oowatie are in Washington. Soon's they get back, they'll report, for your people's gold, your old friend Jackson will betray y'all."

Caesar thought about Tecumseh's visit with the intent to rally the Cherokee to fight the Americans. The Ridge had pulled a gun on Tecumseh and said, "Get out of here you would-be-chief! My people will not follow a Shawnee too weak to recruit most of his own people."

Tecumseh's followers had also drawn weapons but he had held up his hand and said to The Ridge, "All of you are my people. What is more, I do not need to be the war chief to lead us. You may have that honor. All I want is to save our land from thieves."

Not mollified, The Ridge had successfully convinced the vast majority of the Cherokee to stay out of the hostilities.

Caesar thought but did not say, 'You, Jackson's drum, betrayed Tecumseh by siding with the whites and threatening to assassinate the great man. Under Tecumseh's leadership we Shawnees, Creeks, Miamis, Choctaws, Chickasaws, Potawatomies, Lenapes, Kickapoos, Winnebagos, Wyandottes and Cherokees could have whipped the whites. With a few more good men standing beside him, Tecumseh had the ability to bring in the Sauk, Fox, Ojibwe and Seneca, maybe even the Dakota, Osage and Cheyenne. You, my great uncle, took the Cherokees to the wrong side, and we'll never have another chance to win.'

Aloud he said, "The white man never says 'sign' and gives a fair price. Even his claim to be buying is a lie. I didn't agree at the time, but the Shawnees and the others who sold our land did it 'cause it was the only choice we had. We took what they said rather than take nothing. Acceptance as an equal ain't something you going get. Your turning into a red/white man ain't the answer."

"Nephew, you seem to got a hundred whoas and not one giddyup. What would you do in my place?"

"I'd be me and not somebody Jackson wanted me to be."

A Creek captive interrupted by bringing in a fresh baked apple pie, which she held with a red, white, and blue towel. As The Ridge admired the pie as though it were as much a power symbol as the buffalo headdress, Caesar recognized the servant as a distant cousin whom The Ridge had captured as a girl following the battle of Horseshoe Bend. "Will you resist being overrun?" said Caesar in Cherokee.

Also in Cherokee, the Ridge said, "You have no discipline." He watched the slave cut the pie, switched back to English and said, "Whatchou think I'm doing?"

DISPERSED

The reading of Nathan Prescott's will gave flesh to my parents' greatest fear. In many ways I feel blessed because I had escaped north with my brothers Robin and Dan. Watching my parents and their children sold in auction to the highest bidder might have broken my heart for all time. Some five years after both the escape and the dispersal, I found myself in the same room with Zephyrine. I was 18 and she a year or two older. Despite the fact that we had grown up together, often even sharing the same shack while my pain was at its highest level, keeping my distance from her had been a priority just behind breathing. A bullet that lodged in my brother Dan's back while he fled slave catchers had drawn us into a room that was even smaller than the slave cabins we had called home.

I was silently praying when Zephyine said, "Though both Mama and Esi each had long lost sisters, Mama considered Aunt Esi a sister." Her face was hidden in the deepening darkness broken by a single candle. On the chance she might have something to say that could distract me from the fear my brother would die, I looked up to see where this opening might lead. "I didn't particularly care for you and your freckle-faced self," said Zephyrine in her graceless way, "but some of us chillen was like cousin/brothers or sisters, and you already know Dan was the only man I'd let touch me. Any other male could expect to get cut everywhere except under his toenails."

I could not fathom what Dan had seen in her beyond carrying herself like a queen walking with such deliberateness that crass men drooled, being tall and having skin tone that when in later years we had become closer, I admitted was luminous. I never told him, but I considered Dan a bright man who should aspire to more than physicality.

"When you three runned away and then the rest of y'all got sold, it was a great sadness fell on Fruits of the Spirit. Who would've thought that after the next harvest, the great heifer would call us to the big house? Preacher said 'Jesus wept' was the shortest verse in the Bible. Miss Anne matched it when she said, 'Y'all free,' and went back into the house."

"What are you talking about?" I said in shock. "I assumed you had run away as we did."

She continued a story that today, almost 30 years later, mystifies me. When not slaving for Prescott, Kofi, my father, had worked decades trying to earn our purchase price. The only way any of his family found freedom was through escape. Those of who broke the laws of the land that he held sacred and successfully stole ourselves, have spent our lifetimes valuing our free papers more than we do our right hands. A black person without a passport might as well surrender all semblances of freedom.

Zephyrine said when Miss Anne announced their emancipation the Fruits of the Spirit slaves laughed, sang, danced all day. When evening came they had no place to go. Her mother said to her husband that now was his chance to be a man. Gabe had said, "Eula, we got seven chillen, no money, and ain't been nowhere off this property but to Reverend Stringfellow's church!"

She had ordered him to go to the big house and tell Miss Anne those exact words, "And tell her most of us done worked all our life for the Prescott family, making them rich. Don't give her a inch to squirm in. I want some answers up in here."

I knew Eula well. We had even grown up calling her "Aunt Eula." I could imagine her voice and knew that was just the type of unreasonable statement she would make to her timid husband.

Nightfall quieted the slaves. No one knew what to do next. To the surprise of many, Gabe called a council of both married and single men. When Eula tried to insist on attending he said, "You is many things. One of 'em ain't a man."

"Mama was surprised at his new found gumption," said Zephyrine. "I always knew Daddy had it in 'im."

While the families slept in the woods because they were afraid to use their former domiciles since they were refugees and no longer slaves, the men conferred throughout the night.

When morning came Gabe led a deputation to the big house. Miss Anne herself came to the back door and said, "I expected sooner rather than later you Nigras would see something was missing."

Zephyrine said none of the men spoke until she called each by name and handed them free papers for themselves and their families, if they had one. Since she had never called a black person by name they were surprised that she knew that much about them. I suspect she had a ledger on which was recorded more information than any would want known. Instead of moving on they stood their ground. There had to be more…a mule, farm tools, seeds, twenty acres, bags of money, an apology?

"Those who wish to stay may be sharecroppers under my protection. You work my fields and harvest the crops. In turn I will rent you cabins and advance you the necessary food and clothing until you have earned money. As for those clothing you are wearing, you may keep them as a gift. When your debts are subtracted after the harvest, you will have money, and you may go wherever you please. What the law says you cannot do is stay here in Virginia as freedmen without my protection."

All of them had friends and many of the men had families living on nearby plantations. The members with wives who had also been freed by Miss Anne repeated her words to them. Trapped, there was almost universal agreement with the stated terms. Eula was the exception. "I'd rather drink muddy water and sleep in a hollow log than trust that heifer to do right."

"But ain't she just freed us without making us pay her a coin?" said Gabe.

"Is you really that simple minded?"

"Simple can't get no free paper. Kofi was smarter than a whip, but he come up empty."

Eula sighed and said, "Free ain't free. You and them men best come up with another plan."

Unfortunately all of the others were convinced that the only sound option was sharecropping, which Eula declared was almost like slavery. I judged Eula as being filled with incredible anger. But most of the time I also agreed with her assessments.

I was jolted from contemplation by the sound of snoring. "Surely that is not all to the story!"

"Gotcha." Zephyrine chuckled more to herself than at her victim.

I was thoroughly embarrassed to have been so easily duped by someone who I thought of as an inferior. Thankfully she chose not to tease me but proceeded soberly to speak of deprivations experienced early in their exodus. I had never missed a meal because Prescott insisted slaves be fed almost on par with his horses and pigs. Like them, we represented capital that at the time of his choosing should bring maximum price. From what I saw of him, he enjoyed buying and selling all of his possessions even more than he appreciated the company of his wife. Aside from Fruits of the Spirit Plantation, I had been well fed while living with both the Pools and the Fergusons, two well established sets of Quaker farmers. As well, my escape had been led by Caesar and Monni, two Shawnees who constantly lived off the woodlands' abundance.

"Mama was the only one of us born off Fruits of the Spirit," said Zephyrine.

Indeed it was Eula's first ten years that may have saved them from starving.

Zephyrine explained that before Eula's Cherokee father had died, he had taught his children—mixed as well as those of his Cherokee wife—how to find food where others saw barren wilderness. When Eula's father had been killed in battle, his principal wife spitefully had sold Eula's mother and her four children each to a different buyer. Hunger pangs helped Eula recall lessons long shelved.

"You didn't know yours ain't the only family that done been broke up?" said Zephyrine.

"I knew we weren't the first to be dispersed, but because she never found occasion to speak of it, I did not know that Aunt Eula's had also been dispersed."

"'Dispersed' you say? That's a high sounding word for straight up evil. Mama took it hard watching your people sold to whoever. Anyway, we walked north star then sunset west. We thought we was moving well when we come across a Paddyroller on what should've been the good side of the Ohio River. He was looking to collect bounties. He thought we was a gang of runaways 'til Mama pulled them free papers out her bosom. His eyes nearly popped out. Then he tried to act nice and drew us a map to Cincinnati. Only problem was he left out the creeks, swamps, mosquitoes, and rain. A few days later Daddy cussed and said, 'To Hell with this. We going south.' Mama 'bout had another baby and she wasn't pregnant. Then he said, 'I don't mean to slave territory, the north side of the big river.'

From then on we followed the Ohio. That's how we ended up here in Cincinnati."

"Are the others nearby? I'd love to see them."

"No, they all went further west. Daddy hated his job killing hogs all day, and Mama and Mae felt boiled down being maids for whites living two steps higher than Virginia white trash."

I was certain she had come to the end of what she intended to tell me. After a long silence I said, "So Aunt Eula led all of you here from Culpeper."

"I didn't tell that lie! Mama saw to it we ate, but Daddy led the way. But them berries and roots Mama showed us how to find wasn't filling, and we got tired of fishing. We ain't had no gun but some nights Daddy would lead my brothers off to raid some white folks' farms."

"You stole?"

"I know you got book learning, but sometimes you ain't got a drop of mother wit," said Zephyrine. "Daddy said, 'Them white folk done took everything from us but our skin color. Taking enough food to fill the belly ain't no sin.'"

The candle had extinguished itself, and here I sat in a room with a woman whose major tie was known but unacknowledged. The same rapist had hurt to the core the men we called Daddy and dispersed our mothers' joy.

THE STAND

Years after my brother Dan Crispin died, I am using his journal to write this story.

Dan told his wife, Zephyrine, that he considered opening a stagecoach line between Cincinnati and Detroit. I have less reason to believe my brother's surface explanations than does his wife. I knew from experience his words often stopped well short of the whole story. He visited me in Waynesville on his way north. I said, "Is it not true thy ex-lover was living in Detroit?"

"It is certainly possible but unlikely. She is a Wyandotte, and her people have been driven out of the city."

"Since thee left her with child I doubt thee would want to face them."

He was decidedly displeased with my observation and said no more about the topic. Upon his departure, he was still upset. We had been there before. In fact, we both knew that as had been the case with Esi, our mother, pricking his conscience was one of my life's purposes.

◊◊◊◊◊◊

In Dayton Dan searched for and soon found a white family desiring transportation to Detroit. Their fare more than paid for his round trip. The first time he had traveled through the Great Black Swamp he had used the Corduroy Road built in 1825. Now it was graveled leading him to truly consider extending his stagecoach business into Michigan.

The Lion and the Lamb coach arrived in Detroit on the afternoon of

Wednesday, June 12, 1833. The passengers had spent each of the nine nights in the beds of various inns. Dan, a racial outcast, had slept seated in the coach or, when weather permitted, in a bedroll beneath it. With his passengers delivered, he changed into his best suit of clothes and went to visit old male friends to ask about Mariah Chene, his former lover. Over a year ago, the last time they had been together, he had not come home for two, or was it three nights? When he had walked in, she said, with tears in her eyes, "Where have you been?" In his mind, the free papers in his pocket meant no one had the right to ask that question. The next morning he had quit his job and left town thinking, 'Soon you will learn what true loneliness is'.

◊◊◊◊◊◊

Dan dropped by the various places of employment of his old male friends. Each was suitably impressed with his new prosperity, but none claimed any knowledge of Mariah. He turned to Mariah's friend Caroline French. When she answered his knock he took off his hat and said, "Good morning, Miss Caroline."

"Mrs.," she said icily. "I'm grieved to see that a wish-he-was-a-king snake like you would dare knock on my front door."

Suddenly the sky opened in a downpour. He was exposed on Caroline's townhouse stoop. Involuntarily he leaned his head toward the inside but almost jumped back when she said, "If this was Sunday or my husband was at home, I'd invite you in. It's Thursday, and he's at work. Good-bye, Mr. Crispin."

Hospitality demanded more than she admitted, but all Dan could think to say was, "I'm looking for Mariah Chene, ma'am."

"You've come late to your senses?" She paused the closing door. "You should have married that child in the first place. Instead you took complete advantage of her. I know your devious ways; you come with a shiny poison claiming it's an apple. Answer me yes or no without any of your sweet words: did you think it was all right to abandon her because she's an Indian?"

It was an unanswerable question, but clearly Caroline expected a confession.

"I don't know that I took advantage of her."

"That's neither yes nor no, and if knocking up and leaving behind is not taking advantage, heaven help us all. Shameless men may not stop on my stoop." She slammed the door as though he had rudely disappeared in the mist.

The streets were filled with runnels of rain water. In a pair of fine boots made by our brother Robin, Dan tiptoed through the mud, dodging deep puddles, splatters from passersby and cursing the fact that slush obscured fresh horse paddies. The trading post where he had been employed was a few miles away. At the rear door he used a fallen branch to clean his boots, knocked twice, and entered. A few workers loading incoming bundles of beaver furs and barrels of pork greeted him briefly. The supervisor was a woman he had known well.

"How are you, 'Lissa?"

"Who let you back in town?" Shocked by the reaction, Dan said nothing. "When you left here, was I the only one you told?"

"No, I told Mr. Livernois. He even gave me a letter of introduction."

"But you didn't tell that Injin girl you was living with?" When Dan did not answer, 'Lissa said, "I guess because of that time she caught me leaving y'all's house she thought I might know something. She waited four full days after you'd left and then came here looking for you. She was crying right in the store! Mrs. Livernois happened to be here. You know Madame is half Injin herself. The child had *her* crying. I almost lost my job just because I'm black too."

"Have you seen her?"

"Madame Livernois is in the front if that's who you mean, but no, I ain't seen your wife."

"She was not my wife."

"You could've fooled her. She sure 'nough thought she was."

"Goodbye, 'Lissa." Dan turned to leave.

"You got a place to spend the night?"

Recognizing the tone, he paused. His conscience checked him, "I'll sleep in a field if necessary."

'Lissa smiled and said, "It ain't."

"Have a nice life." He left without a true farewell.

◊◊◊◊◊◊

Dan decided to search for clues of Mariah's whereabouts the safe way, in a saloon. He nursed a bottle of Bulleit's and waited out the storm asking questions of a few men refreshing themselves before night shift labor. None could help him until Fleming Denison arrived. He did not know Mariah's whereabouts but there was another pressing matter that held great promise.

"Mr. Denison, you were a slave here in Detroit, just out of curiosity, why didn't you run?"

Fleming took a sip of the Bulleit's. "You was a free man here in Detroit, just out of curiosity, why did you run? I mean from that child carrying your baby?"

Thinking the question oddly invasive for a man he had treated to good whiskey, Dan pretended not to hear. Fleming bore into his eyes until Dan said, "Some things have no good answers."

Fleming laughed. "There's your answer."

"What do you mean?"

"I've spent the better part of my life asking myself the same question you just asked me. You should do the same thing, young fellow."

Uninvited, Fleming poured another drink. The two men drank in silence. Dan thought, 'I had a chance to stand that's as gone as last year's snow. My father would have stood.'

Before leaving Fleming said, "This may not suit your ears, but here's the price of whiskey: I was born just after the cutoff date. So according to Judge Woodward back in '07 I had to do 25 years as a slave and would be free in 1821. I knew Detroit and nowhere else. I stayed because I was and am a Detroiter."

"Who do you think I should be?"

"I ain't your daddy…and neither is the white man. That's a question for you and you alone to answer."

"We were not talking about whites."

"We weren't? Long as you black on this side of the Ocean, when you talk, you're talking about whites. Judges, Presidents, slave masters, don't matter. That's all any of us talk about because when you get right down to it they rule and most of us play the mule or the fool."

The bartender called for silence. He announced that on Saturday two slave hunters had convinced the authorities to arrest a fugitive couple named Blackburn and an assembly of colored people was gathering at dawn at the jail to assist them.

◊◊◊◊◊◊

Dan was in the forefront of the crowd when from the rear a voice called out, "Men talk; women do."

Caroline French came to the front and said, "Friends do not abandon friends to the savages of this country. Unless you grumblers have a better idea, I am going up to visit the jailhouse and switch clothes with Ruth Blackburn."

A few men offered reasons aimed at discouraging her, but Caroline dismissed them as cowardly.

Caroline and Ruth successfully executed the trick. Ruth Blackburn disappeared and Caroline waited several hours before disclosing the ruse. If she had not been from a family with important connections among the white power elite, and most Detroiters not been opposed to slavery, she might have been sold into slavery herself. Instead, she was released from jail on a *writ of habeas corpus.* Dan insisted on having the honor of rowing her across the river into Canada until life in Detroit settled.

On the far side of the river Caroline said, "It would be my guess should the Detroit whites change their mind, the Canadians will not extradite me to such mean-spirited ruffians."

"Then all is forgiven me?" said Dan.

"With this small kindness you have done yourself proud. However I'm not so impressed that I will tell you *Miss* Chene's whereabouts. Good day, Mr. Crispin. Say hello to your new wife from a should-be admirer, and continue your self-improvement work. Unrealized potential embarrasses the race."

◊◊◊◊◊◊

Thornton Blackburn was still in custody. Someone tried to curry his favor and warned Sheriff John M. Wilson, that Detroit people of color were going to storm the jail and rescue his prisoner. When the informant was seen sneaking out the back door, he was beaten into a confession and told life was better in another place. Grateful he had not been tarred and feathered he fled to parts unknown.

The slave catchers and deputies moved quickly to plan safe passage to the docks and drag Thornton downriver to Ohio and back into slavery.

The plans were not finalized when those outside the jail began singing,

"Across the Ohio
and up the River Raisin.
We the strong
is damn sure amazin'.

Mess with our people
and law or not
we'll reshape your noggin
into a warped steeple."

Off to the side, a man who had learned drum playing in the Old Country began a war song whose words he sometimes sang. My brother thought he recognized Fante pronunciations, but like me, Dan had never bothered to learn our ancestral language.

The sheriff was unmoved by words in any tongue. He said in Thornton's hearing, "My riding whip will scare every nigger in Michigan."

Dan stood among the leaders when the sheriff had Thornton brought to the door in leg irons. Wilson waved his whip menacingly as though he were heading for The Promised Land. "Okay you niggers, this is my country. Part and let us through."

Dan shouted to the crowd, "This charlatan doesn't look like Moses to me! Will we stand together with our brother?"

A roar of solidarity as several colored people rushed forward carrying every manner of weapon from broom handles to guns.

"Back! Back I say!"

Men who had been assumed a race of cowards surged forward chasing the sheriff, his deputies, and the slave catchers back inside the jail with the prisoner.

Several times the sheriff conferred with his associates then attempted to cool the crowd. Consistently he was shouted down. The final time the sheriff came out he said, "This is a country of law and order. I am the law, and I order you to stand back."

"Is you blind?" shouted a young man near the front, "or just plain deef?"

The sheriff visibly tried not to wring his hands when Dan said, "Sir, we hold the best ground and unless you intend to be ground meat, give up the prisoner."

The lines were drawn and intently staring at each other waiting for the other to charge. The still-shackled prisoner said to the sheriff, "I like peace as much as the next man."

"What are you saying, boy?"

"Slavery ain't so bad. Let me talk to the crowd before somebody gets hurt."

Dan had placed himself next to the door and was about to lead a charge. Suddenly, from the lawman's blind side, someone handed Thornton a pistol. The prisoner cocked it and pointed the weapon at the chief deputy.

"I'd wade in blood as deep as Hell before going back into slavery," said Thornton. "Unless you want this man to be blown through, I suggest you join the men at your back."

Thornton eyed the sheriff. The deputy in question dove through the doorway to safety. Dan waved the crowd forward. Immediately at least four hundred colored people from throughout southeastern Michigan and nearby Canada moved as one. Thornton was snatched and placed into the coach intended to transport the prisoner, the sheriff, and slave catchers to the dock.

The crowd moved toward the sheriff who had elbowed to the rear of his deputies and slave catchers. His associates hastily retreated past their leader. The sheriff removed his gun from his holster and got off an indiscriminate shot before Dan struck his hand. Releasing rage that in some cases had been pent up and passed down for ten generations, the mob knocked out several of the sheriff's teeth and fractured his skull.

Ignoring the splattered blood on his best suit, Dan said, "Let him live!" then pulled off two youths bent on killing the man on the spot. "If he dies, some of us will probably be hung."

Thornton was quickly ferried across the river into Canada.

◊◊◊◊◊◊

Four years earlier whites in Cincinnati had attacked colored people in one-sided brutality. Many of the colored people who participated had been driven meekly north and wound up in Detroit. Following the Blackburns' escape slave sympathizers attacked the colored community burning down more than three dozen buildings, beating a number of innocent colored people senseless.

Dan joined the Cincinnati refugees many of whom he had known for years. They began chanting, "Never again," and were soon joined by hundreds of colored people who had long been Detroiters and had their own grudges to settle. In the midst of what had become a race war, Fleming Denison said to Dan, "This may be your fight but it ain't your city. Everybody knows you by that white suit. Get while the getting is good."

Dan still had no idea where Mariah and his son might be. Denison said, "That girl is long gone like a turkey through the corn and being hung ain't likely to make her show up."

Reluctantly Dan headed south. He was more frustrated than ever but proud that he had made a stand in the same city from which he had fled.

THREE-FIFTHS

In my younger brother Luther's years on Bob Carver's plantation, nothing galled him more than an incident in which the master had degraded the woman whom he looked up to as surrogate mother. Guests from the three county area had been arriving throughout the day, and Carver had failed to ask neighbors to rent enough slaves to staff his party. Bustling about trying to make dinner guests content, Cora had overcooked a pie. In front of guests, the inebriated Carver backhanded Cora in the face. As she attempted to rise, he spat tobacco juice on her as though she were a muddy patch of earth.

Although most doubted the two happenings were related, on the heels of Cora's humiliation, her health faded. One night Luther came back from the fields, and a house servant said, "Cora wants you. She bad sick, Luther. You better hurry."

He found her in the little room in which she slept surrounded by canned goods. The slave acting as her nurse silently excused herself.

"I'm so glad you made it, Luther," said Mama Cora. "For nigh on seven years you been like a son to me, and I ain't got long to stay here."

Crying, he kissed her sweaty forehead. "I don't know how I can make it here if you die, Mama Cora."

"That's just it, son. Mama Cora don't want you to stay here. I been selfish, and I'm confessing my sin. The last time they caught me running I was trying to get to the Seminoles. I still know the way. Them white mens talk 'round me like I ain't got good sense. They describe every way our folk be running, who tell on 'em, where the dogs catch 'em, why any fool would've tried another way. Listen and I'll tell you what it took me years to figure is the best way out. I was right that last time: it's south."

"But I thought the Seminoles don't like us. I've heard they cook and eat us."

"That's just white folk lies trying to keep us apart. Now hush and listen."

Luther listened to the directions as though each of her words were worth a million dollars. Then she said, "Look for berries and fruit and greens, take from any field that come in sight, but to stop from starving, go to creeks and seek out fish you can catch by hand. You still remember what I taught you about making fire?"

"Yes' ma'am, but because you always made the fire or stood correcting my mistakes, by myself I haven't tried."

"You was watching close and did it right more than once. I ain't worried 'bout that. Make a good one and unless you somehow got a pot or a piece of tin to cook 'em in, put the fish or whatever meat you come across on the coals and stand over the fire with a big stick."

"What if I can't get a good knife, Mama Cora?"

"The only thing easier to get than a knife is dead. Once you got it, hongry done helped many a child aim straight and stab right. Don't forget there's rattlers and moccasins down that way. But don't none of 'em scare half as much as slavers. Stay clear of *all* folk 'til you meet up with the Seminoles. Some coloreds will turn you in quicker than you say, 'roll that marble'."

He kissed her again. "Sleep now and take your rest."

He did not realize how much energy she had expended trying to save him.

◊◊◊◊◊◊

Luther knew many stories of horrid punishments for failed escape attempts. He was still contemplating Cora's words when Jeremiah, the slaves' favorite preacher tried to run north but was captured before he was out of state.

Once brought before an assembly of other slaves, Master Carver said, "Jeremiah, you call yourself a preacher. What verses you got for what I'm about to lay on your black ass?"

Carver had his ankles shackled while the other slaves were assembled to witness Captain Ellis, the overseer, deliver 20 lashes just after dawn. At the noon day break for water and food, in front of his peers, Jeremiah received 25 more lashes. An hour before dusk, the slaves stood stone-faced or weeping as Ellis gave Jeremiah an additional 30 lashes. Afterwards the others were sent back into the fields with instructions to be silent until the sound of the night bell.

A few days later, when Jeremiah had healed enough to join the field work, as a cautionary example for friends and relatives, he did so with the same shackles tied one to an ankle and the other to a wrist. Sometimes he lost his balance and fell to one or both knees. No one was permitted to help him back on his feet. In time he learned to work limping hunchback. For two terrible days his torture went on simultaneously feeding Luther's determination to run and making him fearful of being caught.

The day Jeremiah's shackles were removed, Cora's death watch also ended. Immediately following her after-hours burial while others stood around the grave weeping or covering the body, Luther slipped away. First he sneaked into his master's library and grabbed the first two books he touched. Then he went to Ellis's shack far off from the big house, between the slave quarter and the southern fields. Lying under a tin roof, across the overseer's wood pile was an array of whips swaddled in dirty cloth. In the full moonlight Luther searched until he found the one that he was sure had been used to beat Jeremiah. It had more weight than appearance suggested. Recalling that our mother would have called it cursed, he almost dropped it, but said in a whisper, "An eye for an eye."

Screaming, "This is for Jesus's third cheek," he burst in upon the sleeping overseer and beat Ellis until the overseer passed out. Then he fled without a single look back. South to the Seminoles.

◊◊◊◊◊◊

In February of 1835, Luther crossed the unmarked border into the last of the Seminole territory yet to be appropriated by the Federal government.

There, as a runaway, he joined hundreds of Florida, Georgia, Alabama, and South Carolina former slaves who pledged themselves to live as freedom-loving patriots known as Black Seminoles.

◊◊◊◊◊◊

As a man who was both literate and filled with rage, Luther's services were invaluable. After a year, when the need arose he served as an interpreter. Almost immediately he proved himself a warrior as well. In between skirmishes Luther befriended Luis Pachecho, a slave whose mistress apparently enjoyed owning him more than she had a need for his labor. The intelligent, handsome, and multi-lingual Pachecho was given such impressive freedom of movement that he often spent weeks with the Seminoles. Pachecho relished having one foot in each camp. He even flirted with Juana, the sister of the Black Seminole chief named John Horse. One day he proposed a tryst if not marriage. Juana said to him, "I will not tie myself to one who only thinks he's free."

Pachecho was so irritated by her poor taste in humor that he said to Luther, "She is a great jokester. I prefer my women more serious. You may have her."

Luther knew this was an overstatement but approached Juana as an equal. In time they became lovers, and she assured him that when the war was over she would marry him.

To Pachecho's chagrin, following a long visit among the Seminoles, Major Francis Dade purchased his services from his slave mistress for $25 a month. On Christmas Eve 1835 Dade declared it was time to end the war. He sent Pachecho ahead alone as a scout.

When an officer protested the risk, he dismissed the concern. The expense was with government money. Even in the worst case scenario, a dead colored scout was one less mouth to feed in a war in which the soldiers often went hungry. Pachecho took note of his value and completely crossed over to become a resistor.

◊◊◊◊◊◊

Luther came across two anhingas drying their huge wet wings in an attempt to warm themselves. He wondered if they were preparing to fly further south. Perhaps it was already too late in the season. Killing was wearing business. If not for Juana, he too might have headed further from this American life. He quickly dismissed a possible metaphor intended to inform his day and continued on his mission. His orders were to immediately report back where the American soldiers were pretend to be a slave who had been stolen, allow himself to be captured, gather inside information, and escape. Proceeding with extreme caution, his path crossed with Pachecho's. A night full of nearby wolf howls and war calls had apparently disarmed the slave-scout. He almost tiptoed along the muddy road and prayed that if he came across a Seminole warrior he would somehow be remembered as a friend. Pachecho was so fearful of his predicament that the 15 mile head start he had been given over the army had dwindled almost in half.

Luther stepped into the open. Pachecho was relieved, albeit his orders labeled Luther as enemy. Luther explained that for several days the scout could have been killed.

"You know me, Luther. I'm really on the side of the Seminoles—black and red. The army's behind me."

"We know that."

"Do you know they have 110 well-armed men planning to kill all of you? Should any survive, red or black they'll be made slaves? No mercy."

Luther left Pachecho, made his report, and was reminded he too should play turncoat.

◊◊◊◊◊◊

Luther disarmed and pretended to be an innocent Seminole slave leaving his lover's village. While casually walking he "accidentally" ran into the army and allowed himself to be captured. He was brought to Dade. "You, nigger, walk beside me."

Later that day, the army caught up with Pachecho who was put on Dade's other side. Laughing at his humor he said, "If we are attacked, you two will serve as *3/5 a man* shields. My men will cover what you lack."

Dade left to relieve himself, and Luther said to Pachecho, "What did he mean '3/5 a man'?"

"Haven't you heard? The American Constitution counts a black man as 3/5 a human."

Behind the trio came the troops and officers in double file. Keeping them company was a small band of musicians alternately playing martial and jaunty tunes in what Dade described as "a most delightful program." The entire unit had their coats buttoned over their cartridges against December's chill.

Long before noon a sharpshooter hit Dade right between the eyes, killing him instantly.

Suddenly war calls surrounded Dade's men. In less than a half hour the battle was over. Only two U.S. soldiers survived the attack. Luther stood over Dade's dead body. "I guess your 3/5 a man measurement fell short."

WHERE LOVE RULES

My sister Fannie and Val Lucky arrived at the 1836 Rendezvous with their trapper husbands, the twins Marshall and Scipio. With them were Val's daughter Sally, and two new babies, her son, Kofi and Val's son, William. The older five had attended the Rocky Mountain trappers' gathering twice before. Rendezvous was always Scipio's and Marshall's favorite time of the year. For men who spent most of their lives working in solitude, functionally, Rendezvous was all of the holidays wrapped into one. The men briefly mourned those killed by Indians, grizzly bears or starvation; drank; caroused; cursed and lied while measuring each other to see if one grew stronger, another faded.

"I love you, Val," said Fannie, "but another woman's face, if not her company, would be welcome."

"Why don't you just come on and say it. We *both* get bored with each other from time to time."

I was Val's only female company in the years that she had spent as an Ohio slave of a master pretending that his three farm workers were servants. After she became pregnant by my brother, Dan, she had left the state with my sister.

At the final rise in the land, Fannie rode her horse forward to speak with the men. The party of blacks silently admired the valley of the Green River. Val said, "Butterflies far as the eye can see. Ain't we the lucky ones."

"Us Luckys make our own luck," said Scipio reveling in his wife's joy.

The Lucky families rode into camp and found that a wagon train led by missionaries was already present. The weary travelers sat on their India rubber ponchos and ate a meal prepared by a colored male cook. Rumors claimed that a quarter of the white travelers had died of cholera shortly before arriving at the Rendezvous. In 1832 Fannie had lost two children to cholera. Had it not been for Val, she too would have died. The women saw to it that their tents were set up as far from the whites as possible.

Men from a myriad of Indian tribes walked around the campgrounds along with more than four hundred scruffy looking trappers, few of whom had washed in anything other than falling rain. Most of the white ones referred to themselves as Americans, Canadian Frenchmen, or English. A few claimed to be Dutch, Scots, or Irish. Perhaps a third of the trappers were sons of Indian and white liaisons. Since intermarriage was common among all of the 20 or so tribes represented, what mattered was lifestyle. The smallest group was the colored, some runaways, others born free, and a few who had found ways to purchase their own freedom. In the eyes of the Indians, unless a man of African descent lived within a Native village, he was a black-white man. Many black men protested but to no avail: in Indian eyes a man was what a man practiced.

Like their white counterparts, most with African ancestors were married to Indian women and included such skilled trappers as Moses Harris, John Brazeau, William Clamorgan, Allen Light, Hosea McKinney, Amos Reese and Jedediah Ranne. They came together as often as they deemed safe enough to avoid the risk of being segregated. Back in the states, in all measurable areas, they were assigned the lowest rung on the social ladder. The western frontier was beyond the reach of politicians, courts, judges and lackeys. In the Rocky Mountains no one asked about free papers, and black folk dared to expect fair treatment. White trappers tended to judge men primarily on their competence in the field and fighting ability in a pinch.

"This territory is not America, but by how we live it's more American than America," said Fannie.

"You got that right," said Val.

And yet, the Luckys each knew, white or colored, trappers judged women first on their availability and next on their physical appearance. "Stay close, at least 'til everybody here know you belong to us," said Scipio as he brushed away a swarm of huge horse flies. "Out here y'all too fine for yo' own good, and some of these men is new."

"Don't let nobody think you're loose," said Marshall.

"These wild men don't bother me," said Val. "What bother me most every time we come to Rendezvous is the m'squitoes, confounded flies, body smells, and pot-boiling over cussing."

"Look at how many tribes these Indian women represent!" said Fannie. "Their dresses are in so many styles! They're as beautiful as anything I've ever seen."

"'Cause of raiding and such, their women outnumber the men," said Scipio.

"I guess y'all know, some is wives and some's been corrupted," said Marshall.

"Corrupted women is a man's idea," said Fannie. "Are these scraggly men supposed to be pure?"

◊◊◊◊◊◊

A contest was announced offering two Comanche horses to the couple whose woman's dress was judged the most attractive. Driven by vanity, some men made Indian women happy by spending a year's earnings on dresses they had made to sell for the competition or for village celebrations. Scipio said to Val, "Let me dress you up, darling."

"I ain't pretty 'nough to get out there with them women," said Val.

"Who told you that lie?"

Fannie quickly said, "I'll watch the children while you sashay around."

"You ain't going get in?" said Val.

"Sally and me need to practice our Fante," she said with a smile.

Actually Fannie knew her own beauty and did not want to risk winning a victory that she did not need for self-validation but which might further lower Val's self-esteem.

Val almost skipped beside Scipio as they went to purchase a Bannock dress. Marshall, who had been off with friends, ran up to their campfire. Before he could say a word Fannie said, "Please don't ask, honey. I don't care what your friends think about me. I'm married to Marshall. What do you think about me?"

"Ain't none finer," he said. "Well, since my wife ain't in it, I guess I can see if I can be a judge."

"Maybe not, honey. Val is your sister-in-law. That should disqualify you."

"I wonder if I'll ever get to vote on something?" he said half-joking.

Fannie pretended that his words did not place a new rent in her heart. She turned to Sally. "Let's play paddy-cake in Fante."

Marshall sat down cross-legged to watch his wife play with Sally. Occasionally he gave simultaneous pushes to the baby cradles made of vines and bark. A whirlwind entered the campground. "Look!"

Fannie stopped long enough to watch the whirlwind swirl about then leave, "Aren't we blessed," said Fannie, "that we don't have to spend our days that way?"

Marshall had been born a Mississippi slave and fallen in love in St. Louis. He had left that slave city then discovered the thrill of freedom in the Rocky Mountains. He finished his pipe just as Jim Beckwourth, one of the Luckys' oldest friends, found their campsite. "There's a horse race scheduled in an hour. Your horses look fresh. You care to run?"

"You're not racing?" asked Marshall.

"No," said Beckwourth. "Today, aside from the tomahawk tosses, I'd rather wait and size up the opposition before I risk my racing reputation."

"The last time you raced me I won," said Marshall.

"Didn't I spot you about ten yards that time?" asked Beckwourth, trying to cover for his horse's slow start. Beckwourth's vanity would never allow him to be contradicted in a woman's presence. Marshall let the matter drop.

"I see my brother and his wife coming back. I'll race when I learn what happened."

"You shoulda seen her," said Marshall. "She looked and walked just like a queen."

Val could not contain her smile. "You won?" asked Fannie.

"No chil'," said Val. "Some of them gals wasn't half-past ugly but I weren't concerned 'bout that mess. All I cared 'bout was Sip's eyes when I come down that gauntlet shaking to the east and shaking to the west, shaking to the very one I love the best."

Everyone but Beckwourth laughed. He was uneasy because he had already bet five horses on Marshall. The time for the race fast approached.

"Let me go change back into my work clothes," said Val.

A group of Frenchmen rode up fast with a few Nez Perce. They drove over 100 horses that they had just taken from a nearby Bannock camp while the warriors were out hunting.

"Them Bannocks have more horses than God knows what to do with," said Marshall.

"Let's put the race aside 'til I mosey over there," said Beckwourth. "I need to see if there's that horse that was stolen from me a few months back. Marshall, why don't you come with me?"

"I'm with you too," said Scipio.

Beckwourth produced a fresh bottle of cheap whiskey, and the men on horses dismounted. The others happily passed around the bottle as he examined the horses. This time none was his. The twins left to go play poker while Fannie and Val prepared a lamb that they had purchased from a Nez Perce woman.

Fannie held it tightly so that Val could slit the docile animal's throat. Although it was killed instantly, it flinched a few times. Fannie held on. Blood spurted and then bubbled on her dress. It was only a day before they planned to do the laundry; with the cool nights the smell would not become overly rancid in the interim. Val broke the lamb's front legs at the knee and Fannie tied a three foot long trimmed sapling between two small trees. Securing the lamb's hind legs to the sapling to drain blood from its neck, Val cut and punched off the skin. Meanwhile Fannie gathered wood.

"This ain't like fixing chickens," said Val.

"It'll taste better than chicken," said Fannie. "But I have to admit sometimes I miss Cincinnati's markets and the comfort I had having servants to do the hardest work."

"I done plumb clear forgot everything about Cincinnati except I ain't going back. With the men we got out here I can say for sure: the west is the best, the east is the least."

"They are good to us, aren't they?" said Fannie silently comparing Marshall with Ethan Jefferson, the cruel dairyman who had been her first husband.

They laughed together as they worked. The lamb's skin removed, Val sliced through the sternum and cut the lamb into pieces. Fannie sorted through the cuts, keeping the more choice ones and discarding the others. A pack of camp dogs waited patiently for what they assumed was their fair share. The canines were thrown intestines and stomach.

"What about the liver and kidneys and the heart?" Fannie said to Val.

"You know I likes all of them. The brains too!"

"You can have them if you're cooking them. I only like muscle meat. There's so many dogs here that maybe we'd better give them a little something worth the wait."

"Meat is meat," said Val. "I'll eat anything but grass, and that ain't meat. These dogs don't need nothing from us. They ain't doing nothing but begging; we doing the work."

Fannie laughed, "Val, you are one of a kind. So unlike my sisters, so much my sister."

"It feels like we's in a place where love rules."

"I wonder why all those men are gathering over there." Fannie pointed toward center camp.

"Have mercy! It looks like some mess is 'bout to start!"

◊◊◊◊◊◊

"Here comes trouble!" Scipio threw down his cards. He held neither aces, kings, nor matches of any sort.

Marshall said, "I finally get a hand worth playing and like always, crap shows up."

Scipio grabbed his rifle. Without knowing the source of the danger, players and watchers, whites and blacks, peace loving and stone cold killers alike reached for their weapons.

Into the camp, at full gallop, rode 25 Bannocks led by a war chief named Gray-Eyed Cougar. Each of the Bannocks was armed with bows and quivers of arrows still tied to their waists. Before anyone could comment, Gray-Eyed Cougar demanded of a group of trappers, "Where are our horses?"

Within seconds they were surrounded by 200 men with drawn rifles.

"If I were you, I'd quick-teach my horses to tiptoe their way out of here," said Beckwourth to Gray-Eyed Cougar.

One of the younger Bannocks reached for a prize calico. Before he could grab the reins, he was gunned down. Between saddle and earth his falling body took six additional bullets. Weapons still at their waists, the other Bannocks bolted. As though they were a herd of four-leggéds, a dozen of them were shot on the way back to their camp. Fist fights ensued over the dead men's scalps. Some trappers pursued the remnant while others plundered and burned their camp. They shot unsuspecting old men and assaulted any woman unfortunate enough to cross their path. Seeing their families imperiled and themselves badly outnumbered, the remaining Bannock warriors scattered in all directions hoping to draw their adversaries away.

◊◊◊◊◊◊

"I think I hear wailing," said Fannie.

"Maybe it's only the wind," said Val.

It was keening, an all too familiar sound among both Africans and Indians. 'If that's the wind, it's Nyame crying,' thought Fannie in Fante. 'Mama and Aunt Eula both made it when death came to call.' "Forget this lamb; leave the children with Beckwourth's wives," she said aloud. "Let's go see if we can help."

"We know good and well our men is mixed up in this mess."

"What we know even better is we must answer for ourselves."

The two colored women ran all the way to the ravaged Bannock village. Fannie had seen her mother repeatedly raped, her family sold apart, and witnessed a friend's lynching. Val had watched her mother and grandmother sold away and had been deliberately burned with a clothes iron filled with hot coals by her mistress. Nothing had prepared them for this day.

People were scattered dead, dying, wounded, and in shock.

"All over horses?" said Fannie in disbelief.

"This kinda hate ain't 'bout horses," said Val.

Until dusk, they tried to bind wounds and comfort women and children. They tended to everyone who seemed to have a chance of survival, expressing compassion for the grieving and repeatedly apologizing for deeds they had not executed.

DANNY BOY

In the minds of many I was one of the successful few. I had married a white farmer and owned a seamstress business but most years we lived hand to mouth. The economy was in serious downturn in the year 1841. The colored folk on the bottom wondered if we would ever be included in the American dream. Because Ohio law did not recognize my marriage to Charles, I had to carry a free paper and no woman could vote. I had no illusions that I was somehow a member of the ruling class.

Then spring brought a change for us colored people. In March, the United States Supreme Court freed slaves who rebelled on the illegal slave ship *Amistad*. In Cincinnati, less than a month later, Salmon P. Chase won a case on a technicality that earned the release of a woman defending herself from a former slaveholder who for ten years had sought her following her escape. In May, the Ohio State Supreme Court ruled that any slave brought into the state by an owner was automatically freed because the United States Constitution only addressed fugitives and Ohio was a free state. We people of color believed the arc of justice was bending our way. We also knew enough to brace for push back from the lower class white people who would be encouraged by the upper classes to keep us down.

Following the same script used prior to the 1829 mob attack that had driven over half of the colored population from the city, newspaper editorials fanned enmity by claiming colored people stole white rights. Ministers in pulpits and bully boys on the streets increased attacks on the ones without rights. Then nature seemed to join the conspiracy against us. A horrendous drought dried up black hope. Disproportionate numbers of colored seasonal pickers lost their jobs, and produce prices increased. An August heat wave compounded the tension. Ohio colored people were a few miles removed from slavery but well primed for pain.

Small, commonplace incidents of whites disrespecting colored people multiplied. The colored community argued over strategy, some saying, "Ask King Jesus to bring us mercy," and others, "Let them attack. I got something for 'em they didn't see when they kicked us out of Cincinnati in 29." Bethel African Methodist Episcopal Church noted that the visual odds against colored people were 10 to 1 and took out a newspaper advertisement in the Cincinnati Daily Chronicle promising to strive "in the future" to be more "orderly and industrious." Weary of kowtowing, the more militant colored men mimicked whites and purchased more guns. Ignoring the possibility of a congregation split, some members of Bethel African Methodist Episcopal Church chose Major James Wilkerson to help them organize. Wilkerson's first name hearkened to a non-existent military rank while announcing his parents had reared him to stand and fight.

◊◊◊◊◊◊

My brother Dan had offered Paddy Throughstone, a down on his luck Irish-American blacksmith, a position working for his stagecoach line. Paddy shoed horses, fixed cart wheel rims, and did all manner of repairs to keep the stage coaches in superlative shape. We were all surprised that Paddy continued working in Dan's employ despite some calling him "White trash" and others "Nigger lover." On Friday, September 3 Paddy came to work and said, "there'll be trouble tonight."

"You did give the taxman the money I left?" asked Dan.

"Sure as Belfast is north of Madrid, although I find it hard to believe with your children barred from the public schools you accept taxation without representation and pay as much taxes as a white man."

Looking around and seeing that there were no other employees or customers, thus there was no need to remind him that "Mr. Crispin" was the better way to address him, Dan said, "What is the source of the trouble?"

Paddy explained that the local bully-boys were mad because when Jacob Burnett was caught sheltering a runaway, the sheriff had stopped them from burning the German-American's house. Those with Burnett's background had learned to hate oppression in Europe. So many of them assisted runaways that they were in danger of being ostracized. "If the sheriff had not come when he did the potatoes would have been in the boxty."

"I'm missing something."

"They figure the sheriff is pushing the edges by protecting Germans. If he wants to be reelected he'd better look the other way when you coloreds get attacked and abolitionists try to get in the way of justice. They're planning revenge, and their cousins from Kentucky also are not a forgiving lot. There's no mystery to their favorite party guests. Certain bodies might wish to be elsewhere than on the street after sundown if not before."

Dan chose to risk continuing his normal business for at least one day. Life became complicated when the driver of the original route to the docks sent a note that he was sick. Instead of sending the normal replacement, Dan used the opportunity to reconnoiter the city. He criss-crossed both of his holsters, cleaned his pistols and checked that there was ammunition in his shotgun. Then he made four round trips between the docks and the hotels. With each trip the groups of bully-boys grew. By the time he made the last trip he had counted almost a dozen groups, some of which had as many as one hundred whiskey drinking, profanity spewing men.

All colored people and intelligent whites became scarce. Oblivious to their responsibilities, the sheriff and his deputies chatted with the crowds, lit cigars, shared snuff cans, and accepted sips of moonshine.

◊◊◊◊◊◊

The Lion and the Lamb Stable was closed for the day when Dan returned from the last run. "It's almost sunset, Paddy. Unless you are working on a special customer's job order, you need not stay on."

"I suppose I oughtta go home, Dan m' lad, but unless this a private fight, I thought I'd stick around in case you need help."

"You cannot be serious."

"Danny boy, here I am, offering you my services. Let me make myself useful." Dan hesitated. "I'm sure you know my Baker's Rifle waits near the forge. It's not there just to keep me in old memories. It may help me make some new ones."

They had worked together for years but never had they had a man to man conversation. Dan forced himself to say, "If I were under attack, you'd go to that extent to help me?"

"The angels may not have done their bidding protecting martyrs, but God has been known to send devils to do his bidding. Here I am, and happily I'd help a bully boy find Hell."

The first guns went off in the near distance. Within twenty minutes several rounds were fired into the fronts of businesses owned by colored people. Dan and Paddy were well armed behind bales of hay and waiting for an attack. A cloudburst brought rain that the people had been praying would break the drought. Dan said, "It might be safe now."

"Safe to do what, walk home amidst all those guns?" Paddy ended being coy, "Danny, I wasn't always a blacksmith. I fought for a time with the British Auxiliary in Spain before coming to America."

"I know you hate Brits. What does Ireland have to do with Spain?"

"Nothing. But who do you think fights the wars in Europe? I can tell you from experience, it's the castoffs. We were always led by noble sons of leeches out of the inheritance loop. They'd never admit it, but they were but castoffs like us. Unless they have a death wish or need to prove something to somebody, not enough men with futures go looking to be shot at. I was a mercenary making better money than the Brits would let a man make at home."

"You think we're in a war now?"

"From what I can tell, most of the firing is one way."

"How do you come to that conclusion?" asked Dan.

"If it were two ways, the sides are so unequal we could hear screams from a massacre. Intimidation is fundamental to creation. The bully boys are mostly acting for show."

"I hope you're not holding that gun for show. If they charge, I'll discharge."

Paddy chuckled. "I'm glad to hear you're not given to being massacred, Danny Boy. It pleasures me to stand shoulder to shoulder with a man who ain't suicidal." They both laughed.

"Why are you, a man of means, here in this madness? You could have paid your employees extra to guard the premises."

"For generations we have pulled tobacco and picked cotton, cleaned up their messes, and nursed their babies. Paddy, I've only met a few men my age who know their way back to Africa."

"Say more."

"I know I'm Fante, but who knows how many tribes are mixed in most Africans here in America? I want to be a gentleman and—even though I'm here ready to blow someone's head off—an American gentleman who protects his property. It's that simple. Now my question and your answer: why are *you* here?"

"You, Danny Boy, are my friend. It's that simple." He paused because he knew that was not the whole truth. "But even if you weren't...do you know any Irish history?"

"Beyond that the British disrespect your homeland, I have little knowledge about your people. I read newspapers, Latin, and fiction."

"Forgive me, Sir Scholar, but I will not comment on your choice of reading material. In America it seems colored people are divided: the Indian like your friend Caesar the Shawnee, don't want to forget and the blacks want to catch amnesia. Those of us from the Emerald Isle, rank history with bread, potatoes, comely lasses, and good whiskey. Listen to this well, for should you chance to include history on your reading list, I doubt you'll come across it. Men and women, children and criminals, have been taken from all over Ireland for about 200 years. They've been sent to America and the West Indies."

"What do you mean 'taken'?"

"They were indentured servants serving for 5 or 7 or sometimes even 12 years."

"This is not the first time I've heard rumors of white slaves."

"I said 'indentured servants', but yes, if I got trapped into a confession I'd have to admit they were slaves for a period and forced to do hard labor without rights or pay. On both sides of my family I have aunts and uncles, cousins, a grandfather even a great grandmother who arrived here in such a state. Thousands of Irish have arrived on these shores as stolen people. Germans and Scots too—"

"Now three good people have told me colored people have not been alone. The fiction I have read never mentions this."

"Good? Did you just call me 'good'? I'd sooner share a cup with a Cromwell than have my brothers know you'd call one such as I 'good'.'"

"Name yourself, but I do appreciate you."

Paddy laughed and explained that the notion of an oppressed man being alone in the struggle was a bald faced lie. It took Dan several minutes to digest this information. Meanwhile sporadic shooting and the sound of rain broke the silence. Paddy spoke next. "I had a…friend when I was in Spain. She watered canons, washed and sewed clothes, cooked and…other things. Not a prim and proper woman but I favored her. So did others. One was a captain. She wasn't blind, this woman, and if she'd taken a bullet in her head I suspect her brain was bigger than a pea. The captain was son of a peer, and I was the son of a…Irishman. The world's an unsettled place, Dan. I'd prefer it was civilized, a place where a good man has a fair chance at praise even if he didn't have one at birth."

"Injustice is vice."

"The priests talk a lot about vices. What's your religion have to say about them?"

"I don't practice any religion other than the golden rule."

Paddy tried another route, "All my life it's been vices that confound me. They say that before Miss Zephyrine you were a lover."

"I still am; I just don't cheat on my wife."

Paddy laughed. "With a wife men call 'Queen' a man might be beheaded for such." Although Dan bristled in the darkness at hearing an employee refer to his wife by a nickname not of his own choosing, he said nothing. "How'd you quit the habit of lass chasing?"

"My mother deserved but never got the chance to concentrate on one man at a time."

Paddy was at a loss for words. The two men sat in the darkness and waited for others to determine their next move.

◊◊◊◊◊◊

Intermittent firing continued for three hours. Then there was a lengthy lull. Dan recalled the storm that had enabled our flight from slavery. He told Paddy the story and they discussed the price of leaving loved ones behind. While Dan contemplated far more losses than he had cared to share, the moments deepened. To remove his mind from roads taken that now appeared sacrifices, he changed the subject to the present. "Before it almost seemed like the bully-boys just wanted to be gadflies, but I don't like the silence."

"I doubt that this is silence," said Paddy.

"So far from dawn, and the rain having dwindled to a sprinkle, my guess is this is the calm before the true storm."

Soon a resounding boom went off. "This is America?" said Paddy rhetorically. "Instead of bearing flowers she courts with malice! Danny, it sounds like cannon fire. There it is again. I'm sure that's what it is."

Less than two blocks away, a 6-pound cannon obliterated two

buildings owned by colored businessmen. Dan braced for a shelling to his stables that never came. The bombarding lasted 30 minutes and ended. Paddy said, "I think you know why the biggest downtown colored business is being spared. The esteemed Patience Starbuck protects you. A wealthy white woman's property is beyond these cowards' reach."

"That's a hard, true fact." My brother hid even from a trusted friend he in fact owned the Lion and the Lamb but could not announce it if he wanted whites to do business with him.

After a weighted pause Paddy asked, "Would you be offended if I was to take a little walk around the environs? The Brits would call it a reconnoiter."

"It is too late in the game now to be offended by accepting your assistance."

◊◊◊◊◊◊

Paddy ascertained that the bully boys had exhausted their supply of cannon balls. Their terrorizing had ended with the sheriff yielding to the pressure of businessmen fed up with losing money and a committee of Quakers remembering that once upon a time the Religious Society of Friends had been the despised ones. The sheriff called his deputies together. Their orders were to have the colored men disarmed and herded to 6th and Broadway, "For their own protection." There he appropriated wood from a colored owned lumber yard and had his men select "volunteers" to build their own pen.

From a position of safety, Paddy watched it all. By the time the corralling stopped, Paddy counted more than two hundred men stuffed cheek by jowl. Among them was Major Wilkerson. "So you see," said Paddy to Dan, "unlike me, you're better off hiding in here than traveling the streets even if but to make your way home."

Without speaking a word, my brother hung his rifle on its rack and placed his pistols in a drawer. On the way out of the Lion and the Lamb

Stables he said, "I am not above my people. Be so kind as to send word to my wife the following message: 'Mr. Dan Crispin has been delayed at 6th and Broadway'."

OTHER THAN

In the spring of 1842, the author Charles Dickens came to Cincinnati. One of the most famous men of his age looked on from the deck of the *Messenger,* a steamship that he had described as "negligent and filthy." The "Queen City" spread out before him perched on seven hills just north of the slave line. The beauty of blossoming dogwoods and flame azaleas was impossible to miss. From the dock he saw clothiers, grocers, wholesale merchants, produce stores and, best of all, a coffee shop.

My brother, Dan Crispin sat atop his coach. Although his heart was full of anticipation because of a tip from a fellow Underground Railroad conductor who lived upstream that the great author was aboard, he worked hard to finish reading a chapter. Dickens spied the Lion and the Lamb painted on the doors of the immaculately kept coach. He hailed Dan, who for this special run, pranced instead of walked his magnificent horses to the place where the Dickens party stood.

Dickens turned from the colored porters who loaded the bags on the coach. "At every new temptation I find myself pausing. Can there be any doubt that this fine coach of yours is one such done by the great Quaker painter Edward Hicks?"

"So I've been told, sir," said Dan. "I'm here to serve."

"Gentlemen of education and distinction are rare in these parts."

Against his mentor's counsel, Dan decided that for this particular Englishman it might be worth the risk to resist playing the unlettered Negro and demonstrate a degree of his intelligence. "Gentlemen have other occupations, and I cannot claim study in a school."

"Gentlemen are judged not by oneself but by others," said Dickens. "My personal character is not diplomatical. Speaking plainly, I do not judge a man as superior because he has an Oxford—or Princeton—education." He paused until he was certain the point had been registered that he was not provincial. "I'd rather believe a little education well-seasoned by a bright mind can make one acceptable in all company. Obviously you understand this. Hence you said nothing about my charge that you are distinguished." Ever so slightly, Dan bowed his head in humble acknowledgment of the liberal statement. "I'll not waste another day on unsuitable coffee such as was served on the steamship. I only ask you to wait as truth awaits each good seeker, and point me to an acceptable cup."

"There, sir." He nodded with his head rather than pointing. "I'd wager you'll find something worthy."

By the time the Dickens party appeared on the porch, Dan had almost completed reading his second chapter. Dan saw them exit the coffee shop and jumped down immediately. Moments later he held the door and assisted Catherine Dickens and her traveling companion in ascending the three steps. "I say, chap," said Dickens, "There is gratifying wisdom in good advice and much pleasure in attentive service."

Dan was silent. The coffee shop did not serve colored people. Thus his recommendation had come from several third parties. On the drive, he steered clear of the city's hovels allowing Dickens to admire the broad streets and sturdy homes, some built of brick, and others of stucco and quarried stone. The fear of fires from wood frame houses was ever present in Cincinnati although only the upper classes could avoid building mainly in timbers. Dan drove the coach past numerous churches, the courthouse and two first-quality museums. Everywhere Dickens was allowed to look in the city of 50,000 people he found well maintained stone, shining glass, pruned trees, and weed-free flowers in picture-perfect beds. Hard-working colored servants dominated the mid-afternoon landscape.

By the time they reached the Broadway Hotel, Dickens was in excellent humor. Suddenly he leaned out his window of the slow-moving coach and tapped Dan with his cane. "I was admiring your blue jays so bright that they appear to be flying flowers, when what should I behold but a woman who appeared to be addressing a cross-eyed pig!"

"I try not to judge those I do not know," said Dan.

It took Dickens a moment to understand his driver's retort. Then he laughed in a high pitch voice and said, "No. No. Mine was no metaphor. It was *actually* a pig being greeted by a woman."

Free-running pigs with notches bearing their owner's brand were frequent pedestrians on Cincinnati streets. Dan followed Dickens' eyes. Indeed a well-dressed woman accompanied by her husband was just straightening her back.

"Here we take our pork seriously, sir," said Dan.

Dickens laughed again and settled back into his seat. Dan stopped the coach as two policemen crossed the street without bothering to wait for traffic. While stationary, he heard Dickens say to Catherine, "Unlike the crude, personal-fork-in-common-bowl, taciturn diners on *The Messenger*—a poor excuse for a vessel—this glorious city appears void of flippant conversations. Even pigs are addressed respectfully."

Dan collected his fare and a generous tip.

◊◊◊◊◊◊

The Englishman returned from St. Louis a few months later and found the original Lion and the Lamb coach at the dock to greet him. Instead of Dan, Jerry Riley was driving. Surprised, Dickens asked what had happened to the driver he had met at the docks and sent Jerry back to ask for his presence.

"Tell him Mr. Charles Dickens requests his company."

At noon Dan told the doorman that he had been summoned by Mr. Dickens. A bellhop was dispatched with the message. Dickens met the servant at the door. "Why didn't you send him up?"

"Nigras can't come up here."

"This country is replete with suspense," said Dickens. "Are you not a Negro?" The light-skinned bellhop, who had at least one known African ancestor, could not think of a suitable answer. "This is horribly ludicrous," said Dickens before descending the stairs. Dan awaited on the porch.

"By every means they can compass, the powers seem intent on impressing on the minds of Negroes that they are repulsive," said Dickens. Dan said nothing. "I mean the powers are repulsive, not Negroes themselves." He angrily recounted the exchange with the bellhop.

Dan kept his face inscrutable. "May I assist you in some way, sir?"

"By telling the powers that be not to make an employer come to an employee!" Dan had the good sense not to reply. Dickens gathered himself. "Provided you use the inestimable coach in which I twice now have had the pleasure of being a passenger, I would like you to drive me to Columbus. I cannot brook traveling in one of those 12 passenger monstrosities over inferior roads and with questionable company."

"The 'Original' is available, sir. And the road to Columbus is macadamized."

"I judge from your face there is more. There is always more."

"Yes, sir, but…" Dan's voice trailed off.

"What would be your fee?"

"I hesitate to say. Quoting my dear mother, 'I can't fix my lips' to name the figure."

Dickens laughed. "I love the quaintness in this country. Here is a pen and paper. Write down this mysterious figure that is too ineffable to speak."

Dan mentally measured the amount the original coach usually grossed in a day, the number of days a leisurely roundtrip would take, wear and tear on the coach, travel expenses for food and lodging if a colored man would be fortunate enough to find someone to rent a room, and added 10% for incidentals. Then he wrote the figure on the paper.

Dickens studied the paper, testing to see if Dan would lower the price. Hat in hand, Dan waited patiently. "Well, it seems fair. My party will make a short sojourn in Columbus before moving on to Sandusky. Can you leave Wednesday an hour before first light?"

"I will be here, sir. May I take one or two additional passengers?"

"At this rate?" said Dickens in mock amazement. "I scarcely know what to do with you, Mr. Crispin. You are aware that I have my wife and our two traveling companions."

"Sir, I was thinking of an employee who could sit up top with me and spell me should I grow fatigued." Dan covered up his original hope for a major windfall.

"Profiting by my experience leads me to believe that most country inns delight in such fare as beet roots, shreds of dried beets and cornbread for breakfast and supper. I trust that I need not concern myself with such limitations?"

"No sir." Dan mentally composed a letter to me announcing the coming of Dickens and requesting that I query our wealthy white friend Patience Starbuck about superior inns along a route he had never traveled. This he sent by his next northbound coach that would pass near by home. "And do not invite her to the place where we will introduce you to the great author," he concluded. "Keep ever so quiet."

◊◊◊◊◊◊

The following morning Dan brought Jerry with him. Dickens noted Jerry and the bell boy loading the bags as Dan watched. "This man addresses you as though you were the owner." Dan said nothing. "From the moment of my arrival, I have assumed owners of all that is fine in Cincinnati are white. 'Surely,' I said to myself, 'a Negro man cannot accumulate enough capital to compete when whites are given every advantage.'"

Dan wanted to say, "*Au contraire,*" but instead bit his tongue hoping the moment would pass without being forced to admit Patience Starbuck had financed the initial enterprise. A second question did not follow immediately. Dan assumed that, as with most of his customers, for Dickens the sound of his own voice was sufficient.

◊◊◊◊◊◊

The coach could comfortably average 25 miles a day despite necessary stops. On the roughest roads, and without passengers, Dan had driven much faster. The trip to Lebanon was short and smooth. For the Dickens party, on this first leg of the journey, he drove at the rate of a leisurely 18 to 20 miles. The English tourists enjoyed themselves laughing at this and that, looking forward to supper at a premier hotel. Frequently they peered out on what had been Shawnee and Miami land for centuries. Cultivated farms lay along the length of the road. Many of them were surrounded by woods through which wildlife once roamed and had been established on land cleared by displaced Indians or grazed by bison that whites had exterminated only a few decades earlier. At each small town friendly admirers gathered to wave at the triumphant tourists riding in the resplendent coach.

Dan and Jerry delivered the Dickens party safely to Lebanon's Golden Lamb Inn. Because colored people who were not cleaning or bellhop staff were forbidden inside, the colored men sat under a tree and ate a meal packed by my sister-in-law Zephyrine.

"They call her 'Queen' for a reason," said Jerry. "Miss Zephyrine's Virginia ham slices, hush puppies, and sweet potato cobbler are better than whatever they may be eating."

"I don't doubt your words," said Dan. "It only angers me that we're not seen as worthy of eating inside."

Well-fed and unconcerned with the plight of the drivers, the travelers continued on.

◊◊◊◊◊◊

I had arrived nearly an hour earlier than the coach was expected. While waiting I sat in silence, gathering myself for the momentous occasion when Dan stopped the Lion and the Lamb at Holloway's Tavern. In my bag were notes taken from Patience Starbuck's references of the better inns en route to Columbus as well as hotels where the Dickens family might enjoy an acceptable night's rest. Knowing I seldom left the village unless I was visiting my brother in Cincinnati, Patience had asked why I was interested. I had answered simply that my brother was making a run there. We lived just outside of Waynesville on Caesar's Creek between my in-laws and Patience. The news of Dickens' trip had run ahead after the coach had stopped in Lebanon. Surely Patience had learned through her servants but she never seemed impressed with the famous and other wealthy. I believe she did not press me because she saw no value in standing awestruck at the presence of another human.

After the Dickens party entered Holloway's, I stepped to the rear of the fawning assembly of whites. I grew impatient with my own reticence and pushed forward. The moment seized, I approached the man of the day. "Sir, my name is Sarah Ferguson."

"I am delighted, Mrs. Ferguson. I am Charles Dickens, a visitor to your village."

"Sir," I said boldly, "could you tell me why you wrote *Oliver Twist*? It has a haunting quality that I find strangely ephemeral."

"Perhaps the question is too personal, sister," interrupted Dan, shocked that I was so bold as to approach Dickens without being summoned and allowing him to introduce us.

"*A contrario*. This opulent yet petite beauty is your blood sister?" said Dickens, pretending to measure with his hands the 11" difference in height. I believe our difference in skin color marveled him, deep chocolate man and milk caramel woman.

"Yes, sir," we said simultaneously.

"Aside from speech, one could hardly tell you are brother and sister." He turned to me. "To the question: I am repelled by this world's cruelties and use my pen to speak out. I submit that it is a part of our moral nature to look at evil and long for goodness." He waited for a comment or second question, but because of Dickens' fame, I had spent hours reducing all I might ask into a single question. The gentleman rescued me. "I know that this is Quaker territory and see you dressed like a Quaker. Is it possible that you might know the esteemed William Bassett?"

"I only know him by reputation," I said. "Few Quakers can publicly accuse other Friends of 'moral cowardice' and remain unknown."

"Then you are a Quaker?"

"Family members are; I am only an attender."

"Might *thee* attend a second question?" said Dickens in a teasing voice.

Determined not to appear what our brother Robin had called 'a one-trick pony', I quickly constructed a second question, "For an Englishman, is there curiosity in America?"

"A briefly spoken, well-aimed and cogent question." He paused. "I had not realized the extent of distress that plagues your country—or should I say 'their country'? I fear America is a verbose ghost with little to add to our understanding of civilization. Unless it is intent upon dying in a sinking flame, it must let its heart be touched. Could you touch it? Are you a writer, Mrs. Ferguson?"

"Please, sir, call me Sarah."

"Then, Sarah, do you have a song of your own? You are the one who should speak for America. An Englishman such as I can only observe. Your story might be compelling. Mine might have a trace of malice. By your bearing you obviously are not by nature malicious."

A growing crowd surrounded us, but I pushed myself to a new height, "Having thee as a model, I could not dare place pen to paper. I find one of thy greatest strengths to be where Shakespeare often left off: many of thy characters are multi-layered. How could I develop such talent?"

"Even with the qualifier 'many'," said Dickens smiling graciously, "you had the temerity to mistakenly place my name in the same sentence with Shakespeare. That wonderful compliment has beautified almost to the grandeur of your being. You are not an imitator of intelligence. Do not cage yourself, butterfly. Should you choose to write, never dream of stepping away from the child that first sparked your mind. Your sable eyes, observant of ivory society could give new meaning to America, the Pretender." Then to my amazement, he bowed his head slightly and kissed my hand.

The mayor of the town cleared his throat. Introductions of important citizens and their wives were made. Amidst a mixture of glares and reverent looks, I retreated to my brother's side.

"All that is seen is not all there is," I whispered to Dan.

"For a moment I feared you might go too far. And yet Dickens made it clear that he sees to your heart. I am proud to be your big brother, and Mama would applaud your behavior."

"Thy kind words deserve a gift." I handed him the travel instructions given by Patience atop a picnic basket. He peered inside the basket and found homemade pork sausages, two kinds of muffins and a whole egg custard pie."

"You do know how to show your love, don't you?"

"Was thee showing something less by alerting me of this opportunity?"

Back at the coach, Dickens said to Dan, "Both you and your sister could have easily played buffoons."

"Why would we have done that?"

"I know your fee, but you know gentlemen give something extra. As for her, currying favor is usually the way to impress neighbors. Instead she tossed caution away like chaff. You two resisted modest improvement of your stations."

"We were reared to be other than buffoons."

THE BROOM

My brother Babatunde knew few 44 year old women who had lived through childbirth. He believed Esi had died giving birth to him. I knew our mother well. I believe Mother had died from a broken heart brought on by living as a slave in America. Had I not escaped I probably would have died at a much younger age. Escape brought me more than enough to live for.

Yejide, Babatunde's surrogate mother, the woman others called Judy, died of old age. Some said she might have been 40. That was years ago on July 4th. Her biological children enjoyed saying, "Mama's sure enough free now," but the man everyone knew as Tune disagreed. 'Mama,' he said to himself, 'now that you can't stop me from calling you that, you was always free in your mind. Wheresomever you may be, it's more of the same just not so much work, chops instead of fatback, and no white folk in sight. I ain't gonna simmer in my misery worrying about missing you, but I sure do miss you. Mama Esi done me a great kindness giving me to you, *Mama* Judy."

"Tune," said Eliza Bailey, the 36 year old cook, "are you talking to me, Aunt Judy's ghost, or to the wind."

"Tune just talking to hisself."

"Then is you going eat my pone and my Grandma Betty's sweet potato recipe, or can I pass your'n on to some little one?"

With two massive bites, Tune gulped down the last of his food.

"You is a mess, Tune," she said with a smile.

"Eliza, I don't know why, but I been thinking about my kin."

"I never knew my daddy, and I was 11 when my mother died. I haven't seen my brothers Perry and Frederick or my sisters Eliza, Kitty, and Arianna since '32."

"I ain't talking about you, Eliza," said Tune. "It's my folk that's on my mind." He had no way of knowing that I and his other siblings also thought frequently of him, the baby Mama was carrying when the rest were sold apart.

"Get 'em off before they rides you too long, Tune," said Eliza. "Whatchou can't see, 'though it's got you, you may as well not have. Right now you on Captain Carwell Mustin's Green Manor Plantation situated on the border of Tennessee and Mississippi and them kinfolk subject to be near 'bouts anywhere."

He stood up and walked a short distance to stand eye to eye with her. "That's why I like you Eliza, you ain't got no imagination, but you talk straight."

"Don't you try to hit on me, Tune. I'm old enough to be yo' mama."

"You know you feeling it too," he said trying to kiss her cheek.

"Tune," she pushed back and giggled, "my oldest boy be bigger than you."

"Here I am five foot two of seven foot two man. I may be black, almost blue, but—" He searched for the next rhyme, thought she grew impatient, and slightly changed directions.

"Anyway, I'm trying to prove the point that it ain't the size *of* the man's pants, but the size *in* the man's pants." He successfully planted a kiss on her cheek. "You ever heard that, gal?"

"Life's 'bout more than just crowing and hearing. I done been pregnant seven times and seen three grow to walk. I need for a man to *show me* he's a man on this here battlefield not while he lying down dreaming he's a warrior. That water too deep for you?"

He let her go, "I was only funning with you, Eliza Sooky."

"Where that Sooky come from? I ain't got no down home name. I'm a Maryland gal—"

"Who's 'situated on the border of Tennessee and Mississip', on Captain Carwell Mustins' Green Manor Plantation'," he said laughing and running away. "Tune going go play my banjo. It don't never play hard to get."

"Just go on over there and play another song for Irene. This here old lady ain't got time to mess with your young rump."

"Good night," he said to Eliza with a bow that she could not see in what had become deep darkness. "Miss Bailey, sleep and dream of Tune and I'll strum you a king of a tune under a gold coin moon." His was an inside joke. One day Tune, the slave son of slave parents, intended to make King his surname.

◊◊◊◊◊◊

When Tune was in his early teens, Gus, the Mustin's jockey, let him ride one of the horses. Tune loved the experience and rode each chance he got. Carwell saw him riding Cocoa Dust, the sorrel who was the prize of the county. From a young age, Tune had sneaked out on moonless nights and taken horses on short rides around the area. More than once patrollers heard him, pursued, and failed to run him down.

When we met and he told me of these escapades, I asked why he had not fled north with one of the horses. He had looked at me incredulously and asked where might a young colored boy run to and how could he expect to outrun ten million patrollers? Obviously he was exaggerating his dilemma but I understood his point.

By the time he was in his mid-teens Tune's Sunday afternoon horse performances on the plantation track caught his master's imagination. Tune had an uncanny ability to sit silently and barely move the rope as he guided a horse left, right, clockwise, counterclockwise, forward, backward, horizontally, and diagonally. Moreover, when he raced horses around the plantation track, Daphne Mustin called him, "a black unicorn."

Mustin went to Tune. "I've seen you horseback. You got more horse in you than Gus. I'm going to sell him off while he is at his highest value and invest in you. Yes, I'm going to give you a chance to be a man. I pronounce you a jockey and every time you win, I'll give you a dollar a day until the next race. Lose and you get nothing. It's kind of like, what the Good Book says, 'for whosoever hath, to him shall be given; and whosoever hath not, from him shall be taken even that which he seemeth to have.' Gus will lose his luck. I and you will make the best of this situation."

"'I and you'?" said Mustin's wife, Daphne. "They already speak worse than white trash."

"Keep the world order straight, wife, and there will be peace in the valley. First comes us then comes others."

◊◊◊◊◊◊

In 1845, at Nashville, Tennessee's Easter races, Tune, the first-time jockey, watched white men bet huge sums of money, slaves, even their entire estates. He thought, 'And I'll get a whole dollar a day if I can win. Watch the tune I play.'

He surprised nearly everyone by taking two third places and a second. He rode to win and was disheartened not realizing that all-out sprinting from start to finish seldom won professional races. Mustin had displayed business acumen by betting on other jockeys to win. His increased wealth may have helped him show compassion. He broke his promise and paid Tune a single dollar from his own winnings. Tune smiled at holding the first dollar he could call his own. "Potential counts, boy. Never forget it. Become more and earn more."

Racing and training to race became Tune's livelihood as he was released from the drudgery of paying constant homage to cotton. When at rest he mentally reviewed what he had learned from the other jockeys. Although Mustin was not ready for Tune to appear again as a jockey, the master allowed him to sit on the sidelines and watch local races. Most of the winners paced their horses in degrees varying upon the track conditions, the opponents' skills, and their horse's temperament on a given day. Each of the better jockeys mastered becoming at one with their mount. Tune the avid student, applied lessons learned. He synchronized his heartbeat with that of his mounts.

To further motivate his jockey, Mustin built Tune a humble house of his own. There my brother often sat with his banjo while others were in the fields or left late to handle the best of Mustin's horses until he stopped on his own time. Best of all, from Saturday night through Sunday evening he relaxed with his great love, Irene, a slave on an adjacent plantation who he had met at the local church.

◊◊◊◊◊◊

Irene lay across his legs. They were in the westward leaning umbrageousness formed by a triangle of disparate trees: maple, willow and red oak, each shedding autumn leaves one at a time. He plucked a medley of slow songs, kissed her thick braids at intervals, and played with lyrics as they came to him. The lovers acted as though Sunday's sun would never set. Unfortunately, time is not as kind as soft words and tender strokes from rough hands. Before the sun disappeared, their afternoon of enjoying each other's company ended.

The plantation where Irene was in bondage was claimed by the state of Mississippi while Mustin's was claimed by Tennessee. On the walk back to Judge's plantation she said, "You want to jump the broom?"

He squeezed her hand. "What would it prove? Both of us know couples who live on different plantations and others who got broke up by they masters because colored folks' marriages ain't worth nothing in a white man's eyes. Folk know by my songs ain't but one gal for Tune."

"You do love your Irene don't you, Tune?"

What was he resisting, and could he find it elsewhere? When I asked my brother this question he was at a loss for words, and I regretted having spoken my heart.

◊◊◊◊◊◊

The next year Tune won 40% of the races he entered. An Alabama loudmouth said, "The nigger must be part horse!" It caught on, leading whites to call him Tune Pony, a name he silently rebuked. but was powerless to openly decry. "At least it's better than the Galloping Spook," he said to Irene, trying to laugh off the insult. He continued to think of himself as Tune King.

Later that day Tune shared the surface of his pain he suddenly said aloud, "Sooky, Sooky!" Catching himself he said, "Got, to be mo' careful!"

"Careful about what?" asked Irene.

"Dreaming choices when we ain't got none."

"Why don't you choose to kiss me and put that banjo down?"

They ignored the sweltering August night and loved each other as though one of them did not have to beat sunrise home. Tune was sleeping when Irene rose to dress.

She was about to leave for the five mile hike back home when Tune slowly stretched. "You can't sleep either?"

"Either? You been calling hogs as though you was a pig drover. I got to get on back."

He jumped up. "Them crickets almost made me forget my manners."

For a short time they enjoyed the night sounds. "What you thinking now?"

"I'm thinking ain't but two creatures in the world—Irene and Tune. That's what I'm thinking."

"You done forgot both of us is owned people? I guess being a jockey done confused your mind."

He was putting on his brogans when she kissed his neck. "*Now* what you thinking?"

"That my payment for being a song man is I can't think like regular folk. Of course, if Tune was regular folk, Irene wouldn't have no use for him."

She laughed and kissed his neck again. "A regular man could jump the broom."

"Could he?"

◊◊◊◊◊◊

Tune's three consecutive victories in Memphis made him a jockey of note. After a few months at home, where he was treated by the slave community as though he had won a war, Mustin took him off on a grand tour of racetracks. They were away a dozen weeks on a trip that proved once and for all no southern jockey could compare with "Tune Pony, the nigger in gold and green silks."

The first night back, Eliza Bailey finished her chores in the big house and ran over to Tune's house.

"Something bad happened while you was gone," she said to Tune. "The Judge found out Irene is in the family way and gave her to Big Blue."

The shock almost knocked him to his knees. Although Big Blue had never been an official breeder or claimed a child, he was credited as sire of at least 15 children around The Spokes, a set of five adjoining plantations. When Tune regained his breath he whispered, "You was right when you set it up as bad. Ain't nothing pleasing about that, Eliza."

"I just thought you'd wanna know from a friend. Instead of some fool cackling in your face."

"I wish to Hell somebody would get in my face and say something about this mess."

"You better get yourself together before somebody gets hurt."

"Hurt? Did you say hurt?" She was silent. "You reckon I should've jumped the broom with her?"

"That wouldn't have changed nothing. I was married before I got sold here. My thin-lipped master ripped me away from Henry and my first chillen. We dance to the white man's music even if it stays outta tune."

TECUMSEH'S VISION

Following the 1829 forced exodus of blacks from Cincinnati, my brother Dan had spent a few years in Detroit. While there he and Mariah Chene, a Wyandotte runaway had been lovers. Their son was named Tecumseh. I met my nephew when he came to Waynesville for a memorial service. This is his story.

Tecumseh's mother worked for the visionary abolitionist Laura Haviland who had founded Raisin Institute, the only northern Quaker school that admitted colored students. Tecumseh, the most recent Raisin Institute valedictorian, determined to study at the Kalamazoo Literary Institute. He requested a recommendation from Laura. She wanted immediate emancipation and equal rights for us colored people. This radical stance had forced her to leave the faith. Still she clung to many Quaker teachings about academic excellence and wrote the letter. In a few weeks' time, a letter arrived in her care. Dutifully she handed it to her star pupil and waited for him to open it.

"I have been accepted!"

"You expected less?" said Laura. "If Oberlin to our south and east can act civilized, surely Michigan's Kalamazoo to our north and west can do likewise."

Laura made him wait as she wrote a letter of introduction. She explained that it was not as powerful as his free paper but it carried weight among Underground Railroad operatives in the north or south.

Reluctantly Mariah watched misty-eyed as her firstborn prepared to go off on a great adventure.

"This is a great day, Tecumseh. Your namesake never dreamed the white man would really treat us as equals, and your birth father always wanted to be a gentleman but has no formal education."

"What would my Wyandotte ancestors say?"

After a long pause, Mariah said, "I cannot rightly say. I ran away when I was about your age. No one I knew among our people would have dreamed of attending even Raisin Institute."

"What of my great grandfather Chene?"

"Like Dan Crispin, he did not stay around long enough for me to learn much about him. The last I heard, he was going to the Rocky Mountains to trap beaver. I doubt they have literary institutes out there."

Tecumseh closed his bag and stood staring at his mother. "Ask it," she said anticipating a question whose answer he expected to make her uncomfortable.

"My father abandoned. My grandfather abused. My great grandfather abandoned. Is my blood bad? I want the whole truth."

"Then the whole truth is your father's father, though a slave, was a learned man and a true man. He found his way among all manner of evil. In 1850 so can you. We make ourselves. Now off with you. Make Tecumseh Crispin the man he wants himself to be."

◊◊◊◊◊◊

Dr. James A.B. Stone was the chief administrator for the Kalamazoo Literary Institute. "So, you have come all the way from Adrian, and you really believe that if I were to accept you here, you would not be overwhelmed?"

"I don't understand."

"You *are* a Negro?"

Tecumseh had never claimed that side of himself but his coloration revealed otherwise. As well, his mother had said his father's father might be the best role model for his pursuit of scholarship. When he did not answer, Stone said, "I have seen much darker Negroes, but by your amalgamated nose and silence I know the answer."

"Yes sir, my father, with whom I have never lived, had African born parents."

"Then you are a bastard?"

"I am a man…well I will be in a few months, and yes my father was of Africa. My mother is Wyandotte. I am just asking for a little mercy."

"I am not the Pope."

Stone went on to explain he was a committed abolitionist and although Tecumseh did not appear to be a fugitive, he had to answer to a board that was disinclined to accept any students other than whites. One known drop of colored blood closed the door. The other students would feel insulted. At a school that lived precariously, the risk of withdrawals was to be avoided. He suggested Oberlin, a college known for stretching boundaries.

"I have a letter of acceptance for *this* school," said Tecumseh.

"It was issued because you did not fully disclose your identity." There was a long silence that Stone broke, "Do not think that I am unsympathetic to your cause. I abhor slavery, but race mixing is equally unacceptable."

"I have not mixed with anyone."

"Your parents did the mixing."

Tecumseh stood stock still willing himself not to appear a beggar. Finally Stone offered him a position cleaning spaces and maintaining equipment provided he addressed all whites with deference: sir, ma'am, thank you, please, forgive me; refrained from grunts or eye rolls and steered clear of the girls.

As Tecumseh considered the shame of returning home as a reject, Stone said, "If you obey the rules, when possible I will go out of my way to tutor you a few hours on Saturday afternoons. As for sitting in a classroom with whites, I am afraid that will not be possible."

◊◊◊◊◊◊

For two months Tecumseh worked at Kalamazoo Literary Institute trying his best to remember that if it was his lot only to come close to being educated at least he should be as good at standing on the outside as was possible. The students assumed he was just an unlettered and incapable colored boy if they noticed him at all. Never being the first one to receive a greeting and often being ignored when he spoke kindly to another, mostly he was invisible. Yet no one from the tallest to the shortest person minded ordering him to some great or meaningless task. In time he stopped speaking except when spoken to or asking for clarification of exactly where he needed to clean up after someone.

His one joy was Saturday afternoon tutoring sessions. One day Stone said, "I am taken aback by your academic abilities. Surely it is the French blood on your mother's side. Of course she is primarily, and so functionally, a Wyandotte, a people who some whites admittedly have wronged. Not I however. There were no Indians of any sort when I arrived here. If not for your Negro blood, I would be tempted to approach my board to make an exception."

Stone was only musing, with no response desired. And yet he had come to his conclusion concerning the quality of my nephew's mind later than had Tecumseh. While cleaning up around the students it had become obvious to him that he was better prepared than most of the white students and naturally brighter than all but one or two others. One day, he read in his Bible a verse he had seen many times, "Pride goeth before the fall." This time he interpreted the verse, "Given hope and denied opportunity, I have let my pride go and have fallen from possibilities."

Following the next tutoring session he handed Stone a letter. He sat quietly as the elder man read heartfelt words. Stone folded up the stationery, placed it back in the envelope and said, "So, even though I gave you library privileges last week, you were not man enough to make the adjustments."

"I have been making adjustments all of my life, sir, and I suppose more are in the offing. Some are not worthy of respecting."

Stone's face flushed red, and he swallowed hard at what he considered an affront. "Then it is final?" Tecumseh said nothing. "Before you leave I need to make a confession. I have been fascinated with your hair: half Negro and an admixture of Indian and French. Would you do me a kindness and allow me to touch it?"

As though he had grown deaf, Tecumseh silently left the room.

◇◇◇◇◇◇

Instead of going home Tecumseh moved to Cass County, Michigan, a place where he felt certain he would be welcomed. On the way he had new thoughts. Perhaps my brother, his father, had more struggles than he had realized while he had lived in his sheltered place under Laura Haviland's wing.

At Stephen Bogue's house he presented the family with the letter of introduction from Laura. "So thee knows our dear friend?" said Elva Bogue.

"Yes, ma'am. My mother has been in her employ since just after my birth, and I attended her school."

"Then thee also has met freedom seekers we sent her way," said Stephen.

"I have."

Over dinner they discussed the 1847 Kentucky Raid when nine blacks had been captured by slavers. Tecumseh explained that more than that number had stopped at Laura Haviland's. Stephen told him that several freedmen had led different groups to Canada.

"By my count some 50 people, mostly from Ramptown, fled to greater safety," said Elva.

"My wife qualifies the matter because we Quaker leaders in the Cass County Underground Railroad are still in the courts. The slavers are seeking restitution for our aiding those who stole themselves. Those of us who participated in the saving may lose all we own. Laura Haviland assures us we are at no further risk with you, but as for work, we have hired sufficient workers for the coming harvest."

Tecumseh moved on to Ramptown.

◊◊◊◊◊◊

Chain Lake Missionary Baptist Church was newly established. The church sat on a hilltop and was surrounded by oaks and maples, the same trees from which it had been built. Before entering, Tecumseh enjoyed the turning leaves and admired the view of the lake. He remembered when years before, he had come home from school and told his mother that in addition to reading, writing and arithmetic, they had received a lesson on appreciation of grace, Mariah had added, "There are no lines between the natural world and people. That is the Wyandotte understanding. Love all of life. We are all one."

This bright Sunday morning, his heart was filled with hope when he entered a space with more blacks than he had ever seen at one place. As an early arriver he sat to himself but was soon surrounded by worshippers who greeted him warmly. When services began, their animated worship made him feel he was in a foreign land. 'Where is my homeland?' he asked himself.

Just after the weekly collection for the relief of slaves, Reverend Lett asked him to introduce himself. Tecumseh stood. Instead of simply addressing the minister he spoke to the whole room explaining the origin of his name and his desire for work. Immediately the couple Kinchen and Sidna Artis offered him work. He accepted and the congregation returned to the worship service. Before he could leave with the Artis family, a startlingly lovely young woman named Belle Craft approached. "Could you be Stewart come back?"

"Excuse me, but I don't know a Stewart."

She flashed a knowing smile that still haunts my nephew to this day.

Through the next week of work on the Artis farm, Tecumseh could not get Belle off his mind. In due time she was in his arms. I am at heart a romantic and have had my nephew recite the tale more than once. She was his first love, the one who remains as clear as the first sight of Chain Lake.

◊◊◊◊◊◊

Belle asked Tecumseh if he realized the youngest child sitting on her family's bench was hers and not a sister. Without explaining that another young woman trying to win his attention had disclosed as much he said, he admitted that he was aware of the fact.

"It don't bother you?"

"Why should it? Things happen between men and women."

"He's not coming back; don't worry."

"Who your brother Gib? Kinchen and Sidna say he led a group of fugitives to Canada."

"No, I wasn't talking about Gib. My brother told me a secret before he left: being the only boy among six girls wasn't his idea of a good time. I meant Stewart, Bertie's daddy."

"I hadn't even thought of him."

She appeared to relax after this conversation and they became lovers with everything flowing smoothly until one day she said, "Should we name our first child Tecumseh Junior or maybe Pontiac?"

"What are you talking about?"

"I could be in the family way."

Without another word Tecumseh left their hideaway. All week he thought about the implications of his actions and returned to their rendezvous the next Saturday night. Belle was waiting. "I prayed you back, honey."

"My name is Tecumseh."

"I know, but you're my 'honey'."

He wondered if it were all a mistake. Was he misleading her because he was lonely or enjoyed her company after being rejected at Kalamazoo Institute? She gently pushed his shoulders back toward earth, and he yielded through more positions than he cared to recall to his listening aunt. When it was time to return to their respective homes he said, "I'm here to tell you I can't be your honey or your man...let alone your husband." She started crying. "Belle, I do not even know who I am." He could tell she was confused. "Am I black or Wyandotte? Am I scholar or a farmer? I have to know more than that at 18 I do not want to be a husband."

"Ain't that about what your father said to your mother?"

As far as Tecumseh knew Dan had said nothing to Mariah before sneaking away. He was determined he would not follow suit. The harvest was in. Before parting he said, "If I may, I'll be leaving tomorrow."

"Who's stopping you?" she said angrily.

"If you're carrying my baby, I'm not going anywhere."

"Don't worry, my flow came the day before yesterday."

They stood silently searching each other's eyes. Finally she said, "At least tell me you love me."

"I don't know how to love myself. How can I tell you that I love you?" Belle waited for more. "I will resist the temptation to say I may be back some day. I have no idea what will become of me let alone *us*."

"You told me all about your pappy. I'm not your mama. Give me something to hold onto. Lie to me if that's what it takes."

Tecumseh bit his lip and waited for Belle to dismiss him. With a wry chuckle, she shooed him away with both hands. "You are hopeless!"

"I hope not."

NEW ORLEANS

In 1853 Patience Starbuck finally accepted the decades old marriage proposal of her first and only love. Although she had relocated from Nantucket to Ohio a quarter century earlier, she wanted to be married on her home island. Once I had traveled with her through the southlands. Now I was mother of four and did not even consider such an excursion. My widowed sister Fannie had lost all of her children. She accepted an invitation from Patience to be her travel companion. Patience was the daughter of whalers and wanted to travel by water, down the Ohio and Mississippi Rivers into the Gulf of Mexico and up the Atlantic. Most of the journey was through slave territory. As I had before, Fannie traveled incognito as a slave attendant.

Patience's attorney, David S. Dequindre, met them at the New Orleans dock. "Here she is, my good cousin, wearing a fairy queen's skirt that is nearly as wide as the Mississippi, looking more radiant than Bayou sun on lifting fog!"

Dequindre took her hand and slowly twirled her in a circle admiring her lavender satin dress, with gold velvet bows as well as gold lace gracing a neckline that barely skimmed the shoulders. After a reverse revolution, he clapped his hands. "Magnificent!"

Patience smiled girlishly. "I admit I am enamored with the southern belle styles so antithetical to Quaker gray."

"And 'I am enamored' that you have arrived between yellow fever epidemics," said Dequindre turning sober. "Few have such courage in the wake of thousands dead.

"I expect I will have a dramatic death, no commonplace yellow fever or cholera for me," said Patience.

"I see your mood is better than it was at your last arrival," said Dequindre referring to a visit in 1848, five years earlier, when he had left her standing for an hour because he had expected a stereotypically dressed Quaker.

"I am on my way to be married, and the heat is not as oppressive as before." She turned "This is my friend, Fannie Swift Eagle who is traveling incognito."

Without speaking, he tipped his hat.

◊◊◊◊◊◊

On the way to Dequindre's city house on Elysian Fields Avenue in the Fauboug Marginy, he said to Patience, "I'm dismayed that you'll only be with us for a few days."

"Surely, cousin, thee understands that my wedding takes precedence over entertainment?"

"Certainly, but one can easily see you are not opposed to mixing the two."

"Thee is quite the *homme du monde*."

"You know French?"

So did my sister, from her days living in the Rockies where many of the trappers were of French descent. Of course he did not ask her about her knowledge of a foreign language. He presumed her dark skin signaled deep ignorance. Patience said, "I've studied it since childhood. Thee may recall, my mother, who died young, was born in France. Sadly I am not fluent."

"Certainly you know enough for tonight's festivities; we are hosting a ball."

"I'm not given to *saturnalias*."

Dequindre laughed. "This will be more a delectation with musicians prominently displayed." Patience stared blankly. "It may interest you to know that among my guests will be more than a few coon-asses."

"I expect better language from my cousin and employee."

"Then you do not know that 'coon-ass' is a word the Cajuns use for themselves. They both eat the critter and their poorer ancestors and neighbors wear coonskin hats."

Patience suggested that such language was best avoided. Her father had employed a few Acadian people, and she found them to be as worthy as any other whalers.

"As guest of honor will be Judah Benjamin, the fabulous Jew who will soon be a United States Senator."

Patience already knew that Benjamin owned the magnificent slave plantation, Bellechasse. She also knew that he had defended the insurance companies during the Creole case when kidnapped Africans, after slave importation had been declared illegal successfully commandeered a ship.

"He no longer owns slaves. Does that not please you immensely?"

"Are the slaves 'no longer' possessed by any masters, and were they given back pay?"

Dequindre was certain Patience asked more than was reasonable and such counter-capitalist demands gave abolitionists a bad name.

◊◊◊◊◊◊

One of the things I loved most about Patience was her curiosity. I recall the first time I saw her library. It was filled with more books than I had seen in one place. She also had periodicals from cities as far away as London and Paris. Most were abolitionist tracts, but she also had rags from slave apologists. As well, her forays to concerts and conferences that most Quakers thought forbidden were legendary within our circumscribed world. When my sister Fannie told me that Patience had changed her mind and come down the Dequindres' long winding staircase wearing the violet dress that I had made for just such an occasion I clapped my hands and laughed.

"As you know," said Fannie, "we wear the same size, and she asked me to wear the ivory gown."

Patience led them to where Dequindre was smoking a cigar and holding court. "Why here is my visiting cousin with her trailing servant," said Dequindre.

"I thought you said she is a Quaker," said Judah Benjamin.

"Have you ever known me to lie?" said Dequindre with a smile.

"Thankfully our distinguished founders saw fit to write the Fifth Amendment into our Constitution," said Benjamin, causing the small circle of men who had surrounded Patience to offer light applause for the repartee.

"I assume you are the 'distinguished' featured guest," said Patience.

"You may call me Judah."

"Were thee the President of the United States or the King of Siam, I would still call thee Judah."

"From your lips to The Holy One's ears," said Judah.

"Which would you prefer, President or King?" said Louis Duchamps, Dequindre's principal associate.

"Why not both?" said Judah.

The small crowd was still laughing. A few men were even toasting when Patience said, "Judah, if thee truly believed in 'The Holy One', never would thee have kept slaves."

The room grew momentarily silent until Dequindre's wife Daphne appeared quite suddenly. "Daphne, I am assuming my cousin surreptitiously summoned thee," said Patience.

Daphne's face reddened. She looked toward her husband for guidance. "My wife is not as diplomatic as you, Patience," said Dequindre, throwing Patience temporarily off balance.

"I have been called many things, but diplomatic is not on the list." Addressing the circle of men, she said, "I see your wives are sequestered elsewhere. Perhaps I am expected to join them." There was an audible sigh from a few of the younger men. "However, I will not. I have seen what I came for."

"And if I may ask, what was that?" said Duchamps.

"How thieves of humans look when they are dressed in civilized garb." She paused and looked them up and down as though she were observing slaves on a block. "Clothes do not make a human." She turned. "Come Fannie. The air is fresher on the floor above."

◊◊◊◊◊

Little was said over a sumptuous breakfast of beignets, caramelized apples, and mandarin crepes. Dequindre's baby rested in a magnificent cradle that had been designed by the Goddards and was purchased to become an heirloom. The little girl sighed, and her mother motioned to a servant who went off to bring in the Irish wet nurse.

"When she's fed, may I hold her?" Fannie asked the baby's mother, Daphne.

"I love your voice," said the startled woman who may have assumed my sister was as mute as Ama, the midwife on Fruits of the Spirit Plantation, our first home.

"Thank you, miss."

By the time Patience and Dequindre were ready to retire into his library, the wet nurse had returned and Fannie was rocking the momentarily content baby.

In the study, Dequindre lit a Cuban cigar and Patience said, "David, please understand me. I am opposed to all that slavery brings."

"Mostly whites are in my employ, and every darky who works for me has free papers."

"Colored is a much more suitable word. For a well-educated man your language is abysmal."

"I sit corrected," said Dequindre laughing. "I presume the black as midnight beauty serving you has her free paper?"

Patience ignored the question. "Thee represents slave-free trade interests and should not profit from slave money. I have a sense that this opulent house has some shadows upon it."

"Please be kind," said Dequindre with a smile. "I'm a New Orleans attorney. But even for a man with my predilections for swearing off owning slaves, it is a struggle to separate money into two types. Does it spend as intended? That is the more manageable criteria."

"How thee separates wheat and chaff ultimately is between thee and the Creator," she said icily. "I recently spoke with the Brandeis family of Louisville Jews."

"I have never heard of them."

"The point is Jews are not one people any more than one-time Quakers are one people. The Brandeis family also considers Benjamin's behavior reprehensible, shameless, and damning. People who know the Lord, know the Lord, not just the money they call lord."

Dequindre was being chastised in his own home, but he also was being paid well by the one wielding the scourge.

The heat was mounting, and Patience continued waving a hand fan while Dequindre was being cooled by an Irish servant using pheasant feathers.

"Before we turn to the business that is my occasion for stopping in this torrid, horrid city, I would like to speak with P.C. Richards," said Patience.

"P.C. Richards? Last night when I hosted a distinguished politician who is not a slave owner, as well as a score of his peers, you refused to be seated at the same table. This morning you ask me to send for P.C. Richards?"

"You are in my employ, David. I have not *asked* anything."

He was surprised but not enough to protest her candor. "I'll have him here tomorrow. For timing how does the rise of dinner sound?"

"I want him here *at* dinner. It would gratify me to know that the lead New Orleans attorney for the Slave-free Trade movement is easy having a black man at table."

"Southern etiquette prevents—"

"Cousin," interrupted Patience, "that is a good place to end the sentence. Thee was born in the north—"

"Excuse me, Patience. I was so young that I don't even remember Nantucket," daring to break into his employer's conversation.

"Thee hast implied that Richards can buy and sell Benjamins. I want that particular colored man seated at the table, in a position worthy of what should be his station. "

◊◊◊◊◊◊

Dequindre spoke privately in his library with P.C. Richards before Patience and my sister arrived. Patience entered the dining room dressed in a scarlet and white silk gown with a basqued bodice and three flounces. I had made it to her specifications and she looked as fine in it as any model in Godey's Ladies Book. When Dequindre introduced her to P.C. Richards, although all in the room doubted he would have done so with a southern white woman, he took the opportunity to kiss her hand. From an awkward silence she said, "Sir, your silver fine redingote is of cotton?"

"Yes, it is. The finest the south has to offer. I thank you for the compliment, Madame. I try to be presentable. But you, your dress is magnificent, and you are a Quaker?"

Patience only smiled before turning to Fannie. "Allow me to introduce you to my friend, Fannie Swift."

The methodical care in which Richards had taken Patience's hand and lightly kissed it was missing when he held Fannie's. With her, there was a restrained roughness accompanied by an air kiss.

The featured entrées were mainly seafood dishes prepared by Dequindre's Parisian chef. Dequindre boasted that the chef was a man who had arrived as an indentured servant but soon would complete his five years of service and open his own restaurant backed by his "employer's" financing. The first three courses passed smoothly. The conversation remained at the level of weather, flora, and fauna with the Dequindres dominating the conversation, Richards speaking when spoken to and Patience keeping her conversation to a one or two word

160

comment. Then without warning Patience looked at Richards and said, "Is your God Comfort?"

Richards swallowed hard, caught off guard by the tone of her directness, visibly composed himself and said, "Here, in New Orleans, a man is known by his wealth not his comfort. The road to wealth goes through slavery. I am a man who understands hard labor. There's nothing illegal about slavery."

He believed that he had covered all bases and ended the conversation because for the next few minutes Patience continued eating as though there was nothing more to be said. Meanwhile table banter continued between husband and wife as well as Dequindre and Richards.

Plates were removed in preparation for the next course. "You speak of legalities," said Patience as though much time had not elapsed between sentences, "and we do share one of America's finest attorneys." Both men showed surprise that she realized this fact.

"How else could my cousin have guaranteed your presence at tonight's dinner? But sharing is not the subject, and my concern is not about what is legal. The Creator has only me for this assignment. I believe there is that of God in everyone, including you slaveholders, but I ask you, what is moral about your keeping slaves?"

"My understanding differs from yours, Miss Starbuck. Perhaps that is because even my church owns slaves."

"Doesn't there seem to me a misstep here? Jesus, who it is written came to set men free, is being used as a shield to make men prisoners?"

"Pardon me, but that is a Yankee understanding."

"I doubt that Jesus was a Yankee," said Fannie speaking for the first time. "In my understanding of geography The Holy Land is a long way from any part of America."

Richards did not know how to respond to what he considered an intrusion, so he simply ignored the observation.

"We have our own rules," said Richards to Patience. "We will defend our rights to maintain them."

Fannie was not to be denied, "You use the word *we* mighty freely, Mr. Richards. I and my whole family were slaves. In your mind, who is 'we'?"

Again Richards ignored Fannie. Patience continued the line of interrogation. "Since 1850 the Louisiana legislature has been unilaterally reducing free black privileges. Can you reverse your losses by voting, sir?"

"I cannot, but neither can women anywhere. Yet, you are a citizen. I too am a citizen. You have your rights. I have mine. Should we not be at peace?"

"Peace without justice is best understood as war…even when one is a citizen and the other a *resident*."

Dequindre's throat clearing went unheeded.

"One day we'll all be free," said Richards with determination.

"While you have this dream," said Fannie, "you maintain others in slavery."

He turned red but continued his refusal to look at her.

"Which are you, Mr. Richards," said Fannie pressing, "a man or a slaveholder?"

At last he turned his eyes to the much darker woman and said, "I am a man *and* a slaveholder."

"I don't know that you can be both," said Patience.

Behind his napkin, Richards bit his lip rather than say something that might have been taken as disrespectful to a white woman.

"I tried to warn you of an ambush, Phillip," said Dequindre.

Turning his head ever so slightly Dequindre signaled the Irish butler. "Dessert is served."

GOOD MATERIAL

Just across the North Carolina/Tennessee border my long lost brother Tune spied seven or eight blacks at work in a field. No overseer was in sight. He stopped to watch them and judged by the deliberateness and laughter coupled with joyful singing that theirs was free folks' labor. He rode Cocoa Dust up toward the man who appeared to be the oldest. When he explained that he had not eaten in almost a day, the farmer looked all around, fearful that here was a runaway. Being observed might jeopardize his family. A man two counties away had been lynched for such. Tune explained he too had a free paper and would not put a man at risk in broad daylight. He was told, "Ride on over to my house. Tell Frabbie that J.C. said to feed you. I'll be in directly myself."

Frabbie fearfully said, "We helps runaways but not when the sun's up! I know the Scalfs down the road a piece. They ain't no slave people and more than one runaway stopped there with them. I can't risk my family for no runaway."

"Ma'am, I told your man I got my free paper," said Tune. "What I don't got is food."

Frabbie apologized and invited him in. When her husband arrived with the others they all enjoyed soup and cornbread. They also quizzed Tune about lost relatives, many of whom they thought had been sold further south to places where, as an ex-jockey, Tune might have met them. To no one's surprise, he could not verify that he had encountered a single person with a given name. The absence of surnames was a further hindrance.

◊◊◊◊◊◊

The sun had disappeared by the time, guided by the house lamps, Tune stopped at the Scalf home. He tied Cocoa Dust at the stall and headed around the back to knock on the rear door. Malachi stuck his head out a window. "Someone appears to be walking on my property. Can I help you?"

"Mister, I ain't on the run, but I could use a friend," said Tune.

"Your accent isn't from around here, but in Carter County we use front doors. Especially when there is no back door. That way leads to the root cellar, friend." Malachi laughed and waved Tune to the front.

The family was about to eat supper. "Will you join us?" asked Diannah.

Tune had never eaten at the same table with whites. The fried chicken, green beans and potatoes looked scrumptious. Still he said, "I just ate."

"Eat again," said Malachi pointing to an empty seat between his sons. "This here is William, the other boy is Jim, but his mother calls him James."

"That's because his mother named him James," said Diannah with a smile. "We like to keep a little friction between us. When kept to tiny bits, it keeps the sparks burning."

"The sprite next to her mother is Matilda. I am Malachi and last—"

"But the Queen of the tribe is me, Diannah, wife/consort/chief adviser to Malachi Scalf. You sir are?"

"Tune, ma'am. Tune King, free paper and all. I ain't no runaway...at least not all the way."

"I have no idea what that means," said Malachi. "Nor do I want to. We Scalfs welcome all folk but slavers. You say you are free which is more than many can say when slavers rule the earth. You are not a slave owner are you?"

"Well, no, sir, I ain't," said Tune taken aback by the question.

"We have known more than one colored man, and Cherokees as well, who owned slaves."

"I ain't no slaver."

"You heard the man, Malachi," said Diannah. "He's a freedom seeker like us."

◊◊◊◊◊◊

As Diannah cleared the dinner dishes, Malachi said to Tune, "Stay a while, friend. I need your help."

"I may not be on the run, but I gotta cross that river up north."

"I'd hoped we too would move north of the Ohio," said Diannah.

"If it were the Jordan instead of just the Ohio, I'd agree" said Malachi. Diannah let the chance for argument pass and Malachi said, "I'd like to believe you're safe here. Few undesirables come this far out in Carter County; that's why we moved here."

"I don't know that word," said Tune.

"It means slavers and slave loving fools who don't see that slavery hurts everybody black and white. Their absence and the fact we have dozens of kinfolk within a few days drive and nobody up north."

"I heard tell I got folk in Ohio," said Tune.

"You may want to go hunting there one day, but again I'm asking for your help. My boys are young, and I have to get this work done or risk losing part of my crop."

Diannah placed three pamphlets in front of Tune.

"I can't read, miss ma'am."

"These are abolitionist papers."

"I can't rightly say I know the word."

"Abolitionists are people who are trying to win colored folks' freedom. The sheriff could put Malachi in jail just for having these papers. He could also put my man in jail or worse for inviting you inside before he saw that free paper you say you have."

Tune offered to show them his free paper, but they shook him off and pleaded again for help with the harvest.

"How long will it take?"

"Three days tops if you help," said Malachi.

"You got yourself a nigger."

Malachi extended his hand. "No. I have myself a *friend*. And I'll pay you good for your time."

"I got money."

"The good book says a worker is worth his wages," said Diannah. "We don't give free labor, and we don't take free labor."

"Thank you, Miss Diannah. I'll take that teaching to heart."

"My guess is you had no idea the Bible says that," said Malachi.

"If the preacher back home had taught that lesson, he might've been tarred and feathered. He was as much in the masters' pocket as we was."

"That's the problem with most preachers I've met," said Malachi. "They know the truth but tell only the part they think the big men want to hear. Most are as slimy as a snail in a jar of molasses."

◊◊◊◊◊◊

Tune was assigned the guest pallet in the sons' room. William, a quiet boy, rarely spoke to anyone other than his parents. Perhaps he resented being replaced as youngest even before he was able to walk. Tune had seen that reaction among others he had known. On the other hand, unless told otherwise, Jim was Tune's shadow. Jim moved his own bed nearer to the visitor's, showed him the quickest route to the outhouse, and tried hard to keep up with him as the family harvested a vast field of corn.

Early the third morning Malachi said to Jim, "Son, we're scheduled to help your Uncle Ben with harvesting tomorrow. How about you riding over and telling him we could use a hand over here for a few hours today?"

"I'm sorry, Mr. Malachi, if I've been holding you back," said Tune.

"You're a jockey not a farmer," said Malachi. "I feared I'd bit off more than we can chew before you showed up. We'd be way behind without you."

Tune smiled. "Jim, I done seen you admiring Cocoa Dust. What say you give her a little stretch provided your uncle ain't far off?" Putting a condition on a white person felt amazingly good to Tune who had never had the pleasure.

"Ben's just over yonder hill and down the road apiece," said Malachi to Tune. Then he yelled after Jim. "Don't go riding like a bat outta Hell, boy! Tune's a Jockey. You ain't."

Jim came to an abrupt stop and turned around. "No sir, I'll ride as slow as if he was a mule."

"Cocoa Dust got feelings, Jim," said Tune. "Don't go treating her like no mule."

Even William laughed.

As Jim left the front gate, the sheriff rode up. "How'd you get a horse like that, young Scalf?"

"You got a horse, sir."

"Yes, but I ain't poor as church mice." Jim said nothing. It was not the boy that the sheriff had come to see. "I hear tell you got a nigger on the property."

"My daddy don't like you but he never called you that."

"You're a smart mouthed one, ain't you boy?" Jim said nothing. "Did you hear me asking you a question?"

"Well, sir, if you were asking me true, no I'm not dumb. Daddy doesn't like dumb people."

"One day I'll meet a Scalf with enough sense to respect the law." The sheriff wagged his finger at Jim. "You tell Malachi the circuit judge will be here day after tomorrow. I'll be back here with a warrant and a posse. Can you understand all that?"

"I told you, I'm not dumb…sir."

The sheriff rode off disgusted with the exchange. Jim's quandary was who to obey first, his father or the law. He chose a third path and returned to tell his mother about the sheriff's visit.

She had Jim hitch the wagon, sent Jim to her brother-in-law's as he had been told before telling Malachi about the sheriff and took her daughter Matilda with her to town. Diannah entered the sheriff's office holding her daughter Matilda's hand. Sheriff Landon had his feet on the desk, while sipping from a cup something that had more color than pure water.

"Abe, you and I both know you're not an honest man."

"No 'good morning'?"

"It hasn't started out that way, so why should I lie?"

He placed his feet on the floor. "What bee's in your bonnet, Diannah?"

"Jenny Potter."

"What about her?"

"She told me you kidnapped and sold that poor free colored man over in Tiger Valley."

He stood up red faced. "Why would that low life tell you that?"

"Is it 'low life' you called her? Did you know her pa is my cousin? Did you know I delivered her baby? Did you know I know you're that baby's pa? No, and neither does your wife."

"You wouldn't!"

"Try me. You haven't claimed the child, leaving poor Jenny to be ridiculed. Should you cross me, I'll post 'Wanted Sheriff Abe A. Landon, man stealer and Jenny Potter's baby's daddy' signs up and down the county roads."

"Is that a threat?"

"That's a vow. And it's not all. Keep off our land with or without a warrant."

"This is 1853, and we're in a free country. The law goes where it chooses."

"Please! And don't think that's all I have on you, Aloysius."

She looked him hard in the eyes. Finally he looked away. "Come, Matilda, we have chores to do and the sheriff is a busy man."

The five year old followed her mother out the door. Diannah reported the entire exchange to her husband and Tune who had to be convinced to stay in the fields and spend one last night with the Scalf family.

◊◊◊◊◊◊

Breakfast was over, and Tune was about to leave the Scalfs. "I'm gonna miss you and Cocoa Dust something fierce," said Jim to Tune.

"I can't stay, but how about you make a offer for Cocoa Dust. How much is she worth to you?"

"Worth? I ain't got but three dollars and twenty cents to my name."

"Let's play a game. What if you was a rich master and said, 'Tune, I'll give you half my money'?"

"If I was rich that would have to be a lot."

"Well, pretend you is one rich somebody."

Jim's mind raced until he said, "Tune, I'll give you half my money for Cocoa Dust."

Diannah walked over to where she was keeper of her son's savings and came back. "Here it is, Mr. Tune. It took my boy almost a year to save this from his chores."

The room was quiet while Tune thought things out further. "I'm gonna need a horse to go away. Jim, how's about I buy *your* horse for double."

"But, sir, that makes no sense. You'll be cheated!" said Jim.

"I ain't no ways rich, but with all the money I got from a dollar a day winnings I saved more than $3.20." Jim stood mystified. "Giving me more money you may be getting cheated."

"No, you wouldn't cheat me. I'll sell Thelma."

The boy looked first at his mother then at his father who said, "Go along Jim. Check on your new horse." The boy ran out of the house.

"I know why you did this, Mr. Tune," said Diannah. "Cocoa Dust will draw attention, but Jim's won't."

"That and your kind treatment. And if somebody ask for papers on the horse—"

"In 'the land of the free' horses don't need free papers, only colored folk do," said Malachi.

"One way or the other, I'm less likely of being stopped for a thief riding Thelma *and* if I got my paper on her. Come to think of it, would you read my paper to me before I leave? I know it's good because enough patrollers made me show it. But I'd love to hear what it say."

Diannah read it. "'Proof of Freedom Paper Tune King. Released from bondage in Desoto County, Mississippi by the Honorable Judge Emery Warren'—I thought you were from Tennessee."

"I am but The Judge ain't. I kinda did him a great favor."

"I won't ask about that. Mississippi has always had its special ways. 'Witnessed by Paul Byas and Frederick Bennett on September 20, 1852. Said Tune King is pure black about 5'2" tall, thin, but solidly built, broad nose, bowed legs. Obvious scars include a large one on the bottom half of his left palm and lines from lashes on his back'."

"That whipping going follow me all my days?" There was silence. "It don't say nothing 'bout who I am as a man?"

"That's all he wrote. Sounds barbarian, but in order to me," Malachi said.

"I see you long faced over there, William," said Tune. "I knows how it feels to be overlooked. I have something in my saddle bag for you." He withdrew the gold and green jockey shirt he had worn for Mustin's Green Manor Stables and handed it to the boy. "My master thought I won because of this shirt. Right or wrong, it's made from good material."

William held the silk in his hand. "It ain't a horse, but I didn't have but one."

William smiled broadly. "Thank you sir, I'll always cherish it."

"And do me a kindness, William," said Tune. "Be a good big brother to Jim and little Matilda here. I'm hoping if I keep traveling north by northwest I'll run into some of my big brothers and sisters and they'll treat Tune kindly too."

WINFALL

My nephew Diego Perez, was the firstborn son of Dan Crispin. He was also the only child of Anne Prescott who had been the mistress of Fruits of the Spirit plantation. Either of them might have been lynched for their clandestine passion. It was Diego's lot never to meet Dan or Miss Anne. After attending his father's memorial service, and meeting several of his father's other children, his aunts, and uncles, Diego had relocated from Cuba and purchased a farm overlooking the Great Miami River in Middletown, Ohio. In the autumn of 1853 he visited me in nearby Waynesville. As his aunt, I was more than happy to play surrogate mother, taking him under my wing and teaching him the ways of the United States. His latest visit lasted for a few days. On the final day he packed up free labor produce my husband Charles had purchased for him from Levi Coffin's store in Cincinnati. Both Charles and I knew that Diego was more than a little irritated that conscience had not allowed my husband to purchase the cases of imported rum Diego had requested. Charles had fallen under the influence of the growing Temperance movement. He had even set aside the occasional cordial for health and had insisted that when I made the yearly crop of cider, none be saved for fermentation. Instead of the requested "Devil's brew", as Charles called the rum, he had searched until he had found a few boxes of Cuban cigars. He doubted that these had been made by free laborers, but he had not asked. When I saw them neither did I. Fortunately for all concerned, Diego's manners did not permit a word of criticism or an expression of disdain toward his uncle. Instead, he received the left over change, they shook hands, Diego kissed my cheek, he lit one of the new cigars, and he was off to complete his trip by purchasing a set of caned chairs that he had commissioned at the nearby Shaker Village.

In the forest, barely removed from the pacifist Shaker Village, slave catchers ambushed him.

"What is the meaning of this, gentlemen?" Diego asked as he stared at three mounted and armed slave catchers.

"Gentlemen? The coon called us gentlemen," said Bacon Tate the leader, as he jerked the cigar from Diego's mouth. He dismounted, cut off the end of the expensive cigar that Diego had been smoking, wiped it on his trouser leg and took a long draw. "Billy Bob, you and Bucky, gag and tie him up and put him in the back of this fine looking rig."

Diego's muscles had been toughened during his formative years as a sugar cane slave. He fought with ferocity, bloodying one's lips and blackening another's eye. Because he was only prized alive and he might shoot the wrong man, Tate could not fire his weapon. When Billy Bob and Bucky were both knocked to earth, Tate smashed Diego's back with a rifle butt, and he too went down. "Why hire young men when together y'all can't handle one nigger?" said Tate.

The three methodically tied up his legs and arms. Bucky went to the wagon. "Uncle Bacon, he's got some supplies back here."

"What he got?"

"He got some coffee beans, fruit, sugar, tools, furnishings…Oh my goodness, Uncle Bacon!"

"Bags of gold?"

"Hell no! But he's got a couple of boxes of them big cigars he was smokin'."

"Can you spell windfall?" said Tate.

"W-i-n-f-a-l-l!"

"Close 'nough. I knowed you should've stayed in school more'n three years," said Tate laughing. "I also knowed when I saw this rich nigger we done right not to wait days hopin' them two runaways we tracked to the Shakers might try to head north any time soon."

Bucky returned to where Diego lay tied and bruised. The three picked up the kidnapped man who was much bigger than any of them. Bucky had half-cleared a space in the wagon's bed. They tossed Diego inside, careless of the fact that under his rib cage was a gunny sack filled with small tools.

"You men gag him and cover him with his blankets," said Tate. "Off we go before the sheriff happens by. Warren County must be the dumbest county between Georgia and Lake Erie. Here they think even niggers got rights."

Diego was still in a shock bordering on panic. Over the rutted road, he jostled with the wagon bed's contents. He was thankful for the two bolts of cloth he had purchased for his wife. Once he had rolled off the tool bag and squirmed his way to lay his head on the only soft thing available, it was easier to think clearly. When he calmed he remembered that he had survived slavery as an orphan. He weighed how to regain his freedom. He had heard that American slavery did not compare to Cuban slavery but the speaker had never been a slave in either country. It was not the certainty of hard work that he feared. The two things that bothered him most were the separation from his wife and child followed by answering to people who had convinced themselves that he deserved nothing of value.

His formative years had been spent as a slave who seemed content even to himself because he saw no way out. Life was different now that he had enjoyed both hope and opportunity. Diego's mother had birthed him in a convent and left the nuns to rear him simultaneously as a slave and a favored pet, teaching him reading and writing in multiple languages. He had thought of studying as no more than an inexplicable set of chores, but his privileges had made him a suspect among his powerless peers. When he understood the alienation, he had pretended not to notice how other slaves saw him and won them over by treating women and elders graciously and steering clear of all unnecessary conflicts. Here was a conflict with no obvious exit. What to do when reason was lacking and good behavior brought bad results? Perhaps he could promise a ransom if he were ungagged. The chances that would happen seemed slim. Prayer? Even when the nuns had suddenly freed him and "awarded" him a small plantation, he could not accept their fickle deity who permitted such cruelty as slavery, rape, and maiming.

On the turnpike south he recalled slaveholding priests claiming only faith in Jesus could bring salvation to even a king. The salvation he wanted had nothing to do with pale angels playing harps. Moreover, he had known countless slaves who lived and died praying to a savior who never arrived. Yet, prayer appeared to be his last best alternative. His answer to the dilemma of feeling the need for supernatural assistance and trusting in none to which he had been introduced, was the memory of my sister Fannie telling him that the name of our ancestral deity in Fante-land was Nyame. He yielded to prayer not for consolation but in desperation. "Oh, Nyame," he prayed, "Confound all opposed to my freedom."

◊◊◊◊◊◊

My brother Dan had been one of the wealthiest black men in Cincinnati, some say in the state. I have no way to measure such a claim. Dan's Lion and the Lamb Stagecoaches ran between Cincinnati and Dayton on two lines, the west through Middletown, the east through Waynesville. He had dreamed of extending the latter up to Detroit and the former to Columbus. An early death accomplished what I believe the railroads would have eventually. By the time of Diego's kidnapping, the future was clear. Whites gravitated toward the railroads as the faster means of travel. Soon colored people would be able to ride inside the stagecoaches because no whites were present to force them outside into the elements.

Napoleon once said an army travels on its stomach. American civilians travel on their dollars. If there were poorer whites needing transportation, without our newfound respect, they would either have to walk or pay more for their passage. As it were, although first my brother, and then his widow, owned the Lion and the Lamb, and I had traveled to both Cincinnati and Dayton many times, in 1853 I had never ridden in a stage coach. Why be exposed to hatred, wind, and rain as an inside outcast?

The contraction of the Crispin family prospects did not matter to Dan's surviving friends Haynes Gates, Minstin "Toad" Hayes, J. "Sweetnin' Water" Fassett, and Enochial "Eat-'em-Up Bransford. In their minds, the big man, Dan Crispin, who had frequented Gates' Saloon, had more than tolerated them. He had respected them as friends. Dan's legend grew, and any relative of his was considered royalty. None of them realized Diego had hated the very thought of his father. Of course, a son's feelings did not need to fit their preferred narrative.

By the time the slave catchers came to the outskirts of Cincinnati, it was an hour before sundown and Eat-'em-Up was getting off work. On his way to find refreshment he recognized Diego's wagon by the two horizontal cigars crossed midway by a third on both sides. Eat-em-Up ran the quarter mile to Gates' Saloon.

"Take a breath dammit," said Sweetnin' Water. "What you think you is a catfish?"

Eat-'em-Up took barely enough time to compose himself. "Come quick! I seen Dan's boy's rig with a big red neck weasel lookin' fool sittin' in it while his partners went inside Zemke's Saloon."

"Is you already drunk before sundown?" said Toad.

"I know what my eyes done seen!" said Eat-'em-Up.

"Don't waste time," said Gates, "You boys armed?"

"Is the President white?" said Sweetnin' Water?

Despite his peg leg, Gates led the rescue party out the door.

Billy Bob was in the driver's seat while Tate and his nephew Bucky were recuperating from the road inside Zimke's Saloon.

"Okay, boy," said Eat-'em-Up to Billy Bob, "you better un-ass whoever you got back o' that rig.

"Who you callin' boy?" Billy Bob reached for his rifle.

"Not yo' mama, this time." Toad pointed his pistol just below Billy Bob's midsection.

While Toad and Eat-'em-Up kept their pistols trained on Billy Bob, Gates and Sweetnin' Water untied Diego.

"That nigger is legal tender," said Billy Bob. "Ain't you done heard of the Fugitive Slave Law?"

Diego kept his free paper tied high up his thigh under his long johns. He reached inside his pants and pulled it out, saying, "Here is my passport."

"Let me see that, nigger," said Billy Bob.

"The only thing you gonna see is a minnie ball in yo' mini-ball," said Toad.

Diego was still trying to shake out the kinks from being tied tightly and jostled for twenty miles. "Are we not going to call the sheriff?"

"Where do you think we are?" said Gates.

"America," said Diego facetiously . "Is this land not ruled by justice? I was just kidnapped."

"There's different sets of laws," said Eat-'em-Up.

"They are like the wind," said Sweetnin' Water.

Eat-'em-Up liked the analogy. He smiled and said, "The prevailin' one would have them thieves off before you could open your lips to whisper 'Sweet Jesus'."

"He's right," said Gates. "They'd claim you didn't show proof of bein' free. Worse yet you couldn't even testify to say they was lyin'."

"How could I show I'm free? They beat me and gagged me immediately."

"I'm not the judge," said Gates. "I'm just a resident."

"They stole my money, and I want it back," said Diego. "I had twenty dollars."

Gates looked at Billy Bob. "That was Bacon. He got it."

"But do *you* got $20?" said Toad.

Before Billy Bob could answer, Eat-'em-Up reached into the slave catcher's pocket and withdrew his wallet. He took all the bills inside, "It's $24 in there!" said Billy Bob. "He said it was only $20."

"Call the other $4 a fine," said Sweetnin' Water. "One dollar for each rescue man."

"That's a thought worth havin'," said Eat-'em-Up.

"No," said Diego decisively. "Keeping the extra might open us to being liable to a charge of theft. In the end we could be jailed and fined much more than four dollars while the thieves go free."

"They goin' free no matter what!" said Eat-'em-Up.

"Nothin' will change that," said Gates, "but how 'bout we take a chance on the good sense this man is speakin'?"

After a short silence Toad said, "That boy's smart like his daddy,"

Diego was disturbed both by being twenty-five yet called a boy and being compared to a man he detested. However, the observer had just helped save him from certain slavery. He let the moment pass.

"Tie him up to that lamp post," said Gates.

A full dark and the autumn wind swirled leaves on the empty street by the time the colored men left the scene.

A TASTE

Family was all to twenty year-old Margaret Garner, called Peggy. In her mind the best families were those living together in freedom. The overall escape plans for a group of captives from Kentucky were hers. She was minimally assisted by her husband, Robert, a man who usually was hired out to Northern Kentucky whites who could not afford to purchase a slave of their own. As did millions of others, he worked from last dark to blinding dark wherever he was ordered to go, knowing he would receive no money or thanks for his labor. He was also under the threat that if he failed to give his best effort he would be rented further and further away, perhaps all the way to Mississippi. Of course, in that case, it would probably be a sale and he would never again see his family.

Originally Peggy had planned for an early autumn escape to avoid the strenuous harvesting work. The conspirators' prayers went unanswered. Robert was not returned to the Gaines plantation until Christmas of 1855. The other freedom seekers wanted to leave, but strong-willed Peggy had refused to give the go-ahead. The plan was hers and she knew the way north. The good people bided their time.

In January Peggy launched her grand plan to end generations of oppression. She passed the signal down the line, "God is right on time." On Sunday morning eight runaways escaped from Archibald Gaines' Kentucky plantation. They met up with another slave named Manny, who led nine escapees from two separate plantations. Their female general led the way north. The men were armed with guns stolen over long periods one at a time from their masters' considerable arsenals. As though going to meet the Lord, each of the fugitives was dressed in their best homespun clothing and shoes.

From the appointed place, in the coldest winter in anyone's memory, they walked across the Ohio River's thick ice.

Once they had crossed, they separated into three groups, one led by an Underground Railroad conductor going northeast through Waynesville, the second led northwest through Eaton, close to the Indiana border. Both were Quaker enclaves with an abundance of safe houses. Peggy's group included her four small children, her husband, and his parents. The children were more tired than expected. Instead of seeking Levi Coffin's store with the expectation of going the central route through Middletown where she had heard there were no Quakers and believed that meant less chance of the circling vultures known as slave catchers, they stopped with Cincinnati relatives for a brief rest.

From memory Robert navigated the family through back streets until they reached a small rented house surrounded by the stench of Mill Creek slaughterhouses.

"Smells like freedom," said Robert.

"I hope not," said Peggy.

"You may be right, honey. Most of the white folks in this town come up from Virginny and Kentucky. But it's a bunch of white folk that came because they hate slavery."

"With or without help from white folk, I'll die and go to Hell before I take one step south."

Ethan Jefferson, a colored milk deliveryman noticed something odd about their movements and informed a white friend. The friend informed the United States Marshal, a known pro-slavery man. He deputized several bully boys to help capture the suspicious blacks who had entered a local cabin. Within minutes of their arrival at the Kites' place, the deputies and pursuing Kentucky slave catchers, led by the Garners' master, surrounded the building and demanded surrender.

Elijah said to Robert, "I ain't nothing but a hog butcher with nothing worth nothing to lose. I'll stand with my kinfolk, if you want to fight back."

"I been iron collared umpteen times and watched my wife took for the last time," said Robert. "Me and Peggy already done decided, ain't no stopping us now."

From separate windows the two men fired at the crowd. While they were reloading, the posse charged. Elijah immediately hid his gun behind a loose board in the wall. Robert had enough time to put a single bullet in his pistol. He shot and wounded one of the deputy marshals with a bullet that entered the assailant's hand first then knocked out several teeth. When the smoke cleared the only armed colored man was Robert. He was beaten to the floor and stomped until his owner halted the assault on his property.

"I don't know nothing 'bout nothing," said Elijah. "They knocked, and I let 'em in."

While her husband was being beaten, Peggy grabbed one of Elijah's slaughterhouse butcher knives from the table. With a single stroke she slit the throat of Mary, the nearest and palest daughter. Without a whimper and with blood flowing like a fountain, the child was sent to what her mother believed would be a better world.

"Help me, Mommy; there's more knives here," Peggy pleaded with her mother-in-law. Her mother-in-law saw her namesake granddaughter nearly decapitated and began shrieking. "We can't go back!" screamed Peggy.

Immediately Peggy snatched the nearest son. She cut his throat. Once. Twice. The carotid artery was missed. Tommy breathed. She dropped the knife and picked up a coal shovel. The survival instinct led the boy to roll out of the way. Sounding like thunder, the shovel struck the floor. There was a second son. Peggy hit Samuel in the head with the shovel. In a whirlwind of activity, before the stunned posse could act, she smashed the infant where it lay in the milk crate serving as a cradle.

Peggy was about to strike again when one of the slave hunters said, "My God, the scar-faced heifer is killing property!"

Peggy spun and lunged again for Samuel. Although dazed, the terrified child jumped back, tripping over the table which struck his head and knocked him out. Archibald Gaines picked up the dead child and began weeping for Mary's loss. A marshal tackled Peggy. Their taste of freedom was over.

Less than six hours.

◊◊◊◊◊◊

In accordance with the United States Fugitive Slave Law, Peggy and Robert Garner, as well as his parents, were to be tried for pilfering themselves. The word of the resistance and capture spread quickly through the city. Soon hundreds of supporters were outside the jail, huddled against the biting wind on a bitterly frigid day. Each time one of the colored people had attempted to enter the building, United States deputies had turned them away. Deputies had received orders to only allow citizens inside the courtroom. This was a euphemism for whites only. As the crowd grew outside, hard drinking, pro-slavery people outnumbered the others. They chased away any identifiable white abolitionist, many of whom were pacifist Quakers easily spotted by their gray uniforms. Other whites had been under surveillance because of publicly expressed anti-slavery statements. The colored people stood in groups, often daring the pro-slavery group to try to remove them from the area. When one ordered them to move along, Major James Wilkerson, whose first name was given as a prayer by his mother, said, "Who the Hell deputized you ne'er-do-wells, and what was he drinking, pig piss?"

"You heard me," said the deputy.

"I heard, and we ain't budging."

"Are you armed, boy?"

"Y'all think we monsters. Yeh, I got three arms."

"You uppity—"

"Let those Nigras alone," said the Marshal. "With any luck they'll freeze to death anyway."

When the lawmen retreated to another area, a colored woman said to Major, "What made you use that word 'ne'er-do-wells' for those fools?"

"I wanted to use it from the first time I heard it. What better time than when it fits?"

The colored crowd laughed until some feared tears would freeze before they hit the ground.

The United States Marshal increased his well-armed deputies to 400 strong. The outrageous expense was funded by taxpayers including colored who were taxed but had neither representation nor anything else bordering on equal rights.

◊◊◊◊◊◊

The Garners' attorney was John Jolliffe whose Quaker father was one of the duped Free Quakers who had broken the denomination's rules by fighting in the War for Independence only to learn that the colonists' victory did not win freedom for all people. A man whose country had betrayed him, he spent the rest of his life showing allegiance only to himself. Jolliffe's mother remained devout and influenced her son to continue the struggle for freedom, but without using the weapons his father had chosen. Jolliffe was also a colleague of Ohio's new Governor, Salmon P. Chase, who he believed would be compassionate with the Garners if only the Commissioner could be persuaded to accept the premise that they were humans instead of property. That would require a charge of murder which he assumed was considered more important than theft.

That Jolliffe had lost 16 of 17 his cases defending our people did not lower his position in our hearts. We colored folk admired his commitment to justice and spunk. Neither colored people nor our allies blamed Jolliffe for the ways in which people were cheated out of their natural rights.

◊◊◊◊◊◊

Levi Coffin, often called "The President of the Underground Railroad," entered the courtroom wearing his Quaker silk hat. The federal prosecutor pointed to the hat and demanded he remove it for Commissioner Pendery. "Before thee arrived, I did not remove my hat for these drunken citizens, and they are as worthy in the eyes of The Lord as he who hears the case. I cannot remove it for him."

"But I can," said Deputy George Bennett, knocking it to the ground.

It is said that Cincinnati's cantankerous, government-hating citizens form a higher percentage than in most American cities. Supporters of the Garners hissed and booed and were surprised that some known pro-slavery people joined them. Bennett quickly retrieved the hat and held it out to Coffin.

Coffin said, "Gentlemen do not offend. Until thee hast earned enough to buy thy own, keep the hat as a gesture of my Christian charity."

The courtroom erupted into laughter. Bennett dropped the hat to the floor and retreated to his seat.

The proceedings began. Because they despised every word that comes from an abolitionist's mouth, most in the courtroom sat as though there was no logic when Jolliffe said, "If Congress forbade reading the Bible, all men would realize it is unconstitutional. Likewise, if we are forbidden from practicing Biblical commands it is unconstitutional."

Jolliffe valiantly argued that the Fugitive Slave Law attempted to force people, such as Quakers, to desecrate their consciences. If they supported the law instead of God, who is a Lord of freedom, how could they expect the Lord's mercy?

The first day ended without resolution in sight.

◊◊◊◊◊◊

Zephyrine, my brother Dan's widow, had met Lucy Stone a few years earlier. She also knew Jolliffe through years of working in the Underground Railroad. With Chase leaving town to become governor, she had made Jolliffe the family's only attorney. When Lucy returned to Cincinnati she asked Zephyrine to introduce her to Jolliffe. Zephyrine put on her best dress and drove from Bluestone Road into the city with Lucy.

"Mister Jolliffe, this here's my good friend, Lucy Stone. She helped my niece when she was at Oberlin, and is about as good a white woman as I've come across."

"I have not had the pleasure of meeting you, Miss Stone, but your reputation grows."

Lucy was not given to flattery even when its truth was indisputable. "I am not here to worry patience. All I want, sir, is to see your client Peggy Garner."

Jolliffe asked Sheriff's Deputy Jeff Bridgewater, a known abolitionist, to grant Lucy's request. Although Bridgewater knew that the United States Marshal might resent him facilitating the meeting, he accompanied Lucy to Peggy's cell. When they came to the cell, the Marshal's deputy standing guard said, "Who says this woman can visit?"

"I do, Ralph," said Bridgewater. "I suppose you remember me from the last time I arrested you for being drunk on the street and fed your wife and baby while you kept the rats company."

The second guard, probably also a reprobate, given the poor quality of the new United States deputies, laughed, and the door was opened for Lucy.

"I'll be walking the streets, Miss Stone," said Bridgewater. "You're on your own."

"I've always been on my own." Bridgewater tipped his hat and left.

Lucy adjusted her eyes to the dim light in the room behind the barred door. Peggy was seated on the floor. Her sons napped on either leg. The infant nursed. Lucy was famous for inability to make light conversation. She searched for words, then said "Why this cell is as small as a Boston maid's room!"

"Is it? It's a bit bigger than where we all slept in Kentucky." Lucy was flustered until Peggy said hopefully, "How is Robert?"

Lucy's visit lasted for nearly two hours. Afterwards she went to see

Peggy's attorney. She had barely accepted a cup of tea before she reeled off a stream of profanity to Jolliffe about the Garner case. When she had exhausted her vocabulary, she exhaled a great puff of air, and Jolliffe said, "We cannot simply dismiss the arguments of our Southern brethren."

"Right is on our side."

"I am a patriot and dare not argue that fact. I am also an attorney and dare not ignore that power is on their side. Consider their arguments, Miss Stone. First, the Founding Fathers owned slaves. Second, the Constitution gives them the right to do likewise. Third, their slaves were purchased legally—they may even possess bills of sale—"

"If they do not?"

"Law says it is for blacks to prove themselves free. None of the Garners has a free paper."

"You mean a passport. I have none nor do you."

"We are white."

"That's an answer?"

"That is the *law,* and I am a *lawyer.* I was not finished with their well-buttressed argument. Fourth, Gaines and his supporters will claim they feed, clothe, and house their 'property' better than northern poor whites are treated in our cities. All in all they will claim the white man has made this country great."

"Were the slavers honest they would admit who has picked the cotton; pulled the tobacco; planted, cultivated and harvested all the fields; cleaned their houses; washed their clothing; groomed, herded and killed their domestic animals; built their houses and roads; nursed and raised their children; cooked their meals. Do they make such an admission?"

"Your question is beyond the task before me."

"It is not beyond mine. Should we end slavery—and we will—the worker bees in the slavers' imagination will be those poor deputies and their kin as well as the hordes of poor whites in and out of the courtroom. These, the duped, will be expected to help the masters maintain their wealth now and into the 24th century. For this labor they will be tossed crumbs that fall from overloaded plates, and they will be looked upon with disdain. As for the Garners themselves, if you lose we can expect them and their kin to be worked to death or sent back to Africa, Mexico, or South America."

"They are American born."

"That is my point, Mr. Jolliffe."

"While we sit philosophizing I have a case for which to prepare."

"I am not philosophizing. I am dealing with the real world in which black people are dying and dreams are being killed."

"I will not argue with you. We *are* on the same side. I know that slavery is a form of cannibalism: eating the souls of slave and master alike, consuming the heart of the nation."

"Earlier you called yourself a patriot. What will you do? Paul Revere trumpeted, 'The British are coming.' Sir, 'The Slavers are already here'."

He said so calmly that he almost sounded patronizing, "I have hit upon a strategy. In a two pronged attack I will attempt to have Peggy tried for murder instead of theft of property which will see her as human and give the state of Ohio primacy. This will allow Governor Chase to pardon her after serving five or so years. If that fails, I will point out the Fugitive Slave Law forces moral people to act against their conscience."

Lucy doubted that a moral argument could be efficacious in a country that trusted so heavily in wealth. Jolliffe insisted that the law places murder above theft, even self-theft.

"They call this justice?"

"They call it America."

◊◊◊◊◊◊

I had a dream in which my deceased, hard-edged brother Robin spoke to me. "Sarah, you know I got killed from shots I took from slavers chasing me in Cincy. The least you can do is go visit that sister in jail. She ain't been shot yet, as far as we know, but she done suffered the same way our mama did. She might as well be kin."

In life I would have found some point to dispute with Robin even if all he had said was "Soil is dirty." As an angel, he helped me understand something even more important than the need to visit Peggy. People like Peggy and my brother, and yes me, those rebellious souls were both fighting slavery and helping to keep it alive. If we had remained in the slave states, our non-acceptance of the status quo would have made Haiti's rebellion look like one of Patience Starbuck's tea parties. Once melted into the northern pot, our power was dissipated, mainly by contentment with having a little more than bondage: the illusion that equality was just around the corner. We were not truly free in the north, and Peggy Garner deserved my attention.

I enlisted my sister-in-law Elizabeth and had my husband Charles drive us to Cincinnati. It was there that Zephyrine told us of Lucy's meetings with Peggy and Jolliffe. I looked at Elizabeth and said bitterly, "There can be nothing more evil than forcibly separating lovers, let alone husband and wife." There were layers to my anger including the fact that I had momentarily overlooked that she who had told us about Lucy's encounters was a widow. I glanced quickly at Zephyrine. She obviously had not mistakenly applied the words to herself. Indeed, being a woman of uncommon faith, she no doubt assumed God's taking Dan was somehow an act of compassion.

That night in our bedroom Charles said he understood my passion because I had parallels with Peggy. I waited for more. He was either fatigued from a day of doing his morning chores then driving for hours through the frigid air over treacherously icy roads or felt his meaning was obvious. He dropped off to sleep. After giving him a peck on the forehead I rose to sew a small hole in his mitten. While doing so I contemplated those parallels to which he had alluded. I too am a fugitive from injustice. In fact, I am still a fugitive because my free paper is forged. Like Peggy I have children and a husband. That thought took me inside to a deeper kinship. I wondered how clearly Charles understood the breadth and depth of my love for him. Did my actions make clear words that I rarely spoke outside of the midnight hour or said as he left the house with little more passion than I might toss quilt on a bed? I put out the lamp, undressed and gently motioned for him to turn that I might hold him spoon style, tiny woman to overlarge man, emanating an endless desire. Peggy might never again hold her husband, but mine was in my loving arms. Because our marriage was not sanctioned by the state of Ohio, we had to hide our love from some, but at least most of the time it felt like we owned it.

◊◊◊◊◊◊

Elizabeth and I secured a note from Judge Burgoyne. A block away from the jailhouse, I asked Charles to let us off so we could walk the rest of the way. Our black/white marriage was illegal. With hundreds of hateful new deputies on duty to enforce the Fugitive Slave Law, we might actually be arrested for believing we were married. He protested but in the end yielded to my request. Elizabeth and I arrived at the jail that was holding Peggy and her children. Setting aside my own preference for gay colors, we were dressed in identical Quaker gray dresses and white bonnets. Also matching were our gray caped coats, worn against the worst cold spell I have ever seen. The night before my husband drove us from Waynesville, our thermometer had registered 28 below zero.

Outside the building I said for the third time, "Elizabeth, unless you do the talking, I doubt that we can get in."

Elizabeth was known for her reticence and had never exchanged words with authorities whose rank was higher than that of a Quaker elder. On this day she was determined to be defiant. Without bowing her head, she handed the judge's permission slip to United States Deputy Bennett.

"Please, kind sir, I assume this is in order."

The judge's handwriting was lustrous, but Bennett struggled to read it. Finally he said, "Looks like we're having a parade to see this child murderer. It grieves me, but I gotta search you." He turned first to me. I submitted inhaling as his hands passed with dilatory deliberateness over my body, pausing at places that no man other than my husband had touched. If Charles had seen his actions I have no doubt that Bennett would have regretted the previous sunrise. My husband's maternal grandfather had been sufficiently wild to break Quaker discipline and fight in the Revolution. Charles' mother often said he reminded her of his grandfather.

Elizabeth steeled herself for her turn, but Bennett said, "You look like a Quaker and y'all can't lie. You got any knives or guns or such on your person?"

"No," said Elizabeth more embarrassed than relieved at the reprieve.

"Just so you know, Judge Burgoyne has nothing to do with this case," said Bennett. He turned to me. "You, Nigra Sarah, show me your free paper." I had prepared for this certainty. With a still hand I handed him the forged passport. "Seems in order, but that's not going to get you inside. Miss, today only white ladies is permitted in."

"If she cannot I will not," said Elizabeth.

"Please, Elizabeth," I said. "I will remain outside. Our sister inside needs the visit."

"A good spoken Nigra," said Bennett. "I don't like good speaking Nigras." I held my peace, and Bennett said to Elizabeth, "Come with me, ma'am."

He made a bow with his arm expecting to squire her inside. She ignored it and walked alone in his wake.

◊◊◊◊◊◊

As the door opened Peggy rose from her place on the floor. Daughter of a seamstress, Elizabeth sized up her bearing. She was wearing a new dark blue calico dress that Jolliffe's wife had given her to replace the blood splattered one she was wearing while arrested. A white handkerchief around her shoulders might have seemed simple to an untrained eye but

Elizabeth pronounced the stitching "exquisite." Peggy's visible clothing was completed by a scarlet turban-like head wrap and over-sized well-worn shoes. She also noticed the black woman was average in height. Her nose and lips showed clear signs of Africa although her skin was lighter than most salt-water Africans. Elizabeth tried but was unable to mask being startled by the two scars on the left side of Peggy's face.

"Same white man, diff'rent times," said Peggy simply and sat down. "You ain't who my prayers said would walk through that door. You got business here, ma'am?"

"If you'll have me, I came to call."

"I'd offer you a chair if I had one to give."

Peggy sat on an end of one of two pallets shared by the four members of her family locked in the cell. Elizabeth was about to sit on the cold floor when Peggy said, "It's room for two grown folk if you don't mind touching colored."

"My sister-in-law is colored. She'd be here as well, but the guard forbade her."

"Is 'sister-in-law' another word for your brother's woman?"

"No, ma'am. They're married," said Elizabeth sitting down on the other pallet and smiling at the boys. "Would one of you care to sit on my lap?" Samuel accepted the offer. "My name is Elizabeth but I think of myself as 'E'."

"I'm glad of that," said Peggy. "Master's wife is named Elizabeth. Her 'gander months' caused me the most misery."

Later I had to explain to Elizabeth that the gander months was the time before and after a white woman's labor and delivery when her husband was most likely to commit adultery, usually without a hint of criticism from his wife. Most colored people considered the majority of white women accomplices to the crimes.

"Master named me Margaret, but I call myself Peggy. I suspicion that like Miss Lucy, you got some questions. If I'm right, address me by my chosen name."

"As for questions, I'm a Quaker. My mother taught me to listen, Peggy."

"Then it don't scare you that except for being a new hand at it, I would have sent all my chillen to Jesus then followed 'em."

"I am a woman who does not pretend to be a god."

With Elizabeth's eyes closed in contemplation and Peggy's warily open, they sat in silence for a full five minutes.

Peggy broke the silence, "I can't understand why they're so scared of me. Even big heavy set men wearing guns be shaking around me. Aside from my dress, all I got is this here little finger ring." She extended her left hand. Elizabeth, a woman who had never worn jewelry admired its simplicity. Timidly, the woman accused of murder whispered, "Can you help me ma'am? I mean with a satisfactory explanation, not the offer of a little knife to use against pistols and shotguns?"

Elizabeth heard the question in its fullness. "I can't give you anything more than my love." She offered a smile. If I guess right her smile bordered on innocence and naiveté but embodied neither.

"I guess they figure any woman who'd kill her own chillen might not value anybody's life." Peggy watched Elizabeth's face. In time she said, "They made me suckle the master's chillen while my own was weaned way too early. They wanted to make sure my flow would keep theirs happy but any fool knows a woman who can satisfy one can satisfy two. Why can't they understand my own chillen is myself, and the only reason I killed once, and would kill again, is because I value their life? Why can't they understand that all my life I've had only one choice: run or stay. Once I chose run, how could I go back to staying a slave?"

This time Peggy closed her eyes, and Elizabeth followed suit. Elizabeth prayed for healing in a wounded world.

More than thirty minutes later, the sun crossing the cell started at hiding the scar and darkened Peggy's face. She looked at Elizabeth and said, "They say y'all Quakers have a heart for us colored folk, and y'all don't believe in killing. That said, will you answer this one question?"

Elizabeth agreed to do her best. Peggy asked if she had been wrong to kill her own child. Elizabeth explained she was certain that God never withholds love from loving mothers.

◊◊◊◊◊◊

When Elizabeth returned I was waiting outside the jail, sitting huddled, back against a Buckeye tree. I stood up and knocked the ice from my coat while saying, "Thee was inside for almost two hours. That was quite a surprise as soft-spoken as thee is."

"Is thee using 'soft-spoken' to mean 'soft and weak'?"

"We have known each other too long for me to think of thee as weak. There is a fine suppleness to thy being, and it took great strength to go as a friend to a stranger kept in a dungeon." I paused. "I also remember the great friend thee has been to me since the time of my escape."

"Forgive me. I was defensive perhaps because I can think of no good defense for that harried woman."

We walked against the wind a mile to the Lion and Lamb stable founded by my brother. Charles was waiting. To protect him, I mentioned nothing of my ordeal with the deputy. Instead the two of us listened to Elizabeth all the way to Zephyrine's home.

◊◊◊◊◊◊

On the final day of the hearing, white women had risen and cared for their families so early that they made up the majority of the courtroom audience. Also most people who were nearest the door were women. The largest number had come to bolster the strength of a woman who almost certainly would be crushed by men who neither understood nor cared about the reasons that might have driven her to cross a forbidden line. Although both Elizabeth and Lucy Stone had arrived early enough to be seated, they remained outside with Zephyrine and me.

We heard the call, "All rise!" A black man standing near us said, "What the Hell you think we're trying to do?" A hush fell over the shivering crowd, and Lucy said to my sister-in-law, "E, would you hold my coat?" It must have been nine below zero when Lucy left the outside crowd.

Predictably, Commissioner John Pendery, a lawyer whose appointment was aided by his sister-in-law's husband, Supreme Court Justice McLean, remanded Peggy Garner and her family to return into Kentucky slavery. A second later, Lucy Stone walked through the door theatrically dressed in a black robe that without explanation she had asked me to make, "Of the cheapest material available."

She elbowed a guard aside and said loudly, "Here comes the real judge!"

Although flabbergasted, Commissioner Pendery said, "This hearing has ended, but if you would like a word with those assembled, be my guest."

He walked out of the courtroom while all others sat wide-eyed with curiosity. Lucy advanced to the bench with an exaggerated rooster-like step and plumped down in the chair where Pendery had been seated. Surveying the assembly, she gave an impromptu speech that was recorded in all of the city's newspapers. "I know it is not proper in this border town for a woman to address you but I live by what is right. With your ministers strangely silent I have no choice but to speak out against this deep rooted evil. I am especially addressing my sisters who sit in conscious security while one in six of our darker sisters are subjected to uncivilized outrage.

"We had a grand opportunity to improve our country. Instead, this has been a carnival not a trial. It has sickened my sensibilities. Where was Peggy Garner's trial by her peers? Her peers are slaves. Millions of them live just across the river. Their relatives stand outside in the freezing cold because they are not permitted to sit among so august a body of white skinned people. Where is her judge? She has a commissioner who the government pays double for a conviction over what he receives for an acquittal. If ever there were a set of conflicts of interest, it is the infernal rules of the Fugitive Slave Law. A woman who has walked on water has not been given even enough freedom of speech to testify in a court on her own behalf against kidnappers. In the place of justice we, who are in the process of stealing a continent, and have already stolen millions of Africans, have accused good people of stealing themselves! An escaped Kentucky slave, her little ones, and husband have spent weeks enslaved in a 'free Ohio's' jail cell. Have we no shame? We should be fining their slave masters for their years of service and then transferring the money to the rightful owners."

She paused. The audience seemed transfixed.

"A mother is lowered while a rapist is exalted. God has not wrought this man-made injustice. I will not say 'Father forgive them' because they do know what they are doing."

She brought down the gavel so hard that for years some would claim they felt vibrations in their hearts. "You are dismissed."

Only southern Ohio chivalry that honored a white woman's skin saved her from being lynched by the men who felt outraged.

THE GOLD CIRCLE CLUB

The well-dressed women arrived in small groups, usually driven and left by a husband or a son. Dusk had yet to fall so a few who lived within a mile or two walked. They believed in being on time. Once inside Zephyrine's house, each woman placed a gift bag of food for the hungry in the foyer. Before taking a seat, they deposited papers in the "Hope Jar." Thirty minutes before the official gavel was struck the vast majority were seated around my sister-in-law Zephyrine's outsized parlor. This was her third two year term, each separated by the Gold Circle Club's Constitution that did not permit consecutive terms. It was not her social high rank among colored folk that brought her to the presidency. She had been assured of the first term as President when in 1848, she had organized and led other women armed mostly with rolling pins, fireplace tongs, butcher knives, shovels and washboards against a much smaller group of well-armed slave catchers who had surrounded a house where fugitives were holed up. The slave catchers had decided bounties were not worth limb or life and retreated on the run.

My sister Fannie, who was also sister-in-law to the hostess, entered the parlor five minutes before the announced starting time. She introduced herself to a stranger holding a baby on a love seat and sat down next to her. At precisely 7 pm Zephyrine struck her gavel, and the work began.

Zephyrine opened the meeting with a reading by the deceased founder, a woman who would have been a minister if such had been permissible by those in power. It spoke of Jesus calling the disciples with

"Come and follow me," then went on to explain that what he really wanted was consistent love and compassion, the desire to think new thoughts, and commitment to die that the slaves might be free. Zephyrine offered a prayer whose preamble was a petition for the freedom of the slaves. It segued into praising The Lord, and ended with a request for the strength to prove themselves Christians. It was accompanied by several encouragements of, "Amen," "Come on up, sister," "Jesus be praised" and "Bless His holy name." Then she led the singing of the club's theme song,

"We are Gold Circle,
special ladies of the Lord.
We give our very best
helping our kin pass the test.

"We are Gold Circle,
special ladies of the Lord.
We give our very best
helping our kin past the test.

"If you don't know the way
watch how we be stepping.
It's about our work,
no games and no play,
freeing our people
each and every day.

"We are Gold Circle,
special ladies of the Lord.
We give our very best
helping our kin past the test."

Zephyrine said, "Devotions, prayer, song and right actions all make a circle of gold." Empowering formula complete, the women who had not already done so, smiled greetings and touched hands with each other. Zephyrine's servant came in with coffee and poured them each a cup from a wondrous set that Patience Starbuck had given the hostess.

"My name is Zephyrine Crispin. I am in the first year of my term as the President of this esteemed gathering. This is year 15 of my membership. I was born in Culpeper, Virginia. I am widow of Dan Crispin, father of three boys, Queen Mother of The Lion and the Lamb Stagecoaches."

Her words brought both laughter and pride. "One of my deceased husband's sisters is in town as our guest. I'd like for her to introduce herself next, and then we'll introduce ourselves around the circle clockwise."

On cue Fannie said, "My name is Fante Swift Eagle, mother and wife, visitor." She stopped abruptly and turned to her left. Length of membership ranged from three months to Keziah Boyd's 29 years as the only living founder of a resistance group that had originated when whites had run half the blacks out of Cincinnati in 1829. Most women mentioned their birth states, husbands, and children. Some spoke of their outside profession as a laundress, seamstress, cook, or servant. As a vestige of slave days, the more prestigious the white family someone served, the more likely their name would be mentioned in the introduction. The wife of a wealthy colored man named Robert Gordon spoke of their business as a joint enterprise. One who followed her said, "Our family owns The Wright Blacksmith Shop." The next woman shared that her family owned a barbershop. No doubt their husbands would have claimed total ownership, but the men neither cleaned their business, fed themselves, did their own laundry, nor were responsible for childcare. As much as Gold Circle's Constitution detested all forms of oppression, it prized truth bearing. In their minds most of America was living in a matriarchy. Also, unbeknownst to many a white man, through being the hidden central figure in a household, colored women had usurped much of the masters' power.

Before speaking, the ninth of the 16 members stood and walked over to Fannie. My sister also stood. They embraced each other warmly. Without either speaking a word, they returned to their seats. "My name is Priscilla Carter Jones. I have been a member for seven years. I was born in this city. I am a housewife and I keep a journal."

"It seems you and my sister-in-law know each other," said Zephyrine. The statement was too obvious to merit reply. Introductions continued until each woman had introduced herself. Immediately the members brought out current sewing projects that would clothe runaways passing through Cincinnati. Having been forewarned, Fannie worked on a coat Zephyrine had begun the previous month.

Zephyrine announced the agenda and asked if adjustments needed to be made. With no suggestions, she read one by one notes from the Hope Jar. Omitting duplicates, the jar held the names of businesses and farms known to be hiring. Those who could write scribbled pertinent information down. Those who had yet to master letters, had enlisted others to take notes for them or committed information to memory. The members trusted that the drive for everyone in the community to survive would let nothing and no one fall to earth.

Following a brief silence, Zephyrine asked for attendance reports from local churches. The numbers were noted and compared both to the previous week and the corresponding week of the previous two years.

"Thank God we are growing in faith, growing in power. Now for the vote on whether to change the titles of the cabinet from Secretary of State, Secretary of Defense, Secretary of Peace and Secretary of the Treasury to Vice Presidents. In keeping with our Constitution, if there's a tie, as President and the trusted one with the most responsibility, I break them all."

There was a spirited debate before the women voted, eyes closed. "Usually the President does the counting but, Fannie, as a neutral party, would you count up the votes?"

"By my count," said Fannie, "It is 10 for Secretary and 6 for Vice President."

"Any fool could've told you that would be the count," said Sister Sally Sue Boston.

"There are no fools in this room," said Zephyrine. "Now the Secretary of Peace will give her report."

The woman seated to Fannie's right held that office, but she was also trying to readjust after nursing her baby. "Mrs. Swift Eagle, would you hold my chile?"

"I'd be happy to," said Fannie accepting the infant and beginning the burping process while the mother reported on two funerals and a marriage.

Someone said, "I knew Allen couldn't raise five li'l ones by hisself. Jennie must be more desperate than I thought. She must be half his age!"

"Jimbo Allen wouldn't know a pot from a bayou," said Sally Sue, "and he think soap was made for other folk. However old the woman is she's got her work…and her nose cut out for her."

Someone said, "Tell the truth, sister!"

"I was born the truth!" said Sally Sue.

Zephyrine brought her gavel down hard, "Ladies *we* have work to do."

"I never dropped a stitch," said Sally Sue.

The Secretary of Peace continued with a report on who was sick, duly noting that the city appeared to be cholera free at present.

Zephyrine said, "Secretary of State, are you ready to report?"

Keziah Boyd reported that two families had made it safely to Canada, a family already there had a son as "smart as a whip and can already read and write—he took dictation for this letter."

"Praise the Lord!" said a chorus of voices.

Yet another family was enjoying life in Detroit as was one in Cass County, Michigan.

"Praise the Lord."

The next item in her report was the capture of a man who had fled through Xenia and been captured by the hateful Bacon Tate. He had been advised to go through Middletown on his way to Dayton but had said he was right handed and had right in his favor.

"We guess, and sometimes we guess wrong," said Zephyrine. "The Devil is also guessing."

"Then he should've took the guess out and prayed," said someone. "King Jesus *knows*."

"If you don't mind," said Zephyrine lifting her eyes up from the pants leg she was hemming, "we'll let the Secretary of State finish her report, so we can move on to our other business and not keep your men waiting and getting upset."

The Secretary of State shared *sotto voce*, that William Casey and some of the dockworkers had sneaked two stowaways off a steamboat the previous night. Calvin Fairbank had risked himself again for the cause of freedom and justice by sneaking them onto the steamship. The husband and wife were in hiding until the appropriate time.

"Fairbank is a gentleman to John Fairchild's wildness," said Zephyrine. "We need both types of white men or we cannot win in this lifetime, and win we will."

The names of the Iron Chest men who were on first alert to help fugitives were given. Finally Keziah said, "There is no news on the repeal of the state's Black Codes but we remain grateful that we no longer have to post bond just for being colored."

"Little by little," said someone.

"Too damned little!" said Zephyrine before exaggeratedly placing her hand over her mouth as though she had accidentally spoken the profanity.

The meeting continued with the Secretary of the Treasury reporting on the amount earned at the annual Freedom Fair, the timing for the next bake sale, and the overall state of the finances. She concluded, that Gold Circle was not in business to make money but to help the needy, especially the enslaved. Since the Freedom Fair had placed them over the 'threshold of civility,' in keeping with The Constitution, the excess would be used to feed and clothe the hungry. The committee of non-office holders were called on to compile a list of needy and each member would see to it that the treasury was at a more respectable level by next month's meeting.

"Praise the Lord!" echoed around the room.

The Attorney General spoke next telling who colored was in jail and which court cases involving colored people had been decided. In her opinion, with Salmon P. Chase governor thanks to the vote of New England born people populating northern Ohio, John Jolliffe was the only trustworthy attorney in town. She warned people that after the Peggy Garner case, half the judges hated the ground he walked on.

Priscilla said, "I wish John Mercer Langston would come home to practice."

"If he did," said Sally Sue, "them low down judges and juries would hate him more than Jolliffe."

"Attorneys do more than go to court," said the Attorney General. "He could help us stay out of court."

"Long as we black, white folk going pull us into court where we can't testify against 'em or sit on a jury," said Sally Sue.

Zephyrine said to the Attorney General, "Thank you. If life were fair, you would have made a great lawyer yourself."

The Attorney General bowed her head modestly but did not dispute what everyone knew to be true.

"We have two more pieces of business before my report."

The Secretary of Education reported on the state of the schools, each of which remained separated by race. She reminded members that the main item on the agenda next month was for The Gold Circle to choose a slate to run for Colored School Board.

"We must make certain that this time whites do not control our board," said Keziah. "If we leave our education to them, we will be taught that we are a race of thieves and slaves."

"Don't worry, Keziah, the men we recommend will be worthy," said Zephyrine.

"That's part of the problem, Madame President," said Priscilla. "You and Sister Keziah could serve us well. After all, it is the women who are the educators in the home."

"Amen! Ain't it the truth!" were exclaimed around the room.

"Our time will come," said Zephyrine. "Madame Secretary of Defense, it's your turn."

She began by giving the names and descriptions of known slave catchers who had been seen in the city since the last meeting. She followed the list with a shorter one of suspected spies. When she concluded her report, Sally Sue said, "Robert Shines is a known spy. A friend of mine seen 'im taking money from Deputy Bennett, and he ain't put nothing in Bennett's hand but air custard pie."

"Even Cincinnati courts could not convict a man on that, sister. But it is worth noting," said the Secretary of Defense. She continued, "I've inventoried 12 outfits for girls and boys as well as 14 outfits for women and men… What's been completed tonight?" The women went around the circle reporting on completed clothing.

Zephyrine said, "For my report let me say simply, the resistance to the 1850 Fugitive Slave Law continues all up and down the north. Not just colored folk, white folk too is saying just let slave catchers come up in here. We'll do the same as we did in '48."

"We should have done more for poor Peggy Garner," said Sally Sue.

Suddenly there was a commotion at the door. Deputy Bennett strode in with three other men.

Zephyrine stood. "Who gave you the right to enter my house?"

"The law goes where we want especially among women who are known contraband hiders," said Bennett. "Okay you men, look through the house. See if them runaways is in here somewhere."

The Gold Circle women protested at the intrusion but Zephyrine held up her hand, "The sooner these…gentlemen—"

"Gentlemen?" said Sally Sue.

"I am giving these gentlemen permission to see how the other half live," said Zephyrine. Bennett turned red. "I have never seen his house but I know from others that it is a humble dwelling near the slaughterhouses." The four white men went all through the house, found nothing and slammed the front door.

They had removed themselves when Zephyrine said, "I supervised the building of this house using one colored crew and one Irish crew working side by side. The next week I had the colored crew come back and build a special hideaway. There's a couple in it as we speak."

"It's not in my report," said the Secretary of Defense.

"If I told all my business it wouldn't be *my* business," said Zephyrine.

"That's a questionable precedent," said Keziah.

"It ain't a precedent until we vote that it is," said Zephyrine smiling. Most women laughed. "Besides, more of our men have been approached to spy on us after Peggy Garner's case. Not that I suspect any of your men would sell us out, but I'm trusting you Gold Circle women to keep buttoned up about this whole affair, at least until my boys get these good folk off and heading up north."

At last Sally Sue was at a loss for a retort.

Zephyrine reported that she had met in her home with the Presidents of the other colored sewing circles and at the main meetinghouse of the Religious Society of Friends with both the presidents of the regular white women's abolitionist clubs and the Quaker committee. She reached for the gavel, but before she could call for a motion to end the meeting, Sally Sue said, "In two months we have elections. Can I run for President?"

"First, my term just started in January. Second, the Vice President is like an Apprentice President."

"Whoever heard of a colored apprentice? Them whites don't allow such in their mechanical associations."

Keziah said, "The Gold Circle is constructed as life should be."

"The Constitution says you can run for Vice President or a Secretary position," said Zephyrine. "We all believe if you do, it's because you wanna work."

"I'm steady as Black Betty," said Sally Sue. "The last time I didn't work Skippy was a pup and I was still crawling."

Zephyrine brought the gavel down. "Madame Vice President, please close this session."

The Vice President ended with a long emotional prayer in which she called on Moses and King Jesus before reminding the women of Moses's black wife, Zipporah, and that Mother Mary gave birth to a baby with hair like lamb's wool who was loved by his father.

Afterwards Sally Sue nearly choked while saying, "If I could hear my daddy pray again."

Her sorrow was so deep that time seemed to stop. Amidst an awkward silence the women moved into the dining room.

◊◊◊◊◊◊

Curious women were anxious to delve into the welcoming exchange between Priscilla and Fannie. Seeing the most inquisitive try subtly to jockey for a position next to either woman, Zephyrine said, "Me and my help been cooking all day. We hope you ladies have time to enjoy our best food and know ya'll won't be dipping into our visitor and sister member's business. That would make Madame President very unhappy, and this is a house of joy."

The women laughed and took the nearest seat to where they happened to be standing. Fannie had already observed only a dozen could be seated at the table. She took the corner seat nearest Zephyrine.

"No you don't," said Zephyrine. "You are our honored guest. Sit at the other head, opposite me. That way we can see each other and better enjoy the time together."

"As you wish," said Fannie.

Keziah moved from the seat at the far end of the table. Zephyrine and her female employee had prepared a simple meal of corn on the cob, fried chicken, collard greens, biscuits, and the first stewed apples of the season. After grace was said someone began to gossip, but Zephyrine reminded them spreading rumors at the dinner table was disagreeable to her digestion.

◊◊◊◊◊

After the meal Zephyrine said, "Ladies, please keep in mind that Cincinnati is the kidnapping capitol of the world. It's dark out there. Let me know if anybody's on foot. My younger son and a male servant are in their rooms and know how to drive carriages." People laughed and expressed gratitude for her generosity. "Apparently my sister-in-law and Mrs. Jones have much to talk over. I will see the rest of you to the door and explain to Mr. Jones that in due time my son Abel will drive his good wife home. Selected for the after-meeting private talk is Sally Sue."

"I wish you the peace of God," said Keziah Boyd to Sally Sue.

"Why is it always me?" said Sally Sue.

"Ask yourself, and the answer may become clear," said Keziah. "Good evening, all." She walked out the door.

◊◊◊◊◊

Zephyrine sat in what once was her husband's library. Now it was where she kept the piano Dan had given to her before death and where, in keeping with the Gold Circle Constitution, she met privately with one woman following each meeting.

"I know I'm here to be taught," said Sally Sue.

"We're all here to be taught."

"I mean in this room not in this world!"

Zephyrine smiled and said, "I did too." After a pause she said, "You almost broke my heart the way you talked about longing to hear your daddy pray. What's the *short* story?"

Sally Sue successfully fought back tears and looked away momentarily.

Refocusing, she said, "The last time we was all together Daddy prayed to Jehovah that we'd stay one in heart even if we never saw each other again. He'd hit the overseer in the mouth for some reason. Instead of giving him the lashes, Master sold 'im to a Mississippi slave man. He left 'fore us kids woke up. Before he did he made Mama promise not to cry 'til he was long gone like a turkey through the corn.

"From that day on, every time I saw that big willow where he used to pray for all of us on the plantation, I listened for the sound of his voice. Nothing. At home, not once did I step in the place where he said that last prayer. The hardest part is I thought I had a home 'til I woke up and Daddy was gone."

"My Lord, have mercy!"

"That's mercy's a pretty word. If I ever have a gal I'll name her that. Of course, I hope Jehovah will break me off a piece of mercy before then. Now what you wanna teach me tonight?"

Zephyrine exhaled and took her friend's hand. "Sally Sue, I'm glad you told me what you did just now, but every thought that comes our way don't deserve saying."

"Ain't that what freedom's about: saying what's on yo' mind?"

"I know as slaves we were treated like children—only speak when spoken to and told 'now's the time'—but even as free adults we have to leave space for others."

"In my experience, the more I talk the less chance somebody'll ask what I don't want 'em to."

"So you try to drive people off?"

"Off the scent of my pain, yes."

"Honey, ain't a black woman in this country—slave or otherwise—lives without pain. We don't want to hurt you." Sally Sue appeared unconvinced. Zephyrine turned to another concern. "As for running for office, if I was you, I'd wait a while longer. You've only been in Cincinnati for a few years and this was just your third meeting with Gold Circle."

"Do you think I can really get elected?"

"As we used to say on Fruits of the Spirit, 'Is fat meat greasy?'"

Sally Sue smiled. "You know how long it's been since somebody believed in me? Nigh on four years, and she died dead before I left."

"Then you just circled back to a club of women that practices believing in each other."

◊◊◊◊◊◊

For several seconds Fannie and Priscilla held hands silently.

Priscilla spoke first, "It's been more than 30 years."

Fannie, "Yes it has. The last time I saw you was when you gave me the dress before I swam across the Ohio River. I wore it the first day across the river, on Freedom Day, and as my wedding dress. "

"I had no idea it would be that special! How have you been keeping yourself?"

"I am well and happy with my life. And you?"

"Life is good now, but after I was kidnapped—not far from where we're sitting—I spent years as a slave forced by my master to sleep with visitors. I did what they wanted when they wanted. Most tipped me well. I kept every dollar they gave me. One day my chance came. While he was drunk my master offered a room full of friends a bet on the Kentucky Derby. None of his friends took the bet, but when we were alone I said, 'I have a thousand dollars'."

Her master asked her how she had accumulated so much money, and she said she never spent anything. He made a disparaging remark about those to whom he had given her. She had bet on her own freedom and that of the only son he had let her keep. When Fannie expressed surprise that such a degenerate would allow her the company of even a single child she explained that the special one was the child of a United States Congressman with whom she had slept the last month of his wife's pregnancy and first two weeks after she had her baby. When she proved the boy was his, he told her breeder master it would make him very unhappy if he sold his boy.

"Every now and then he'd stop by 'for old time's sake', see me, see his son. How I wish the three sons Master put in his pocket was his. I'd sleep better."

Fannie knew the idiom 'put in his pocket'. When she and the rest of our family were sold and their worth was transformed into money for Miss Ann that was how we all understood the transaction. "Where's your special son now?"

"Can you keep a secret?"

"Better than you can."

Priscilla laughed, then explained her son who had seven white great grandparents was not only passing for white but a leading Cincinnati bully boy. Her husband Matthew belonged to the Iron Chest and had no idea about her son.

"Unlike this one you and my sister-in-law belong to, this sounds like a lop-sided circle to me."

"Any gold we colored ladies find is gold we make."

FAMILY VALUES

In late December, 1858, Jeremy, grandson of Esi and Kofi, son of Liza Mae Baker and my brother Dan Crispin, made his own path through 8" of fresh fallen and even higher drifts of snow. My nephew knew that he was walking on the blood of others. The trail he blazed was over the two-year old Osawatomie Battlefield. Later, when he told me the stories of both the battle in the summer heat of August, 1856 and on the subsequent snowy journey, he still had not figured out if, with bullets flying, his bowels had released because of fear from the shots whistling around him, being startled by the screams of nearby men who had been mortally wounded, or one of the many agues that plagued Brown's freedom fighters. "I doubt that it matters, Aunt Sarah," he had said, laughing, "but it was for the best cause. Although it was humbling it did not make me surrender or retreat."

I have since learned that Jeremy did retreat along with the others, but only when ordered to do so by his commander. I throw no stones. Some would call my own escape from slavery a retreat. Furthermore, surely he would have been killed or enslaved had the Border Ruffians had their way. As for me, each time I have not confronted oppression, was I not retreating?

I said, "Does it not bother thee how close thee was to death?"

"Like the Old Man, I am willing to give my life for the slaves."

"Thee is a young man."

"Didn't you tell me my grandfather was a warrior?"

"Yes, and so was thy grand*mother* and all of their ancestors. That was not an answer to my question."

"We all die some time. Whether it bothers us or not isn't a question worth asking."

I suppose the young scamp inherited his smart mouth from a mind as active as mine at the same age. I was tempted to bring him a few pegs down from his warrior's stance, but I pressed him no further. He would continue needing a measure of hard-spiritedness to maintain his own pride or, more importantly, for our people to be released.

I said, "Out of curiosity, nephew, why has thee not organized a body of thy colored friends to help with this work?" He did not understand the question, so I spoke more bluntly, "Is it not great risk to trust thy life to whites? Is it not they who oppress us?"

He said, "Auntie, the greater risk would be if I worked with all coloreds. The mob wouldn't hesitate to massacre us. Besides, the Captain and his boys don't know that they're white!" He laughed. At the time I thought he was mistaken.

◊◊◊◊◊◊

Jeremy passed the spot where a good friend had lost most of his head and all of his life. At the time the bullet had struck the friend, he recalled hesitating in mid step as though he might catch flesh in his off hand. Although the act might have been admirable, he had no idea what other purpose would have been served if he had possessed the reflexes of an angel. He fired his next shot before looking down at his friend's lifeless body. Especially for a man who had faith in nothing but resistance, it was not the time for mourning. A few rises in the terrain later he came near where another fellow had fallen with a leg wound and was writhing in pain. He was not particularly close to him and had not even offered him a drink of water. Jeremy never saw him again. Had this man been captured, died of the wound, or been murdered by someone who saw abolitionists as traitors to the Constitution? The Captain's men all knew the risks. What they did not realize was that many of the survivors, like so many violated women I have known, would be plagued with perpetual nightmares of the dead, wounded, and killed.

After four miles of forging his crude trail, he finally came to the Adair family's small log cabin. He knocked several times.

"Who is it?" said John Brown's sister Florella through the barred door.

"Jeremy Baker, ma'am."

"I know no Jeremy Baker."

"Ma'am, your brother Captain John sent me."

"My brother is infamous, but no captain. I have heard liars and ruffians make such statements."

"Would a liar know that your father was a trustee and you and your husband graduated from Oberlin College as did a member of my family?"

"There were no colored Bakers at Oberlin with me, and by your voice I am sure you are colored."

The snow was swirling, the frigid temperature in free fall, and standing still had made Jeremy begin to shiver. He placed his rifle against the wall. For warmth he put his mittened hands inside his fearnought. "Ma'am, my cousin Susan Ferguson graduated in '54, long after your time, and I have a brother Abel at Oberlin as we speak."

Suddenly a voice from behind Jeremy said, "For heaven's sake, dear, let the young man inside, so I may put down this load of wood!"

Jeremy was fatigued and had been so preoccupied with convincing Florella of his worthiness that he had not heard Samuel come through the snow behind him. When telling this story to me he said such an indiscretion among enemies might have been fatal.

At the sound of her unbarring the door, Jeremy quickly cleaned the snow off his coat and buffalo skin cap while stomping his feet to remove it from his boots. The door swung open and he stepped aside for Samuel to enter first.

With the door closed and wood deposited, Samuel said, "Now, my friend, what brings you out here on a cold, snowy night?"

"Reverend, the Captain and us men liberated eleven slaves in Missouri. We need a place to rest. They're not far behind me."

"Surely you jest," said Florella. "The last time my brother was here, there was a near-war and men, including my sweet nephew Frederick, were killed. We have children's safety to consider, yet you sound as calm as if you were saying, 'My mother wrote me a letter'."

"She can't write."

"I am most serious, Sir Puck."

"It's Christmas season, ma'am."

"He's right," said Samuel. "We can scarcely turn them away claiming there is no room at the inn." Turning to Jeremy he said, "Does the 'they' who are right behind you include pursuing Missourians?"

Before Jeremy could answer, Florella said to her husband, "This is a home, not an inn!"

"Dear, if you can turn away fugitives from injustice as well as your own brother, I will honor my marriage vows, grab my rifle and keep them all at bay."

"I did not ask you to do that, Samuel."

"Say the word and I will shoot John between the eyes and order the lot of them into the icy depths of winter!"

Florella's heart was racing. She needed to think things through. Following the battle of Osawatomie the Missourians had broken into her house. Only their commander's restraint had prevented a massacre of innocents. "The others were all for looting or at least destroying everything in sight in this humble dwelling," she reminded her husband who had fortunately been absent during the raid. "As I have told you before, he asked me if my husband is an abolitionist and I said, 'He is a preacher.' Then he asked if I were a free-soiler, and I said, 'I am a housewife who, like others in my class, is in Kansas seeking the prospect of a better life for her children. What can a woman know of politics? Is that not why we are not allowed to vote?' Samuel, such evasive speech satisfied both commander and followers. I dare not consider what St. Peter will think of it. Then he condescendingly said, 'The damn Jayhawks, led by the fanatic John Brown, don't understand they are encouraging nigger rebellion at worst, and at best niggers to dream of seizing power and treating us as the inferiors.' I was given no choice but to listen to vulgar language and vicious drivel in my own home."

"Your brother waits in the winter wind. Did you not say but a few days ago that you wish to speak to him?"

"That is a misquote. I said, 'Were my brother here, I would speak sense to him,' but that was mere daydreaming. I did not want him ever again to set foot in my house."

"I repeat, he is not inside the house God gave to us. He is in the winter wind."

She sighed and said, "We only came to Kansas for the good of the enslaved. I cannot make this hateful place worse by resisting to perform my Christian duty."

As Fannie and I had taken pains to teach our inordinately wild nephew, he told me that he had listened to Florella's speech with understanding patience.

Florella turned to Jeremy, "By what signal will they come forward?"

"A waving lamp from the porch," said Jeremy. "One for the Father, one for the Son and one for the Holy Spirit."

Florella put on her coat, grabbed a lamp, and went out onto the porch.

◊◊◊◊◊◊

The slaves were allowed to enter first. Smiling her greetings, Florella welcomed each of the eleven into her house, introducing herself as Mrs. Adair and training her eyes on theirs, not their thin and tattered clothing. A few looked directly at her with clear gratitude but most did as trained, not daring to meet a white woman's eyes under any circumstances.

Once inside, they huddled together in a congratulatory embrace and offered prayers of gratitude. Learning this, I was reminded of a freedom seeking mother and child that Charles had brought into our home one night. He offered her a place to rest, called me wife, kissed me as though he had doubted he might ever again see me, did the same with our children, excused himself and went across the way to tell his parents he had returned safely. The weary but wide eyed fugitive said, "This is the Promised Land!" I said, "No sister. This is only Ohio." Almost instantly I self-measured, found my answer wanting, and prevented myself from telling her all of Ohio's many shortcomings. "For this moment, thee *is* in the Promised Land. Further north there is even more freedom."

"I thought freedom was whole type thing not cut in pieces."

I could no longer restrain myself, "For us, a piece is all we get. Now, rest with us and let me prepare thee and thy child some plates of warm food."

Although each is unique, there are so many parallels between the stories of freedom seekers that I find the sordid pattern particularly striking.

Returning to Jeremy's adventure, before entering his sister's house, Brown and his soldiers left their pikes, broad swords, and Sharp's rifles stacked next to the door. Pistols and Bowie knives were discreetly tucked in trousers or holsters covered by coats.

"I knew you would help us, sister," said Brown between sips of hot coffee.

"How did you know about me what I did not know about myself?"

"I have only a short time to live. In those moments…days… weeks…who knows…until the end, I am determined only to associate with the best sort."

"You and your words," said Florella.

"Talk is a favored institution of the cowards. I am God's instrument, a man of action." He passed his cup to the next person in the circle, as her husband had passed it to him. Florella filled it and Brown said, "As

a servant, I am here to give a thorough shape to abolitionist theories."
Florella did not appear impressed. "Coffee warms the body, dear sister,
but we have eaten nothing but Johnny Cake. Do you have food for these
good people, and a place on the floor for them to sleep? If the Lord
requires it, my men and I can camp on an ice covered river."

Samuel Adair inquired about the number of men and was told there
were eight. They all would have entered but four were left outside to
stand guard.

"Bring them in. I'll add water to the soup," said Florella.

"I suppose for a short time," said Brown, "we can live without a guard."

Jeremy went to tell the others.

Surely her comment about more water was overstating the problem,
but the family's poverty was well known. According to Jeremy, the only
wealthy people Brown associated with were those who funded the work.
Otherwise he despised them and accused them of benefiting from
slavery.

"We are not totally without our own resources," said Brown, bringing
a dead squirrel out of his bag.

"And I shot a rabbit," said Jeremy on his return.

Samuel said, "We have more than Jesus had at the Sermon on the
Mount."

Brown smiled at Samuel's good humor and asked Samuel if he ever
regretted not pastoring a large Boston congregation. Samuel told him
through his abolitionist work on the frontier he was pastoring all of
America. Brown laughed heartily then said, "There is more truth in your
words than God would prefer."

"Brother," said Florella to Brown, "they say you are bleeding Kansas."

Brown said in a softer than usual voice, "I am freeing slaves held by
Pukes. If some people bleed in the process, blame the Founding Fathers
not me."

"Do I blame them for the dead at Pottawatomie Creek?"

"Life on the frontier is harder for some than others," said Brown. "No prophet has ever been beyond fighting the sin of bogus men."

She scolded Brown for not recognizing the limits of decency, but he retorted that slavery is nothing but a line of limits. He might have added that each one ends in a shallow and premature grave. Instead he stood and said, "Let us pray, dear sister." He bowed his head and prayed earnestly both for the freeing of the slaves and those citizens wed to the slavocracy. "Help these heathens to find their way to the Lord who despises slavery, the sum of all villainies." He ended with encouraging slaves everywhere to seize their freedom by any means.

When Brown ended, Jeremy noted Florella looked as though she had be chastened. Jeremy told me that he could not feel sympathy for her because at times he too had been forced to admonish both his younger siblings and the men in his former gang of bandits—although he referred to them as "friends." He also observed that as a frontier woman Florella was "as tough as uncured leather." I told him that a grown woman should be above being admonished by a brother. He is so much a person of these times that, although he nodded as though in agreement, I could see he was dismissing my point.

Brown had scarcely closed his prayer when Florella said, "The same Pa who taught you to pray taught me to pray. As I recall, he was clear that prayer alone only changes the quality of air around a body's lips. Brother, let me be clear. You have not convinced me that your path is right. I am still opposed to letting killers in my home. I did not open my door because we are kin. It is for the sake of these oppressed children of the Lord that *you* are inside."

The Captain smiled at her and admitted to always admiring her passion, but in taking stock of white Kansas he found that only a handful were as opposed to slavery as those assembled in her home. Others hate both slaves and free colored folks—Indians as well as blacks. He refused to wait for the majority to see the ways of the Lord or the politicians to act like statesmen.

Samuel said, "I've heard it said you do not respect any politician."

"It's gratifying to know sometimes people tell the truth about me. I have yet to see a professional politician who would not sell out the truth for his own advantage."

"Perhaps that is why both sides in power wish you would disappear. Brother-in-law, how is it you have not been shot and killed?"

"I am more likely to be crucified, stoned, or hanged. If half the bullets which have been aimed at me had struck flesh, I would have more holes than Grandmother's riddles."

"I have soup to prepare," said Florella.

◊◊◊◊◊◊

The only time any of the runaways had been so far from where they had been enslaved was when traveling in a chained coffle. Although each step of the almost 50 mile walk to the Adairs' home had been fraught with danger and plagued with cold, snow, and sometimes sleet, it had been as freed people. No one had complained. Now they were overjoyed with the thought that they might be home as free people, never guessing that three months of walking lay ahead. As well, no colored people enjoyed the level of freedom that they had seen their masters exercise. Perhaps for the first time, as children trade marbles, they expressed their dreams among themselves. Meanwhile the soup heated more slowly than anyone desired because the wild meat had been nearly frozen.

Jeremy sat down between Jim Daniels and Samuel Harper, two of the fugitives. Although they had just recently met, there seemed to be a special kinship among the three resistors. He felt that he had found his calling. He was about to doze off when he heard a mother sing,

"You're gone from me
my first born child,
in your ears you heard my plea,
master sold you anyway,
though we was meek and mild."

Jeremy was a fatherless man with no appreciation for a parent's continued pain even when life seemed on the upswing. He opened his eyes and recalled waiting for these same fugitives to be released from work so that he could explain that the Captain and his men were going to lead them from bondage. Listening to how they passed the time in unpaid drudgery singing songs with double meanings had infuriated him. Sorrow songs enraged him still more. He caught their attention and said, "No matter what you've been taught, you ain't livestock." He explained that they were equal to whites, and they needed to compose songs that went beyond mourning. "How about some hope songs?"

They loved their black knight. When he taught them a few hand-clapping songs about people who had found their freedom or were carefree, they sang with passion.

◊◊◊◊◊◊

Brown gave his nephew Charles a hearty handshake and credited him with saving the life of him and his men at the Battle of Osawatomie. The boy admitted his mother had sent him to warn of an ambush.

The abolitionist was bemused that his sister had acted, when no one else had dared. He laughed and called out, "Sister, I'd give you blackberries or a ham. But neither have I." Jeremy saw her hide a smile.

Brown, a very religious man, turned from his relatives to tell the fugitives to love the Lord of Freedom, quote scripture, make mature plans, and beware of traitors because Judas comes in many forms. "Ain't a slave master a Judas?" said one of the women.

"The worst kind," said Brown. "The kind who thinks he owns you and therefore cannot betray everything right and good in the world."

Brown looked up from his place on the floor beside the oldest fugitive and said, "Well, sister, what are your thoughts?"

Instead of asking him to beat his swords and Sharp rifles into plowshares and carpenter's tools, Florella said, "I guess tonight those in the Adair home will sleep cheek by jowl." For the first time in Jeremy's presence, she smiled broadly. Then she referenced the infamous painting of kidnapped slaves close packed on a hateful ship. "But this time the ship will be helping people get to freedom."

"Then your anger has abated?"

"It's the times that make me angry at *you*."

"Praise the Lord for tender mercies."

"If family is divided, we all will surely be conquered." She paused. "In our small outbuilding we have collected extra camp equipment should fugitives happen by, a few knapsacks, blankets, and a tent."

"No weapons?"

"No weapons."

"And all this time I thought you understood that I am a lover of peace but there can be none without justice. If these men and women and their brothers and sisters are ever to be free, it must be by force, probably by spilled blood. This guilty land resists prayer and moral persuasion as much as our father's mules resisted the idea of plowing without being driven."

"Then living by the gun you will probably be shot for treason."

"Perhaps," he paused before saying, "I expect to forfeit my life for being a man. If some call it treason, the law of God does not."

When John Brown prepared his party to go out into the cold, Florella came to his side and the two embraced without saying a word. He turned at the door and looked at his nephew, "Farewell, Charles. Keep an eye on my sister here and remember if you care for those in bonds you too will be free."

Past Titles

Running Wild Stories Anthology, Volume 1

Running Wild Anthology of Novellas, Volume 1

Jersey Diner by Lisa Diane Kastner

Magic Forgotten by Jack Hillman

The Kidnapped by Dwight L. Wilson

Running Wild Stories Anthology, Volume 2

Running Wild Novella Anthology, Volume 2, Part 1

Running Wild Novella Anthology, Volume 2, Part 2

Running Wild's Best of 2017, AWP Special Edition

Build Your Music Career From Scratch, Second Edition by Andrae Alexander

Writers Resist: Anthology 2018 with featured editors Sara Marchant and Kit-Bacon Gressitt

Magic Forbidden by Jack Hillman

Frontal Matter: Glue Gone Wild by Suzanne Samples

Running Wild Press, Best of 2018

Dark Corners by Reuben Tihi Hayslett

Upcoming Titles

Running Wild Stories Anthology, Volume 3
Running Wild Stories Anthology, Volume 4
Open My Eyes by Tommy Hahn
Legendary by Amelia Kibbie
Running Wild Novella Anthology, Volume 3
Running Wild Novella Anthology, Volume 4

Running Wild Press publishes stories that don't fit neatly in a box. Our team consists of:

Lisa Diane Kastner, Founder and Executive Editor
Barbara Lockwood, Editor
Cecile Serruf, Editor
Tone Milazzo, Podcast Interviewer Extraordinaire
Amrita Raman, Project Manager
Lisa Montagne, Director of Education

Learn more about us and our stories at www.runningwildpress.com

Loved this story and want more? Follow us at
www.runningwildpress.com, www.facebook.com/runningwildpress, on
Twitter @lisadkastner @JadeBlackwater @RunWildBooks

CPSIA information can be obtained
at www.ICGtesting.com
Printed in the USA
LVHW110712180919
630972LV00005B/50/P